Copyright © 2019 by Mark Rice

All rights reserved. No part of th
reproduced, distributed or transmitted in any form or by any means, including photocopying, recording, or other electronic or mechanical methods, without the prior written permission of the publisher, except in the case of brief quotations embodied in critical reviews and certain other noncommercial uses permitted by copyright law. For permission requests, write to the publisher.

Publisher's Note: This is a work of fiction. Names, characters, places, and incidents are a product of the author's imagination. Locales and public names are sometimes used for atmospheric purposes. Any resemblance to actual people, living or dead, or to businesses, companies, events, institutions, or locales is completely coincidental.

Ordering Information:

Quantity sales. Special discounts are available on quantity purchases by corporations, associations, and others. For details, contact the "Special Sales Department" at the email address markrice10@gmail.com.

This book is dedicated to the memory of my mother and father whose belief in me was unshakeable.

Day 1

Tuesday 3rd January.
Departure.

I opened the door and found Margaret pulling back the bedroom curtains to let in what light there was to be found at dawn on a winter's morning.

She turned and smiled at me. "You should have woken me," she scolded gently as she made her way to the en-suite. "We'll be pushed to make breakfast."

We are at the start of our journey to England to join the SS Azara that sets sail this evening on a fifty-day cruise. We must reach Southampton by 15:00 and, to do so, all parts of our travel plan have to work perfectly.

Twenty minutes later, we are outside the Conrad hotel in Dublin airport on a dark, wet and cold morning. I glanced at my watch. We'd checked out already and were patiently waiting for the driver of the hotel courtesy shuttle, parked a few feet away. When he finally appeared it signalled the arrival of six other passengers with bags who'd shunned the biting cold wind and had sat in the warmth of the reception. Thus, it was a full minibus that departed for the short journey to Dublin Airport's Terminal 2.

On the bus I glanced again at my wife. Margaret is a totally innocent soul in this venture of mine. We've been married some three years but together for ten years in total. We met through work and clicked with an outpouring of passion, love and lust that had been in cold storage for the previous twenty years. The sliding open of the minibus's door to release the travellers and their luggage snapped me back to reality.

Freed from the cases and with time to spare before the departure gate was announced we shared an Irish big breakfast with a large mug of steaming hot tea. The food stations were buzzing with activity, people who had been on the road for hours to reach the airport, and knew they still had hours to travel, ate heartily.

In England, eight hours later, our journey ended with a short taxi ride to the Octavian Cruise line's terminal building. We arrived bang on time.

The taxi driver, a chatty medical student, pocketed the tip and removed our cases from his boot.

Nearby a team of uniformed workers were unloading cases from the open storage bellies of an endless stream of coaches. They were offloading hundreds of pensioners that were swapping English snow, sleet and rain for Caribbean sunshine.

The SS Azara is a 69,000-ton ship that stands fourteen decks tall and towers over the check-in terminal. I'd spotted it within a minute of leaving the train station, as it was considerably taller than any building or ship in the port. Its sleek white bow stood majestically pointing towards us as the taxi laboured through the midday traffic.

The SS Azara will carry 2,012 passengers and 887 crew and all passengers are boarding today, in fact, within the next three hours. The ship will depart at 19:00 tonight with the highlight of the cruise being a 1,000-mile journey up the Amazon River to visit the city of Manaus. It returns to Southampton on 22nd February.

We'd labelled the cases with our cabin number and this time we passed them to the baggage handlers and rode an escalator to the first floor of the terminal building. There we found about 1,800 people patiently waiting their turn to hand over their debit/credit card details, have their photographs taken and receive a ship account card which is used for everything you buy onboard and for accessing your cabin.

Cards pocketed, we moved onto the security scanner queue, a part of the process we had been through many times before, incident free. I watched the people and bags being processed ahead of us and was already in holiday mode.

"Excuse me, sir, is this your bag?" the cruise line security team member asked me, pointing to one of our hand luggage bags. He'd selected mine and I suddenly feared the worst, that the true nature of my talcum powder container had been rumbled. These scanners may be more sophisticated than I had originally thought.

"Yes, officer, it is." I answered cordially, my senses on high alert "What seems to be the matter?"

"Can you step over here, please?" he gestured me towards a small curtained cubicle some feet to his right and I followed him over. Margaret, now reunited with her bag, stood at the gangplank looking anxiously towards me.

Behind the curtain, my bag was opened and the security man removed two bottles of wine I'd purchased at the airport hours earlier.

"I'm sorry, sir, but the cruise lines rules are quite clear on this matter and you are not allowed to bring alcohol on board. I'll have to confiscate these." In that moment I simultaneously experienced relief and disappointment.

"Of course, officer. You do what you have to. I'm sorry I didn't spot that restriction when I was reading the cruise details."

I was lying, of course. I knew damn well you couldn't bring alcohol on board, but I'd got away with it in the past. I reckon I was just unlucky. If I'd drawn a different security team member, they'd have allowed the bottles to pass without comment. Ship prices for alcohol are not cheap. Well, he was just damn lucky he wasn't actually going to sail with us tonight because if he had been his odds of making it through the night had just taken a dramatic dip. I took the bag from him and rejoined Margaret.

"What was the problem back there?" she asked, so I told her. "Oh, Luke, haven't I warned you about this penny-pinching. Trying to save a few quid here and there always ends up backfiring and costing us more."

I knew I shouldn't have told her. It just gave her the opportunity to wheel out that same old speech again.

By 17:00 we were onboard and admiring the new carpets and swish look to the ship we'd last seen four years ago. It had undergone major refurbishment in Germany last year and it showed.

We found our cabin, F100 on Deck 5, right in the bow of the ship. Persel, our cabin steward, introduced himself with a smile and announced that nothing would be too much trouble for him to arrange for us. Moments later he wheeled the luggage into the room and as he left I accompanied him out to have a quiet word in the corridor. I have found that it's always worth buying a bit of service at the start of a cruise from cabin staff. I mean, it's pretty useless giving the gratuity to them at the end when they can do nothing for you. No, I wanted Persel on my side from day one and he knew the drill.

"Thank you for bringing our cases, it's much appreciated," I said as I pressed a £50 note into his hand.

Persel seemed surprised at the amount and thanked me profusely.

I had a sixth sense that I may need his services in the coming days and weeks and the money would buy me his prompt discreet attention. "I may need your help during this cruise as my wife is poorly," I lied.

He nodded his understanding of my words and turned away a happy man.

To date, I have gone through life as an eternal optimist and have been proved wrong more times than I care to mention. Why do I set myself up for a disappointment? It's an inbuilt character weakness that I have because when I am let down, as I invariably am, I am surprised and angry. Angry because people with a more cynical approach to life are proven correct. So now, finally, I am joining the cynics and my *talcum powder concoction*, for want of a better description, is actually a sign that I am changing my attitude to life. I am becoming less of an optimist, more of a pragmatist. The optimist in me hopes that I will never have to use my concoction, but the pragmatist believes I will. At least this time when incidents arise I have the ability to react and not to just internalise it and let it eat away at me. Not like the last cruise.

With the cabin door firmly closed in his wake, now was the time for us to kick off our shoes and finally relax. The madness of the journey to reach the ship was already dissolving in our minds, as we took in the comfortable surroundings of our inside cabin, home for the next seven weeks.

That's the beauty of travelling by sea. You unpack just once and the world thereafter is delivered to your door and not the other way round.

There was just time for a quick scan of the ships daily newsletter, *Skyline,* which detailed the multiple activities onboard each day from 07:00 to midnight and beyond. After a quick stroll along the deck, we made our way to the compulsory fire safety drill.

Our muster location was zone C, located on deck 7 in the

Pelican Ballroom dance lounge. We arrived and found about two hundred passengers already gathered inside, and an overflow of humanity stood outside or sat waiting in the window wells of the inside corridor. I scanned their bored faces and watched as they interacted with their partners and fellow passengers and crew. None of them would have been any the wiser of my intent, as I smiled and gazed at the people around me.

The crew wore uniforms, with their lifejackets on and fastened. They guided new arrivals to any free spots in the already full corridor.

We were gestured to stand next to the bar counter and that's when I accidentally stepped on the woman's foot. She let out a little cry, reminiscent of a whimper from a small dog, rather than a human being's cry of pain. I turned to apologise but in doing so, managed to elbow her in the right breast.

Her partner, an elderly man leaning on a walking stick, looked sourly at me but didn't move a muscle.

"I'm terribly sorry," I exclaimed, bending down to pick up her shoe which had fallen off.

The situation almost worsened as my downward head motion to pick up the shoe, just missed her glancing upwards to see who the clumsy sod was. Disaster avoided, I slid her shoe back into place.

Margaret then grabbed me firmly by the arm and marched me away. "I'm mortified! You damn near head-butted that old dear," Margaret said, looking sternly at me before giving in to a fit of giggles. "Really," she continued, "I can't take you anywhere."

Around us, the old folk were struggling to remain standing as the clock ticked past the 15-minute mark. Eventually, the voice of the ship's captain, Peter Cox, boomed through the PA system and delivered succinctly the information on health and safety, before handing over to the muster station crew to instruct passengers on how to put on and wear their life jackets. Judging by the hopeless attempts made by some of the elderly passengers, a large number of deaths through strangulation in their cabins will most likely occur, long before the ship goes down.

Today is the 3rd of January and it will be zero degrees at best outside on the open deck tonight. Obviously, we are heading for warmer climates in the coming days and weeks but until we reach the Azores in five days' time, the North Atlantic will be a cold turbulent passage to complete.

The ship's departure today was delayed by the slow loading of passenger bags and we missed the spectacular fireworks display set off on the quayside as its revised commencement time meant it now clashed with our dinner time. We had reserved the first sitting of the evening meal when we booked the cruise, so had to leave the outside deck early to make our 18:30 dinner date.

We appeared a little late, and very casually dressed, in the Imperial Restaurant at table 80, where we met two of the three couples that we would dine with for the next fifty nights, Roger and Rose, and Frank and Jill. Neither couple were overjoyed as their cases had failed to materialize, meaning they'd been forced to attend the meal in their travelling attire.

I sat with Margaret and surveyed our table companions, as I'd imagine Simon Cowell would do when assessing acts for *Britain's Got Talent*. I looked at them somewhat dispassionately to see if they would be good company over the coming weeks, to see if they displayed the qualities I value in humanity, namely a sense of humour, intelligence, good manners and tactile affection. I go by the mantra, *know me by my actions, not my words*, as words are cheap.

First impressions are also important. It's hard to get over a bad start when meeting people for the first time but I was prepared to make allowances tonight as we'd all had a long day.

Roger and Rose were already seated when we arrived. Frank and Jill came somewhat later and I could see his caring manner right away. He helped Jill into her seat before he settled into his own chair.

The conversation was awkward at first as we all sounded each other out on common experiences.

"So, Roger, have you cruised before?" I ventured. He looked a rather serious man, old enough to be my father and evaluated my question for what seemed an eternity before replying.

"Well, Luke, this would be our forty-second cruise in total and we've done all but one of them with Octavian Cruises. We've been on two round-the-world cruises but never been up the Amazon River, so that's what attracted us to this particular one."

"Yes," Rose chipped in. "Roger was in the Royal Navy and had seen most of the world already so it was really unusual to find somewhere he hadn't already visited!"

"Whereas Rose," responded Roger, "...had rarely travelled outside Wales before she met me, so we are filling in her missing life experiences, so to speak."

He gazed fondly at her and she reciprocated.

"That much is true," she confirmed. "Since we met I've travelled the world and can't imagine life any other way."

"I couldn't help overhearing your conversation," Frank sparked up. "So, you were in the Royal Navy? Me too."

Within moments the two men were swapping their naval histories and it seemed that often over the decades they really had passed each other, like ships in the night. However, they did find that they shared several mutual acquaintances. Both had left the Royal Navy decades ago but the nautical pull was strong. They were back now to enjoy life at sea, but this time as passengers.

I decided to build a bridge or two with our new acquaintances and find out a bit more about whom I was dealing with at this table for the next few weeks. I dusted down an old story I could use for that purpose and ventured forth with it.

"My father was in the navy too," I volunteered, "but he was in the merchant navy."

"Makes no difference," said Roger. "A sailor is a sailor and we are all tied together by the love and fear of the sea. If any ship gets into difficulties, merchant or Royal Navy, the nearest ships will always respond and come to their aid. It's the first law of the sea."

"Funnily enough," I continued, "even though he was in the merchant navy, his ship was requisitioned by the Royal Navy during the Suez Canal crisis, back in the 1950s, and it carried a platoon of Gurkha soldiers down the canal to support the main British Army effort." I became aware that I now held the interest of the entire table. "My father went on to tell me a crewman lost one of his hands one night trying to remove a kukri, a lethal curved knife, from a sleeping Gurkha."

"Oh, yes," said Frank, "once the knife is removed from its scabbard blood must flow, or so the story goes."

"Enough now!" Margaret shook her head. "Really, Luke, you are putting me off my dinner."

"What about you, Jill?" I ventured, turning to the slim white-haired lady on my right. "Will tales of blood and body parts upset your appetite?"

"Not in the slightest, Luke. I was a Wren myself for thirty years and worked in the Royal Naval Hospital in Portsmouth for a while. It would take more than a severed limb or two to put me off my food."

The table erupted with laughter at the image she portrayed.

"Is that where you and Frank met then? I asked.

"While you were both in the navy?" Margaret added.

Jill nodded. "Mr Romance over there took my best friend to a dance and came home with me. His ship was just back from action in the Falklands and a lot of steam was let off that night, a lot of beer drunk and a lot of partying had, if you follow my drift. I ended up helping his best friend carry him home and the rest is history. He can't really drink, never could."

Frank grinned sheepishly and gestured to the glass of water in front of him on the table.

"Hey, Frank, he could be your brother," said Margaret, pointing in my direction. "He's great for the lowering of the first pint but you'll find him asleep halfway through the second. He's the cheapest date I ever had."

Frank switched topics and the table conversation continued as we got to know each other. The arrival of wine loosened some tongues, but I noticed Frank and Jill still stuck to drinking water. The small talk was interrupted by the arrival of tonight's starter—bowls of steaming hot Scotch broth which was delivered to our table by Ali and Hamoud. The two smiling, uniformed stewards had to that moment earned plenty of points on my scorecards. Well, that was all about to change. Hamoud stretched an arm across my face to pour coffee into Margaret's cup and my stomach turned at his strong pungent body odour. I could almost taste the sweat rising like steam from his armpit.

Hastily burying my nose in my open shirt, I tried to inhale some aftershave to shake off the foul aroma.

As we ate, I had a chance to gather my thoughts on our table companions. My initial conclusions were favourable and I think we will enjoy their company over the coming weeks.

There are two more passengers yet to join us, but tonight, their seats at the other end of the oval table sat empty. I believed they were already onboard but having arrived late this evening, they had decided to skip the meal.

I wondered what they would be like and who they were? Would they prove as good company as the other two couples?

While we were eating the ship had let go of the mooring lines and had proceeded down the Southampton Waters, passing Hamble, Fawley and Calshot. It transited the Thom Channel and rounded Brambles Bank. Having disembarked the local pilot, the bell was rung for full away on passage, and this cruise truly got underway.

The meal over, we savoured a few moments on deck before walking to the other end of the ship, towards the Gaiety Theatre where Laura Drum the Entertainments Manager, was presenting a *Welcome onboard* show. I saw Margaret safely into her seat and feigned a need to visit the toilet. The confiscated wine played on my mind and I knew I wouldn't relax completely until I righted the wrong. I skipped down a deck or two and swiped my way into our cabin.

I grabbed a plastic bag and travelled again upstairs stuffing it in my jacket pocket. This time I headed for mid-ships and the shops which had opened, now that we were at sea. They were milling with passengers who excitedly wandered between the jewellery, watches, clothing, art, sportswear and of course alcohol on display.

I glanced around and couldn't see any security guards and the CCTV camera had lost some of its coverage with a tall cardboard mannequin of Captain Morgan holding a bottle of rum, obscuring the area to the left of the cash desk. I headed there and knelt down picking up two bottles of wine. I turned towards the cash desk, as though I intended to pay for them but instead I left with the bottles now hidden in my bag. I strolled away, along the shopping aisle, not daring to look back and felt like a naughty school kid, which I probably was, the last time I pulled this sort of stunt. Once I'd offloaded the bag in the cabin, I rejoined Margaret in the theatre.

After the show had finished we met Laura and her team of seven redcoats, as well as the resident dance/singing troupe, Topstars. As an added bonus, Lucy Miller, an ex-West End lead singer was brought forth to entertain us. It was a good show and I appreciated the energy and skill of the dancers as by now our energy was beginning to flag.

It was back to the cabin at to unpack and store away our stuff, which took the best part of an hour. We sipped on our illicit wine, which had been chilling in the cabins fridge. Margaret would have had a fit if she knew where it had come from.

Day 2

Wednesday 4th January.
Heading for the Azores.

The day started at 07:00, a tad too early for a holiday, I felt. The night had passed with fitful sleep. It wasn't my conscience nagging me or my inner self questioning my plans to approach this cruise in quite a different manner to the past. It wasn't the throbbing of the engines or the vibration of the same that had caused any grief. It was the lack of air conditioning in the cabin. We were by change too hot and then too cold throughout the night. We suffered from the Goldilocks syndrome. We couldn't get the temperature just right.

Margaret had taken a shower last night and discovered a leak in the chrome shower cable which meant more water sprayed wildly about the shower cubicle than fell on her head. The bed was also too hard on her arthritic hips and damaged back. We reported the shower problems and sought a mattress topper from Persel, my new best buddy. By the end of the day, any issues had been swiftly addressed, leaving me more than a little impressed, which isn't an easy feat to achieve.

We dressed and made our way to the Palace restaurant for breakfast and met a somewhat odd Scottish woman in her eighties called Laragh. She appeared to be lost. With her shock of white hair standing on end, she reminded me of Dr Emmett Brown from the *Back to the Future* movies.

Wearing only what appeared to be her cotton white nightdress and a light shawl, she strode along the open deck chatting away to Margaret. Having been on this ship before, we knew our way around, so we took her with us to the restaurant.

"Are you travelling alone, Laragh?" asked Margaret.

"Nae, love, ma sister is in the cabin, but she canna be bothered getting up this morning and has ordered breakfast in bed. Aye, no extra charge either but I'm ravenous and decided to get fed now. She could be sitting there another hour before the food arrives and I canna wait. I'll eat my own arm if I don't get food in the next five minutes."

We left her free-ranging in the buffet area and got our own breakfast. As is usual, people race about from station to station grabbing food as if the food may run out. They eventually return to their seats, plates piled high with food which they can't physically eat. Smartly dressed waiters silently move between tables taking unfinished meals back to the bins for disposal, probably to be dumped in the sea.

After breakfast, we took off on a walk around the promenade deck and got a blast of fresh air. A full circuit of the deck is half a kilometre, so we did a few laps before returning to the cabin. Getting around the deck today is like trying to run a marathon while surrounded by hundreds of slow-moving spectators who have stumbled onto the track. Some of them travel in large groups and frequently stop, without warning. Others walk against the flow, going anticlockwise around the deck so in traversing round blind corners you run the risk of colliding with them. God save us! There should be fast and slow lanes painted on the deck and everyone should be forced to walk clockwise. It's not rocket science. I feel my blood beginning to boil.

10:00. Beginners Bridge Class

The class was held in Lawton's room on deck 5, a long bright room near the library. The room's floor was carpeted and laid out with rows of small tables, each with a cluster of four chairs. A whiteboard had been erected halfway up the room and a middle-aged couple stood nearby sorting out boxes of paper and unpacking sets of cards, extracted from the wooden presses that ran the length of the room.

Neither of us has ever played bridge but it's popular in our village so we decided to learn, if only to challenge our brains. We found ourselves a table and were joined by Jimmy and Jennifer, two fellow passengers who arrived separately and asked if they could join our table.

Jennifer was tall, elegantly dressed and spoke with a crystal clear upper-class English accent. Her slim figure and lined face told of a life of challenges. She reached across the table and shook both our hands while introducing herself. A very English and formal introduction, I thought. She seemed quite shy, so I set to finding out more about her.

The class had yet to formally start and a loud buzz of

conversation filled the room. "Playing on your own, Jennifer?" I asked.

She nodded her head in confirmation. "I was widowed seven years ago and have holidayed with girlfriends ever since. Gwen isn't interested in bridge, so here I am, alone again." She smiled weakly but sounded more than slightly depressed by the prospect.

"And very welcome you are too." I said loudly, in a warm and positive voice. "Are you a complete beginner?"

She shook her head. "No, but as good as, I did attend classes on two earlier cruises, but they moved too fast for me and I failed to grasp the basics which led me to drop out. I'm hoping I'll get further this time. And you three? Have you played before?"

I turned around as Jimmy answered first. "I've never been to a bridge class as such, but I love card games and I learned quite a bit in a card school we had at work. My wife isn't in the best of health, so won't be joining us. How about you two?" he said looking at me and Margaret with a wry smile. "Can you play bridge?"

All eyes had turned to Margaret who happily spelt out our experience or lack of it. "Yes, Jimmy, Luke here is not a card player and he won't mind me saying so. I love card games although I haven't played bridge. I'm looking forward to learning it. There's a bridge club in our village, and on our return, I fully intend to pay them a visit."

Our conversation was halted when the teacher clapped his hands loudly and brought the class to order while introducing himself and his wife. On this cruise, Brendan and Shirley Flood would teach bridge to beginners, intermediate and advanced players. Classes would occur only on sea days as most passengers would go ashore on days when the ship was in port.

The first class each morning was for beginners, followed an hour later by the intermediate class and finally, an hour later again by the advanced players who got the opportunity to hone their skills. In the evening a session would be organised by Brendan and Shirley where players of any standard could play together.

Roughly the same approach was being adopted, I later found out, for the ballroom dancing classes which we joined an hour later.

I found I knew a bit more than I thought. It was only in the last ten minutes of the class that an actual game was started and we gathered around the table to watch the four chosen beginners play. We were just about to deal a hand ourselves when time ran out and the next class members, the intermediate class, began to appear. I deemed our first lesson a success, giving us something to build on for tomorrow.

11:00. Ballroom Dancing - Introduction to the Foxtrot

I don't dance. It's a pet phobia of mine. For years as a teenager and young adult, I attended events as the disc jockey, bringing along my equipment and hundreds of records to liven up many flat and house parties. My role as DJ afforded me the opportunity to avoid dancing, yet it was always a tug of war. I loved music and did long to have a secret bop in the corner when no one was looking. I was brutally self-conscious and couldn't just get blitzed enough in the pubs or clubs to let myself go.

But Margaret does dance and is very good at it. Having sat out our previous cruises, I sensed her longing to get out on the dance floor and I felt she should at least see me trying to make her happy, so there we stood, with about sixty others on the large shiny, wooden dance floor in the Pelican Ballroom.

Russian ex-professional prize-winning dancers, Roxanne and Thomak stood in the centre of the floor and took on the mission of trying to teach me some steps. Three steps, as it turned out.

Looking back on it, it was probably too much too soon.

I nailed the first one but floundered thereafter. Then blind panic set in, and I couldn't put one foot in front of the other. It was a disaster. I spent the entire lesson apologising to those I'd bumped into, or to those that had been forced to take sudden evasive action to avoid my size nines.

Even Margaret became frustrated with me.

For the second part of the lesson the instructors used the *watch-and-learn* approach. The men were split from women and taught each of their steps separately, then both were united, to execute the step together. Once the basics were grasped, we danced to the music.

It was all too much for an uncoordinated, stressed novice like me. I lasted another few minutes before giving up. We left saddened and met Brian and Anita, another Irish couple, who tried to comfort me, saying they'd had a similar start.

"Yeah," said Brian. "I'm twice your size and I've left more

pensioners limping in one class than arthritis has managed to cripple in a year. If they didn't move, I just bumped them on a bit, leading with our outstretched arms."

"It's true," chipped in Anita. "I just have to close my eyes at times and allow him to sweep me onwards, as he thinks he always knows best." She raised her eyes to the heavens.

We all laughed. "I saw you both in the Bridge class earlier. Fancy practising a few hands out of class? We could meet up in the afternoons and play for half an hour before dinner?" suggested Anita, as Brian led her away.

Margaret nodded agreement. She clearly thought it was a great idea.

I retreated to our cabin, settled my nerves and changed out of my soaking wet T-shirt before joining the choir in the Gaiety Theatre. I'm determined to stretch myself and take on new challenges. This may have unexpected consequences, but nothing tried means nothing gained and I'm determined to challenge myself on this cruise.

12:15. Ships Choir

We entered the Gaiety theatre and saw the choir had attracted a large number of passengers. The choirmaster stood on the stage next to a black piano with pianist already in position. We slid into the plush red velvet seats normally filled by the audience and received a copy of the lyric sheets for the five songs we were to tackle today.

The plan is that we will put on a performance at the halfway mark of the cruise, then a different choirmaster will set off with new songs for the remainder of the cruise and a second performance will be delivered before we dock in Southampton.

Lorcan Bond, who leads the ships jazz trio, had taken on the role of choirmaster and immediately split the choir into male-female, tenor, bass, alto and soprano. He had roughly sixty women and thirty men to work with.

I sat with a friendly Welshman, whose name I failed to catch, and Arthur, an Aussie who'd only flown into England days earlier to join the cruise.

Arthur, a chunky, bespectacled man in his early fifties, moved along the row to let me into a seat and then handed me the lyric sheet for *Food Glorious Food*.

"Have you sung before, Luke?" he asked.

"About six years ago I joined a local folk group that sang at church services a couple of times a year but that's about it," I said, "How about you?"

"Oh, yes, almost all year round with the Sydney Male Choristers and then on any cruises we take where choirs are formed. I love the coming together of the music, the harmonies and best of all, the day of the performance. My wife also sings." He pointed to a tall woman of a similar vintage seated near Margaret in the ladies group.

She saw him and waved vigorously back.

In the minutes that followed, I discovered Arthur and his wife would be staying on after we disembarked, for the Northern Lights cruise that followed. It seemed they worked six months of the year and cruised the other six. What a great way to live your life. Certainly, money was not an issue for this Australian couple or maybe they just managed it better than most of the rest of us.

Before we could speak further Lorcan got the session going with some breathing exercises. "All together now," he instructed. "Draw in deep breaths of air and sing with me. *I can sing high, I can sing low.*"

We did as he asked, starting at the lower end of the scale and then gradually rising up the scales until the men's singing became more like screeching. The limit had been reached.

Then he launched into the first number and the sound of one hundred voices brought to life the music of George Gershwin and his infectious *I've Got Rhythm* echoed around the aft end of the ship, as the theatre's outer door had been left ajar. When we finished the song, a smattering of applause rose up from the back of the theatre where some masochistic passengers had decided to sit and listen in to our early efforts.

I must say I enjoyed the session and Lorcan seemed impressed by our singing, but then, I'm sure he says that to every class. I felt rejuvenated by the experience and ate lunch a happier man.

Margaret talks to everyone we meet, wherever we are on the ship. Part of the fun of a cruise is the meeting of complete strangers whose life stories are so different from our own. Meetings often occur in the ship's restaurants where you share tables for half an hour and today was no exception. We sat with a blind woman in her eighties and her attentive young husband, a mere sixty-eight-years-old.

Alice sat with Derek in a window seat of the restaurant, her unseeing eyes oblivious to the endless white topped waves that rushed past. Her old thin fingers struggled to find the teacake on her plate. Derek gently moved them into position, and she gathered the cake with her shaking hand and raised it unsteadily to her lips.

"So when I retired in 2014," Derek told us, "we found ourselves rattling round this six-bedroom detached house which was far too big for us, now the children had grown up and gone. We suddenly realised we were slaves to the house and the acre of garden that went with it. Frankly, it all became too much to maintain so we sold it.

Alice added: "I mean, with all the children now in their forties and owning their own places in far-flung parts of the world, we knew they had no interest in keeping the place."

"So we put the money in the bank and have been cruising ever since." said Derek.

"My only regret is that we didn't do it sooner. There is a time in life for everything and we overstayed our time in that house. We had to move on. I mean, you can't take it with you, can you?"

"Now we can visit the kids and stay over for a few weeks before picking up another cruise or flying back to Old Blighty," chipped in Alice. And so we left them discussing their next cruise and enjoying each other's company and the freshly made cakes.

On Deck 13 we played a game of tennis on the netted court

before the cricket gang arrived for their scheduled session. The racquets and balls were freely available and left out in a plastic box for anyone to use. Behind the court, three netted golf driving ranges were in use. We may well be travelling across the Atlantic Ocean in winter, but the ship stabilisers keep the decks on an even keel.

However, an enjoyable tennis session was spoilt by the arrival of a very pushy entertainments team member who marched onto our court ten minutes early and evicted us mid-game.

I didn't protest at the time, but I was burning with rage inside.

"Sorry, Margaret, it looks like we're done for today" I said.

She nodded her head in agreement and we returned the equipment to the nearby box.

I stared long and hard at the short arse with a clipboard. Richard Chad, his name according to his badge, had just qualified for an entry on a most unwanted list. I left him setting up the cricket stumps and picking two teams to battle it out over the next two hours.

Down a level, we finally found the table tennis table deserted, with the daily competition over. We got three games in before quitting for a walk around the ship.

15:00. Ballroom Dancing - Intermediate Foxtrot

We had practised our dancing during lunchtime in our cabin and I had not improved. In fact, I think I was now more confused and left-footed than ever. Exasperation and terror had set in. However, I agreed to attend the afternoon class as the dance instructors did say they would reprise the morning steps before advancing to add another dance. So we found ourselves back amongst a slightly smaller but still considerable number of couples. I'm sorry to say the outcome for the afternoon session was almost as disastrous as the morning's had been. Margaret, God bless her, tried hard to help me and was as sure-footed and supportive as ever. She cut a graceful figure while this wretched limpet hung onto her shoulders and tripped her up at every opportunity. You see, after three steps, my mind freezes and I lose any recollection of what I've been taught. I then cast glances about the room trying to copy what other men are doing, indeed what the instructors are doing, what Margaret is doing until finally I suffer sensory overload and stop processing anything at all. It's truly pathetic but I will persist until she decides enough is enough.

The cruise had its first change to the published sailing itinerary within an hour of boarding yesterday. The captain announced that the US authorities had refused us permission to dock overnight in Fort Lauderdale so it's only one day there, not two. However, today he announced we now have an extra stop to enjoy, with a visit to Cape Canaveral. So, a visit to the NASA Kennedy Space Centre is on. We booked the excursion immediately and threw in another excursion, this time to the Everglades marshes via airboat for the next day.

In the Imperial Restaurant it was a full complement of diners for the first time. Craig and his wife, Mary, turned up to add a bit of sparkle to the table. They'd started their journey from the Scottish Highlands at 02.30 and, as suspected, after arriving worn out, had skipped dinner last night.

Craig was a tall well-built man whose face showed the weathering effects of being out on the land all year round. His wild white hair was a stranger to a comb, as much as his strong white bushy eyebrows were to a pair of scissors.

Mary, a short stout woman with sparkling blue eyes and an easy smile took a seat next to her husband, flipped out his jacket pocket flap and straightened his tie. It was clear from the off that she was the boss in this relationship, a benign dictator.

"So, Craig, tell us about life in the Highlands?" ventured Frank.

"You're a farmer I believe," said Roger.

"Aye, a farmer I used to be, but I'm retired now. My two sons have farms nearby and they now work my land too."

"He didn't stop farming until he hit eighty," said Mary, "and only this week I had to climb up the Shelly Mountains after him, to get him to come home for his dinner."

"He keeps you fit then," said Rose with a smile.

"We're on this cruise so I can stop him working himself to death." Mary smiled. "And yes, he keeps me on my toes. We live in an isolated part of the Highlands and the emergency services would take hours to reach us, so I've done a first aid course myself. We even have a defibrillator in the yard," she bragged, "and I know how to use it. Please God I'll never have to"

Craig nodded.

Our new dinner guests fitted in easily and by the end of the meal we were a single homogenous group. Margaret left the restaurant drooling over Craig and Mary's soft Scottish accents. We took our seats with Brian and Anita, the Irish couple, whom we bumped into again on the walk to the theatre.

In the Gaiety Theatre, the star turn tonight is Richie Rowe, a singer who won a TV talent competition in the 1970s and managed one hit single during his fifteen minutes of fame. At that time, there were only two TV channels in the UK and this show, *Big Chance,* attracted weekly audiences of twenty million viewers. Richie won it fifteen weeks in a row, an unheard of and never repeated achievement. He's made a career as a cabaret artist out of a fifteen-week phenomenon that occurred forty years ago, but more power to him. He seems a lovely guy and was applauded off the stage.

Afterwards, there was just time for a whiskey in the Hawks Inn perched on the front of Deck 13. The ship's seven-piece jazz band played some George Benson and Lee Morgan standards before we retired to bed, our cup overflowing with food, drink and music to feed the soul.

Day 3

Thursday 5th January.
Somewhere beyond the Bay of Biscay.

We rose early, having slept well for the first night in a long time. We caught breakfast in the Palace buffet restaurant which required a walk across the open wet decks in windy conditions. We ate well and popped down to the library to collect some books for Margaret who reads detective and murder novels by the dozen.

10:00. Beginners Bridge Class

This class was one where we were left to play on our own. We actually completed four hands in the allotted time, and I felt good progress had been made. I'm beginning to like both Jennifer and Jimmy who make up our table of four. Jimmy plays a mean hand of cards quickly while Jennifer takes ages to play her cards but invariably plays the correct card and wins her contracts.

I am becoming aware of the next bridge class, the Intermediate players, who are gathering prematurely around our table and are beginning to annoy me.

Why haven't people any patience anymore?

Everything has to be *right now*. I gazed at them with bemusement.

Aren't they the same generation as us?

Did we, not all learn basic manners when at school?

Back in the day, we grew up respecting everyone older than us. God help you if you didn't doff your cap to someone you met. You'd get a clip over the ear or something stronger.

How did this lot not experience the same?

I resumed my concentration on Brendan's words, but one elderly lady stood just to my right and spoke loudly to her partner as if he was standing half a mile away. On and on she droned about their presidential suite and the complimentary flowers that had greeted them when they boarded. My hopes of following Brendan's final instructions evaporated completely when she suddenly sneezed violently and loudly. I felt a layer of spittle spray across my bare neck and head.

"For Christ sake woman will you kindly cover your mouth when you sneeze?" I heard myself shout as I leapt out my seat. "The contents of your nose have just landed on the back of my head!"

I reached up to feel what had actually landed and theatrically removed my hand to display what I had found to a stunned gathering. My palm was now coated in a wet, glistening mass of clear phlegm.

The old dear had the grace to look mortified and chastened before she managed a whimpered, "I'm so sorry." She then burst into tears and was led away, comforted by her equally frail partner. The old witch had played this game before. One hundred eyes followed their progress to the door and then switched back to staring coldly at me.

"Well really?" I stuttered "I mean–who got sprayed with bacteria just now? Me or her?" I swiftly realised I was now public enemy number one. I sat back down in my chair.

Margaret came to my aid and handed me a large tissue which I used to mop up the phlegm and Brendan declared the class over.

I was now grateful for the mindless chatter which resumed with gusto. I was aware my face was the colour of beetroot but I could do little about it. That's how my body reacts to stressful situations. I'm sure my blood pressure had gone through the roof. I left the room conscious that I'd lost the sympathy vote. "Well, fuck 'em all" I muttered under my breath.

11:00. Ballroom Dancing - Beginners Cha Cha Cha

Here was a fresh start on a new but fast dance, so I could safely forget all that I had learned or failed to learn yesterday. I mastered one step and Margaret reckoned we should quit while we were ahead, so, before I got confused, we left the large class to proceed without us. If I can master yesterday's four steps and the simple cha-cha-cha start, Margaret will be happy.

Later that morning, we met another couple who were struggling with the dance steps too. We all felt the instructors had pushed on far too fast and should have spent longer bedding in the basics.

What didn't help was having the experienced dancers attend our beginner's class. They gave the instructors a false impression as to how well the class was coping with the speed of learning. This man had dropped out at the same point as me, but still, being eager to learn, we all stood by the table tennis table as Margaret ran through the basics again.

I feel useless and, if I'm honest, I believe the instructors, Roxanne and Thomak are failing us—the real beginners. I'm toying with giving them two slots on my list of offenders purely because they are crap teachers. It's a hypothetical list of offenders and I enjoy toying with the idea of taking the law into my own hands.

I'm sure they have spotted me on the crowded dancefloor stumbling about and just decided to do absolutely nothing to help me. I decided to give them one last chance to avoid the executioner's noose.

12:15. Ships Choir

Almost one hundred souls gathered for day two of the choir rehearsals and we settled into the same seats and partners as we had yesterday. We ran through three new songs, *Sunrise Sunset* from *Fiddler on the Roof*, a complicated *Lightning Tree* and *Bye, Bye Love*. My two singing companions were already seated when I arrived and had saved me the lyric sheets.

"Sung any of these before?" I asked Arthur, as I settled in my seat.

"Oh, yes, only the *Lightning Tree* is new to me" he replied. "I'll have to concentrate when Lorcan gets to that one because I like to be note-perfect when I sing and I don't even know the tune,"

Arthur answered.

Our Welsh companion, whose name continues to escape me, knew all three songs so I was the odd one out in not knowing any of them. Since he knew the *Lightening Tree,* he sang it through, and I could see Arthur coming to grips with the complexity of the tune. Within minutes the session started and my colleagues sang with heart and brilliance.

The songs that were strangers to me a few minutes earlier have now been indelibly absorbed into my brain. Lorcan, our choirmaster, also proclaimed his surprise with our speedy mastery of the songs but again, being cynical, I think it's just one strand of his clever motivational strategies. I, for my part, was left quite choked up by the beautiful singing and the lyrics of *Sunrise Sunset*. What a moving piece of music. I'll never keep it together on stage when we perform publically. I'll just stand there sobbing my heart out.

A quick lunch was taken before we again nipped onto the tennis court and played for half an hour before the cricket team arrived. Richard Chad was again in charge and once more pushed his luck by lowering our net while chatting to other cricketing passengers, apparently oblivious of our presence.

"Hold on a minute" I shouted and advanced towards him.

He glanced over his shoulder as if suddenly aware of my existence for the first time.

"Yes?" he uttered.

"We are not finished…" I said, squinting at his name tag, "…Richard. I've got 13:52 on my watch. There are another eight minutes before the cricket is due to start."

He had the good grace to look at his watch. "Well, I need time to set up the area for the cricket, so you'll just have to finish up now."

He proceeded to lower the tennis net and turned his back on me. I stared helplessly at him and became aware of the amused look in the eyes of the on-looking cricketers.

"C'mon, Margaret, we'll get lunch," I said, but in my head, I was halving Richard's odds of walking off this ship. We left the netted court and descended to the open deck where Margaret beat me soundly in the table tennis. In truth, my mind was still distracted by Richard. I hadn't envisaged wiping out crew members but sometimes you just have to go with the flow and this guy was clearly being brought to my attention. It was time for a cup of coffee and a bite to eat.

15:15. Harmony Twist in the Pacific Lounge.

It was raining lightly out on the deck but here in the lounge, it was time to remove cardigans and coats. Several hundred passengers had gathered to enjoy the first classical concert of the cruise. Peter Row, a prize-winning pianist from Cornwall, and Olelandi Hala, a brilliant violinist from Ukraine, played some pieces composed between 1755 and 1980. The duo earned the prolonged applause that followed their performance.

We chatted away with more passengers before returning to our cabin to change for the first of fourteen formal dress nights. As an extra bonus, we had an invite to meet the ship's captain. It wasn't a private gathering, but one we were to share with several hundred others, as it turned out.

Margaret visited the toilet before showering. She was a few minutes in the shower before stepping out into a flooded bathroom. The toilet cistern's overflow pipe was pumping out water. Thinking quickly she realized the toilet bowl was full to the brim so pushed the knob and this time it worked. A loud whoosh and the vacuum driven system sucked the water away in a nano-second. She threw down a pile of towels to soak up the water that threatened to overflow onto the bedroom carpet.

We hurriedly dressed and stopped for a few pictures by the foot of the atrium's staircase. Up two flights we climbed before walking along the inner promenade, a carpeted walkway until we reached the Imperial Lounge.

We entered a room sparkling with bright lights, sharp suits and glamorous women. The ship's officers decked out in uniform formed a welcoming line just inside the door, with the captain standing at the end. We shook hands with all in turn and then took a glass of sparkling wine from the nearest waiter.

Looking around at the smartly dressed passengers, I noticed a fair number of them had been in the armed forces, their jacket breast pockets glittering with rows of braid and silver. White-jacketed waiters floated by circulating through the crowd with trays of drinks. It was a scene that could have been played out in any one of the last hundred years.

Finally, Captain Peter Cox took to the stage. He may have been short in stature, but he carried an easy confidence as he spoke off the cuff to the gathered throng.

"On behalf of Octavian Cruises and the ship's officers and crew, I'd like to welcome you all on board the SS Azara, on this her first voyage into the Amazon Basin. This cruise has been in the planning for almost a year and I am delighted to be on board this maiden voyage to Manaus. I was last in charge of the SS Azara fifteen years ago and I must say, following the recent refit, she looks better than ever."

A small ripple of applause greeted these words.

"We are delighted to have you on board and will endeavour to ensure that you have a safe and very pleasant cruise. I checked the weather forecast before greeting you this evening and am delighted to say, we departed just in the nick of time, as heavy snowfalls and blizzards are forecast for Scotland overnight and they're expected to spread across the whole of the United Kingdom by noon tomorrow."

A childish feeling of *na na na na na na* rippled through the passengers as they felt a certain smugness about their decision to book this cruise in the first place and a distinct lack of sympathy for the poor sods left behind.

Captain Cox went on: "The sea conditions for us over the next few days are forecast to be moderately rough, but I will do my best to navigate around any storms that should head our way. Thank you for your patience and I wish you a very happy voyage."

He stepped down off the stage and was instantly surrounded

by fawning passengers who had regressed to being school kids on a day out, staring adoringly at him, hanging on his every word, asking stupid questions and generally boring the pants off the supreme commander of this vessel.

The waiters now disappeared along with the glasses of free wine and the passengers funnelled out of the theatre and off to the first formal black and white dinner of the cruise. We made our way to our table and found our fellow diners already ensconced. The table glistened with sparkly dresses and black suits. Even Craig, our Highlands farmer had dug out a black suit and white silk shirt. He capped it off with a sparkling black and gold dickie-bow tie.

Mary, his wife, wore white pearl earrings and an elegant full-length purple gown hanging bare off the shoulders.

Roger, Frank and Jill all sported military braid on their clothing while Rose and Margaret wore long dresses with faux fur shawls.

"What a sight we all are," I announced, as I sat down. "Well done everyone." I took a chance and tried to find out more about my fellow diners. "Roger, can you tell me about the medals you're wearing tonight?"

For a moment I thought I'd overstepped the mark as he looked somewhat displeased by my question.

"I apologise if you don't want to discuss it, Roger. I'm sorry I brought the matter up," I said. I must have hit a raw nerve. He thought for a moment and waved away my retraction and decided to answer me anyway.

"This one here is the South Atlantic medal and I got that for services in the Falklands in 1982. Frank has one of these too. The others I picked up while seconded to the Metropolitan Police to assist in the Iranian Embassy siege in 1980. I won't say more than that though, as my role is still covered by the Official Secrets Act. I just did my duty and it's a long time ago now."

I made a mental note that Roger was one person I must handle with care. His involvement with the SAS (Special Air Service) Regiment meant he had, at the very least, finely tuned combat skills and a sharp quick mind. Any slip-ups in conversations at the dinner table could prove fatal to me.

Frank lightened up the mood by asking Margaret about the gold brooch she was wearing and she cheerfully explained how my mother, God rest her soul, had pressed it into her hand, as a dying wish that she should keep it and wear it proudly.

"Your mum would have loved this cruise, Luke," Margaret said to me. "If only your dad had shown the slightest interest in cruising…"

"Yes. If only," I answered.

This evening in the Gaiety Theatre the Judy Garland Show was performed by Rita Watson who looked the spitting image of Judy Garland. She not only sang like her but had her manner of speaking and moving down to a T. I enjoyed the high energy performance very much and was amazed that she seemed to sing her heart out, as her performance had to be repeated an hour later for the second sitting audience. All the evening shows are repeated twice each night as the formal dinners, to cater for the two thousand passengers on board are served in two sittings, at 18:30 for the early diners and at 20:30 for the late.

We travelled again to the Hawks Inn to wind down with the Lorcan Bond Trio playing laid-back jazz standards. The room was dimly lit, and a scattering of well-dressed passengers sat in booths listening to a selection of 1920's jazz numbers while uniformed waiters quietly circled taking orders and delivering drinks.

We descended by lift and took a stroll outside on the promenade to experience the offering of a cold blast from a North Atlantic gale. We fought our way along the wooden deck as the ship rose and fell with the waves. We gratefully levered open a door some fifty yards further down the deck and rejoined the living.

It was almost midnight when we slid the card into the cabin door lock.

Exhausted, we climbed into bed after each of us using the bathroom.

A few minutes later, I became aware of the continuous sound of running water. I jumped out of the bed and flung open the bathroom door hitting the light switch to find water again pumping out of the side of the toilet bowl and onto the moulded plastic bathroom floor. At least this time I knew what to do. I punched the button and the vacuum flush drained the overflowing toilet bowl. Now it was just the inch of water washing about the bathroom floor to deal with.

I called reception and within minutes staff appeared and sucked the water up. However further investigation revealed water had filtered under the carpet just outside the bathroom door. This cabin seems jinxed.

We fell into bed again, well after midnight and slept soundly.

Day 4

Friday 6th January.
Closing in on the Azores.

This morning we left the cabin to the maintenance team and had breakfast.

Free to wander, we circumnavigated the promenade deck, clocking up the steps, when we heard the Captain announce another change to the itinerary.

10:00. Beginners Bridge Class

Now we are nine tables strong. Today was all about scoring and bidding and not a single hand of cards was played. Brendan asked if we wanted a recap or to press ahead and the louder *let's press ahead* group won the day. Our table resolved to get a practice game in before the next session. If I was seeking a challenge with bridge it is delivering in spades. My head is throbbing after an hour of concentration. Right now I'd be happy to postpone the actual playing of hand, indefinitely.

11:00. Ballroom Dancing - Beginners Sequence Dancing

Again a large group of dancers materialized in the Pelican ballroom. The Russian instructors seemed more than a little irritated with the crowded dancefloor and excited students. It's obviously going to be more difficult to teach such a number with space at a premium. Roxanne informed us that though less complex in steps, there were many more steps to be memorised in sequence dancing. Also, though no lead and follow had to be catered for, the sequences themselves were quite challenging. We started with the box step, but that's all I can remember of the class.

Within a matter of minutes, I stormed off the floor, red with embarrassment, hot with a fever brought on by my efforts and my frustration with the dance we had to execute. I brushed through the other couples, their eyes burning into me as I went, and I didn't stop until I stood well away from the Ballroom—and far away from the classes probing eyes. I was aware of Margaret standing next to me, who had followed close on my tail.

"What brought that on?" she challenged me.

"You saw it all," I replied, curtly. "I tried so hard, but I just couldn't do the steps and rather than show you up, I cut my losses and ran."

She shrugged her shoulders and grabbed my arm. "Don't worry, love, there is more to life than dancing."

It took quite a while for me to shake off the black cloud that hung over me. We slipped upstairs for coffee and before long, my good humour had returned.

12:15. Ships Choir

My singing buddies were all in place when I arrived. We were still holding steady with the large numbers. We recapped five of the six songs already covered, and, if I'm honest, I thought the singing was of a lower standard than in earlier sessions.

Certainly, there was no sign of praise, heaped on us in earlier sessions by our choirmaster Lorcan. We were making silly mistakes and I feel we were given a reality check. We will have to work harder in days to come. An extremely well known if not boring song, *You Are My Sunshine*, was added to our repertoire, and we finished the class on time.

We took advantage of lunchtime to commandeer the tennis court and had another session. This time we had finished by the time Richard and his cricket cronies arrived. He made no effort at building bridges with me and behaved as if nothing was amiss between us. But there is Richard, and ignoring it isn't going to make it go away. He's just tightened the noose around his neck, metaphorically speaking.

Lunch was small and we ate late and met up with Brian and Anita at four to play a few practice hands of bridge. Upon strong recommendations, we, did not play together as a team.

"Apparently, a man knifed and killed his wife because she played a bad hand of cards," Margaret said. "I heard Brendan talk about the incident today with Shirley. It's a true story as apparently, they both knew the couple in question. "

"Yes," Anita interjected. "Shirley said she never knew what the woman saw in him in the first place. He was one of those biker types with tattoos on his knuckles, you know the sort."

"Not your average bridge player then," I ventured.

"No, quite so, but I can see how it could happen." Brian smiled, casting a sideways glance at his wife.

The session went well, with honours even, 2-2 and we all gained a bit more confidence from the exercise.

We returned to our cabin and its damp carpet, to glam up again for dinner.

We joined our table of fellow diners as the menus were being distributed. The conversation was good, and we appeared to have gelled as a group, even if we don't seek out each other's company away from the table. The food was, as always, very good and the waiters were respectful and courteous. Roger suggested we mix the seating positions tomorrow night and we all agreed. Craig, the Scots farmer, is very nice to talk to, but his accent and voice is so soft I struggle to hear him even when seated next to him.

Afterwards, we rushed to get the best seats in the place to see Richie Rowe's final show. I can honestly say I have never seen Margaret laugh so often and so uncontrollably as she did in the following forty-five minutes. Richie finished off with a rousing rendition of the *Wild Rover* and the audience sang along, none louder than my Margaret who clapped and stood to wave him off stage.

Feeling pumped and upbeat, we ducked in to see the Revolver band, playing the sounds of the sixties, to a packed lounge and then into the Pelican bar to watch experienced ballroom dancers including Brian and Anita execute the correct steps to various dance styles.

Afterwards, we headed to the Hawks Inn where the Lorcan

Bond Trio and the SS Azara Jazz orchestra were playing jazz till midnight.

I ordered a beer and Margaret settled for a gin and tonic while the music washed over us. The night was going well and I was relaxing at last, when I saw Richard Chad appear at the bar. He was off duty and was dressed in a casual suit, but I recognized him all the same. He didn't recognise me, probably because I was dressed in a black suit and not a pair of shorts and a t-shirt.

It was a pure coincidence, that when I headed out of the lounge to the men's toilets a little later, I found Richard on my tail.

An idea began to form in my head, fed by my growing resentment for the small dictator Richard truly was.

I exited the lounge and glanced to my right and yes, there it was, the sea door out onto the open deck. I grabbed the handle and checked it would open. Looking back I saw Richard's shoulder appear, and, in one motion, I grabbed him around the neck and pulled him head-first and out through the doorway. I appeared to have taken him completely by surprise.

He didn't utter a word or any resistance, as I dragged him across the open deck and thrust his slight body up and over the rails, into the turbulent North Atlantic Sea.

I stood there holding my breath, in total shock, as I stared over the wooden rail. In the pitch-black darkness of night and, with the ship travelling at 18 knots, Richard was gone in seconds.

Had I actually gone through with it? I pinched myself, and no, it wasn't a dream. I glanced up and down the deck, relieved there were no other passengers about. It was stupid of me to have taken this chance but then I have a history of procrastination. I endlessly think things over and end up doing, nothing. Maybe it had to be this way.

    I stepped back inside the sea door and closed it behind me, trying to calm my raging pumping heart. I glanced at my watch. The whole episode had taken less than seven seconds. My hair had been blown to kingdom come, so I continued to the toilet where I straightened myself up and splashed a handful of icy water on my face before grabbing a few tissues and returning to the lounge.

Day 5

Saturday 7th January.
Docked in - Praia Da Victoria, Azores.

I had a rough night. The source of my heaving stomach was not the rolling movement of the ship or the murder of Richard Chad, but I suspect the pint of John Smith bitter I'd supped in the Hawks Inn. Maybe the combination of all three had played their part in leaving me feeling quite fragile this morning. I've never before acted on impulse like I did last night. In the cold light of day, I am experiencing some regret but also a measure of astonishment that I found, from somewhere, the steely determination to act. But actions have consequences and I fear I may have jeopardised our future together by this one reckless act.

Our arrival at Praia Da Victoria has been delayed by five hours as we are now due to dock at 13:00. I suspect the delay is linked to the disappearance of Richard.

I'd switched on the TV during the night and took the navigational statistics off the screen. The ship had definitely gone backwards while passengers slept and had only resumed its normal course at 06:00. Presumably, the night search yielded nothing. There was certainly no mention of anything untoward happening, to any of the passengers in the daily newsletter or in the First Officers 08.00 report, delivered over the ships PA system. The captain himself came on at 08.30 and apologised for the ships late arrival in Praia Da Victoria but, tellingly, didn't explain why we were late in.

Hopefully, that would be the end of the matter, but I doubt it.

Margaret took advantage of the delay and decided we would do the laundry instead. The nearest launderette is almost directly above our room and we managed to get a wash on straight away.

While waiting for the laundry, we found a quiet buffet restaurant.

Doing a detour on the way back to the cabin, we loaded our clothes into a dryer. An older woman helped Margaret with the setting. Then they chatted like old friends while I flicked through a few of the complimentary magazines.

A while later, a ship's security officer walked into the laundry and my heart missed a beat. I felt my cheeks flush and I turned away from him until I regained my composure.

He didn't seem to notice me as he retrieved his washing from a washing machine.

"Morning, ladies" he uttered in a Scottish accent, as he shoved his clothes into a dryer. "Have yea got an exciting day planned?"

"Yes, thanks and you?" Margaret smiled.

"Oh, I'm looking forward to a few hours of shut-eye now. I was on the bridge for twelve hours straight last night. I'm completely knackered. The bed is all I'm good for!"

Having gathered her dried clothes Margaret picked up a

handbag and slung the strap over her shoulder and made for the door.

The other woman reacted swiftly and reached over and removed the bag's strap from Margaret's shoulder.

"What the…?" Margaret uttered as the bag was taken from her arms and we all turned to look at her.

"That's my bag, thank you!" The woman smiled, placing it on the chair by her side.

"Oh, my God" blurted Margaret. "I thought it was mine. I have one almost identical. I do apologise!"

Immediately, smiling, the officer produced his walkie-talkie and pretended to speak loudly into it. "Alert all stations. We have a 94 occurring on Deck 9 in the laundry. Please dispatch two armed officers immediately!"

Red-faced but laughing, Margaret took the jibbing well and we left the room pronto.

We took a stroll on deck and watched the docking process. We were berthed in a large semi-circular harbour. The SS Azara was by far the biggest ship in port, the rest being small fishing vessels.

A fleet of shuttle buses were running every ten minutes to and from the town, about a mile further round the bay.

The day looked grey and clouds covered the upper half of the mountains. The captain had forecast temperatures of sixteen to nineteen degrees, but at that hour it looked unlikely and we took cardigans and raincoats.

Emerging from the bus we found the town was filled with

hundreds of passengers. They were everywhere. Around every corner were more and more ancient, slow-moving, cruise passengers. The shuttle bus stopped outside the Santander Bank which offered free Wi-Fi for about fifty yards in all directions so that was where a lot of passengers had headed. Octavian Cruises and their expensive Wi-Fi packages caused many of their passengers to ignore the shops and sights and instead spend hours on their phones and tablets reconnecting with families at home.

It was amusing and sad in equal measure to watch octogenarians produce shiny new tablets, the plastic film still on the screen and watch them trying to find the settings option to connect and send messages home that all was well.

We pressed on into the town after sending our own messages. We walked on down the streets and along a promenade to a sandy beach. Following a steep path past the yacht club and moored boats which led to a cliff top, it was a challenge even for us, relatively young passengers. In amongst the volcanic rocks that made up the steps and walls, thin rock coloured lizards lay warming themselves in the sun. We climbed the zigzagging sets of steps to reach a tall statue of Christ that stood on the hilltop overlooking the harbour. Given Margaret's bad hips and dodgy knee, she did brilliantly, and we stayed a few minutes to enjoy the view and gather our breath.

By the time we had descended the steps we were both melting from the extra layers of clothing we'd worn. We made our way back into the narrow, windy streets of the town and sought out the ancient church in its centre.

The building was lavishly decorated with gold leaf painted walls, ceilings and pillars. There stood multiple statues of Jesus, Catholic priests and monks from centuries past. The baby Jesus was still in his crib by the altar and the Christmas tree still stood in the body of the church. Some Catholics celebrate the Epiphany on January 6th as well as Christmas on 25th December.

An ancient church organ, operated by stops, that were pulled in and out, stood to the right of the altar. A massive wooden chandelier hung from the ceiling half-way down the centre aisle.

I knelt alongside Margaret and said a small prayer of thanks for letting me dispense with Richard Chad in such a speedy and painless manner. I'd had no time to worry or doubt my actions. My victim likewise had been given no time to contemplate his fate. I have to point out now that I'm not religious other than having a lingering fear that there just might be a great all-powerful being, so bending a knee in this holy place, might be a moment well invested.

At the bus stop, the coach was collecting more than dispersing. It was now mid-afternoon and the tired passengers were returning to the ship. We motored back along the flat terrain and I took a few shots of the SS Azara, that being our first opportunity to see her from a distance since boarding and she gleamed in the setting sunlight.

At dinner, the couples split up again around the table and I sat with Roger and Craig on either side of me. I must say the conversation flowed as did the stories and jokes.

"I had to visit my local bank branch recently to collect some cash for this cruise" said Roger, "and I found just a row of machines lined up along the wall. I looked around for a human being, a bank official, but couldn't find one. Now I may be in my eighties but I'd like to think that I'm pretty computer literate. I had a look at the terminals but I was damned if I could find the machine I needed to use."

"So what did you do? asked Craig.

"Well, I stood by the customer service desk and tinkled the bloody bell for a couple of minutes until this young chap appeared and approached me."

"I hope you gave him a right telling off!" I interjected.

"I said I'd like to speak to some human being and not just these bloody machines." Roger gestured wildly as he probably did on the day. "And he said," continued Roger. "You are in a bank sir and not attending a counselling service. Please use the machines provided. If you want to talk to someone, I recommend you ring the Samaritans!"

A collective gasp sounded from around the table.

"I damn near clocked him" said Roger, the colour rising in his cheeks. He took another sip of his whiskey "I was banking with this crowd before he was born, and I told him so."

"Cheeky Devil," Frank added smiling broadly.

Craig then spoke up "Aye, they shut the last bank in our village, six years ago and this year the post office is about to close. If it goes then the supermarket and petrol station's days are numbered. The last thing to go will be the village pub which has been open since 1754. It's only open in the evenings now as it is. It wouldn't take much to snuff out the last bit of life in the village. Sure the churches are three-quarters empty and there are precious few young people staying around the Highlands these days. Rural life is dying."

It was the truth. I could see the same erosion happening in my own village in Ireland. Farming is now a one-man job. In decades gone by, teams of labourers and farm hands would have been employed for months in the autumn during the harvesting of crops. Now one man with a tractor and the right bailing equipment can cut, gather in, wrap in black plastic, and store away thousands of bails of grass for use as fodder for animals in the winter months. Similarly, one man can dig furrows, spread seeds, water and harvest acres of vegetables. Rural life is now a very solitary existence.

"What did you all make of Praia Da Victoria?" I asked.

"We didn't bother getting off the ship" answered Roger. "We've been around the island a dozen times before, so we stayed on board and enjoyed a few hours by the pool when the sun came out."

"You didn't miss much," added Craig. "We ate in a Spanish restaurant in the town, but a lot of the shops were closed. It might have been that they were closed for lunch but we didn't hang around to find out. T'was a bit of a sleepy old place."

Throughout the meal I gently probed my companions to see if any fallout had reached their ears about the missing crewman. It appeared there wasn't as much as a whisper that anything was amiss and I left the table marginally more assured that his absence would be a matter not communicated to passengers anytime soon.

The Gaiety Theatre was eighty per cent full tonight for the first show from a Liverpudlian comedian, Roy Flem. He made the most of his ability to mimic regional British accents and to tell one-liners. Roy came across as very self-assured and motored through the performance never quite hitting the heights that Richie Rowe had achieved.

After the show, we walked with Brian and Anita to the midships Pelican bar and ballroom dancing where the now familiar Lorcan Bond Jazz Trio were playing ballroom dance standards. Together we watched the experienced couples float around the floor, always in a clockwise direction and always looking assured and graceful.

Margaret and I decided on an early night and started off towards our cabin. It was 22:00 and the ship was humming along nicely.

As we descended the graceful swirling stairs of the bejewelled atrium, the sound of a piano being played, a floor above, wafted towards us on the breeze. Another activity-packed day had gone by.

I lay awake in bed thinking, just thinking. Richard Chad was dead, but no one seemed to care. I scanned the newsletter, listened to the ship's announcements and watched the crew going about their duties. I felt sure by now his absence had been spotted, his bunk left un-slept in, his duties undone. The ship's management would have furtively carried out a thorough search of fifteen decks and all storage areas before stopping and turning the ship about. I would imagine a protocol exists for that type of occurrence and in it, orders were no doubt laid down that passengers are not to be made aware of its occurrence, which suited me fine.

I'd done a little research before leaving home and had found, that deaths at sea are rarely reported on in the national press or online websites. Not unless it's truly sensational in form, for example, *Body in a suitcase found floating in the sea, Husband kills wife and is stopped at the airport with kids about to fly home.* No, I am talking about the more humdrum deaths, like the passenger whose body just gave out during the holiday, the heart that stopped beating, the brain that stopped processing, the lungs that stopped pumping. Those types of deaths have never been communicated to fellow passengers *during* a cruise. The cruise lines have taken the decision to keep deaths on board a secret from passengers.

So, the SS Azara, carrying 2,012 passengers with an average age of seventy-three, would surely expect to lose several of them through natural causes over the duration of a standard cruise.

Day 6

Sunday 8th January.
At Sea sailing to Bermuda.

We planned to have breakfast and skip the Bridge class in favour of the church service, but this morning didn't work out as planned. We ended up staying as Brendan Flood covered the scoring mechanism for bridge and boy is it complex.

With my head wrecked by bridge rules and protocol, it was on up to the netted tennis court where three men, Bill, Alan and Phil awaited us.

Margaret played the first short tennis doubles match but didn't enjoy the extra person standing by and watching so she left the court to us four men and sat nearby.

I played rather too long and with no time to change clothes, I attended the choir practice sweaty and with my shirt sticking to my back. It was in the Atlas Lounge this time and Lorcan added two new numbers to our repertoire. A Les Miserables song *Do you hear the people sing* and the Beatles standard *Let it be*.

"I want passion" said Lorcan, conductor baton in hand, leaning out over the podium and surveying the golden oldies choir before him. "Give me passion!"

"Don't we all," muttered Arthur in reply, rather louder than he had intended. It got a few belly laughs from the pensioners around him. Passion is at a premium when you reach deeper into old age. It's a case of saving your supply and using it sparingly. The voices unified and got into the Les Miserables song which was a marching tune, strident and loud. Everyone knew the Beatles *Let It Be*. It's an anthem of a generation, probably looking at this lot, their children's generation!

We changed in our cabin and walked to the pool at the stern of the shop. Margaret went ahead of me and climbed down the steps to enter the water leaving her white towel on a nearby sun lounger. She was a strong swimmer which was fortunate as the pool water she swam in began to change its form and shape dramatically. Looking back on it I can only guess that the ship's captain altered the course of the ship for, without notice, the SS Azara now sailed forward, crashing into the waves and rocking from side to side rather than slicing smoothly through them.

The water in the pool, once calm and placid now massed at one end before rushing to the other like a mini tsunami. It crashed into the far end sending a wall of water high and out of the pool and far across the deck. Then back it came with equal force but in the opposite direction! Another spray of water was flung far and wide across vacant sun loungers.

Initially, Margaret, bobbing in the pool, seemed oblivious to the change of circumstance. Then she sought a safe handrail to hang onto but within seconds she found herself sucked down to the pool floor in a swirling mass of water that was picking her up and slamming her against the sides of the pool.

Margaret managed a startled cry of, "Help!" before swallowing a mouthful of water and being pulled under again.

I ran to the pool and threw her one end of a towel. I retained the other and slowly I pulled her to the side of the pool and then out of the water. Together, shaken and panting, we sat on deck chairs and watched the raging sea that was now being replicated in the on-deck pool.

We returned again to the cabin and got changed for cards with Brian and Anita. The bridge games went un-eventfully and everyone had a moment when they played well. Brian and Margaret are by far the better players, but bridge empowers those with poor hands to make the good cardholders fight for their tricks. We played as long as we could and left to get ready for another formal night of dining. Margaret wore the grey dress she wore at her daughter's wedding last summer. With sparkly grey shoes to match, she looked gorgeous.

We posed for several of the ship's photographers and had shots taken at the table before enjoying the best meal so far. Normally I don't comment on the food. but the main course featured a serving of lamb shank to die for. All eight diners chose it from the menu and weren't disappointed. The meat just fell from the bone and really you didn't need teeth as it dissolved in your mouth. The table continued to change their seating order and the conversation was the better for it. I sat next to Rose, Roger's wife.

"So, Rose, how did you guys meet?" I asked as I stretched

across the table for the wine decanter and refilled my glass.

"Well, I'm sure you'd expect me to answer something like, in a bar, or at a party, or through mutual friends, but we actually met online through a singles club. No-one was more surprised than me that it worked out. My sister had been at me for a few years to get active online and find someone. You're not getting any younger she'd say and I'd fob her off. Anyway, one night when we'd had a few glasses of wine she created a profile for me and there I was, added to this club.

"How long ago was this?" I probed.

"Lord! It must be twenty or more years ago," she answered. She went on to tell me they had both been married previously, for decades, so this story taught me two things. One, never neglect your partner as you age and two, there is always the chance of love no matter how old you are.

"So what is your story?" Rose shot back. "We know so little about you and Margaret. When did you both meet?"

"Oh, it was much like yourselves really," I answered. "We met late in life. I'd been living and working in London for years when Margaret was seconded into a twelve-month IT project that I was already working on. We bonded over many late nights in the office and then, after work, got to know each other over a few drinks and voila! Here we are."

We are served each night by two youthful and charming waiters of Goan descent. Ali, our chief waiter, and Hamoud his junior. It took me many days to realise that these guys appeared in different uniforms throughout the day—in the various restaurants and buffet bars on the ship. They always recognise me before I spot them as their different uniforms throw me. Daphne, our wine waiter, also mans the security desk at embark/disembarkation so they all work longer and harder than I initially suspected.

After dinner, we walked down to the Gaiety Theatre where a female violin duo called Electric presented a modern twist to classical musical standards. They shared the stage with the SS Azara orchestra creating a fantastic tribute to Irish folk music and finished with a medley of James Bond theme tunes. The two young girls were warmly applauded off stage. We passed them outside where they were available to speak with any of the passengers leaving the theatre. Brian gave them our praise for the skilful delivery of the Irish songs, not easy music to play.

We could have sampled the second show from the Harmony Twist (a classical piano and violin duo) but we preferred the Lorcan Bond Trio in the Hawks Inn and Brian and Anita joined us there.

Day 7

Monday 9th January.
Three days from Bermuda.

The clocks have gone back an hour for the third time. I have decided to drop the Russian dancers from my list. I now recognise it's only my own issues with dancing that brought them onto the list in the first place and not some gross act of cruelty or evil on their part. Omission or failure to act perhaps, but I'm big enough to acknowledge when I'm wrong.

10:00. Beginners Bridge Class

The session was notable, only for Brendan's instructions, issued at the end of class. That and the, by now, inevitable early arrival of our table's next occupants, the intermediate class members. They, particularly the women, stood behind my back chatting loudly and drowning out Brendan's voice.

"Please can each table place all the cards back in the plastic trays, as I have detailed, on the board to my right?" He shouted to make himself heard.

"Make sure the cards are in the sequence shown on the board. We will use these sets tomorrow when both the beginner's class and the intermediate class will play an identical hand. Remember, beginners are free to attend the evening bridge classes held in this room each night and can partner up with experienced players."

So tomorrow the intermediate class were to inherit our table and chairs *and cards*, set exactly as we had received them.

This set me thinking. The cards were held in a plastic tray with four sections, North, South, East and West. My table partners had returned all the cards, as originally dealt, and had placed them back in the plastic tray. I offered to return them to Brendan while the other three gathered their things, getting ready to leave. But I didn't pass the cards up to Brendan. I slipped the tray into my bag and then rejoined Margaret outside Lawton's room. I had a plan.

Up on deck the tennis court was set up and ready to use and Margaret joined in with the lads for a couple of games before I took her place. I partnered with a new player, Glen, who was morbidly obese and very slow moving. He'd been watching the earlier games and been encouraged by some of his friends to give it a go.

"I last played when I was fifteen years old," he said to me.

I'm afraid it showed. He even had trouble bending down to pick up the ball so thereafter I made sure to hand them up to him. We did well enough and he played three games in all. He was panting heavily by the end. I guessed he was approximately forty-five years old, but he was in terrible condition for a man of such a young age.

12.15. Ships Choir

I found Arthur in good form and discovered Geoff, the Welsh

singer's name. I wrote it down in an attempt to retain it.

We added a new song to our repertoire today, Bette Midler's *The Rose* and managed to squeeze another, "Gorgeous," out of choirmaster Lorcan before the end.

The choir numbers seemed lower than in previous days, but it was to be expected with the first sustained burst of sunshine appearing out on deck. The sun loungers had made their first appearance too.

We ate a light snack and had a coffee before sneaking up to the tennis court and getting a good game in for about an hour while others took lunch.

That evening we attended the theatre and enjoyed Josh Lacey, the Wisconsin born juggler, who made the very most of his talent juggling balls, cones and hoops while balancing a guitar on his chin. He rounded up several members of the audience for various tricks and he went down well with the audience.

The Captain had been on the PA system earlier warning that we are in for a couple of stormy days and to secure everything in the cabin, such as bottles of alcohol and anything breakable.

Within minutes on climbing into bed, Margaret was snoring.

I walked into the bathroom with my bag and closed the door behind me, switched on the mirror light and donned a pair of disposable surgical gloves. Running the tap, a small pool of water formed in the basin. I tilted the talcum powder bottle and let fall a small quantity of white powder onto the tissue spread across the bathroom counter. Removing the cards and tray from my bag, one by one, I held the cards across their centre, pinched between my forefinger and thumb and ran their narrow edges through the water. I then dipped the card in the powder, rotating it so that each of the four sides was liberally coated by the poisonous substance. Within the enclosed bathroom the cards dried almost immediately. Therefore, I'd managed to attach a small quantity of poison to the edge of each card. Having coated the cards I marked them with a pen, a little dot in the corner and placed them back in the tray. I knew I'd need to find them again after their job was done.

I tidied up the bathroom storing the remaining powder in my Talcum Powder bottle, within my bag. Then I flushed the tissue and gloves down the toilet and far away into the bowels of the ship. Finally, I stored the tray and cards in a plastic bag within my bag and slipped into bed beside Margaret.

Day 8

Tuesday 10th January.
Still at sea. Mid North Atlantic.

The ship heaved and lurched all night. It was like trying to sleep in a flight simulator. Add to that, what sounded like someone at irregular periods banging on a metal door somewhere beneath our bed. The banging was so loud, that the bed and walls of the cabin shuddered and vibrated for many seconds after each and every blow.

That said, I had a relatively good nights sleep, all in all. Margaret appeared to sleep well too, but, when questioned, she claimed to have been awake most of the night.

"Don't you remember me watching television?" she asked.

"No," I answered truthfully.

"Didn't you see the wardrobe doors fly open and the suitcases fall out?" she continued.

I shook my head. "No." I made us both a cup of coffee and wondered how the older passengers would cope with the conditions onboard today. I know this cruise is an adult's only cruise, but that label doesn't quite describe the age profile of a large number of passengers on board. Many are well into their eighties and older still.

In one respect, these adult cruises are actually, convalescent nursing homes, at sea. For us, in some respects, it's as if we signed up to spend seven weeks' in a nautical nursing home. If I'm honest it's also a peek into the future, at what sort of mental and physical shape we may well have ourselves, in thirty year's time.

Remember also, these people we see before us, are life's survivors. Those who have made it this far and can afford on their savings and pensions, to travel the world.

It's now 08:00 and for many of the passengers, taking a shower or walking to the buffet will be a major challenge, as we are still being bounced about this vast ocean like a cork. I felt a bit rough myself and was on the verge of taking seasick tablets.

We made our way to the Palace restaurant for the buffet breakfast. Once inside, I felt much better and had tea with scrambled eggs, sausages and croissants while Margaret managed a little fruit but not much else.

10:00. Beginners Bridge Class

All tables played the same hand, learning how to bid and why to bid the amounts Brendan dictated. A good class was again spoiled by the crowding and loud talking of the intermediate class that hover over me and my chair with at least five minutes of our class left to run. They really are the rudest and most badly behaved mob I have encountered for years.

I just know they will also be the most unsympathetic players when we, beginners, eventually, join a club and start to play for real. They will punish our mistakes, expose our ignorance of standard coded messages and destroy us in games without a moment's hesitation.

Well, this time I was ready for them. While my playing partners were packing up and getting ready to leave the table, I deliberately knocked the tray of cards under the table and while down there I swapped it for the identical tray and cards that I had worked on last night. Straightening up, I slipped my card tray onto the table and, looking around I smiled graciously to the newcomers who barely registered my existence.

Swept away in the crowd, out of the room, into the hallway, I stood waiting for Margaret and Jennifer to collect the daily newspaper from the library.

I'm not quite sure what the effect of the poison I used will have. It's a naturally occurring nightshade flower, ground down with a hint of arsenic added for good measure. Just a little concoction I mixed myself in preparation for our holiday, so I'll just have to wait and see. I had tried it out at home on a mouse I'd caught in a trap and he was stiff as a board when I found him the next morning.

We spent the next hour completing the daily crossword before attending the choir session.

12.15. Ships Choir

Another two new songs were added, *No Business like Show Business* and *Annie's Song*. Several other songs were revisited and yes, we won two "Gorgeous!" pronouncements from Lorcan. Still, there are too few photocopied lyric sheets to go around so I'm without the lyrics, again. A fact that didn't miss Margaret's all-seeing eyes.

When we reunited at the theatre door she said "Why am I not surprised you gave away your sheets? You'd give away your seat in a lifeboat!"

The concert date is now known, as Saturday 28th January but no venue is yet confirmed. We ate lunch and then attended a classical recital by the Harmony Twist in the Pacific Lounge. To add atmosphere to the occasion, the curtains are always pulled across during these performances turning day into night. The small stage was subtly lit with the sleek black piano already in position.

We took a seat near the back and at the end of a row. I sat in the outer seat.

Margaret's eyes closed as she let the music waft over her. She slept through most songs, occasionally roused by the applause of the audience, before resuming her deep sleep. While she slept through a particularly long Wagnerian piece, I slid out of my seat and revisited the now empty Lawton's bridge room. I slipped on a pair of disposable surgical gloves I'd brought along and retrieved the marked poisoned cards and tray from the unlocked cabinet.

Exiting the room I threw the poisoned cards and tray into a litter bin outside the men's toilets and covered its contents with a few reams of scrunched up toilet paper. I was back, seated by her dozing body within minutes and caught the final notes of the piece.

The afternoon found us meeting Brian and Anita for another

round of mini bridge. This time we swapped partners and Margaret and I played together for the first time. More to the point Brian and Anita, forty-seven years married, played as a team and, frankly, it was touch and go as to whether they would complete one hand together, they bickered so much.

Margaret was still feeling the effect of seasickness and we dropped out of the evening meal and opted for a light snack in the buffet restaurant.

Day 9

Wednesday 11th January.
At sea and two days to Bermuda.

It was another rough night. but we were so exhausted it didn't take long for us to drift off.

10:15. Beginners Bridge Class

We were a player down until near the end when Jimmy appeared, clutching an invoice from the medical centre. His wife had a fall in the cabin some days ago and her condition had worsened. He explained she has chronic obstructive pulmonary disease, thanks to a lifetime of smoking, and the fall had exasperated her condition. The doctors in the medical centre had now placed her permanently on oxygen. She has a cylinder and facemask in their cabin where she will spend her immediate future.

The class was interrupted when the captain carried out a turn for the ship and announced that, at last, we were over the worst of the weather and were heading towards Bermuda and smoother sailing conditions.

The class continued and as the clock slowly ticked around to 10:55, I was curious to see who would turn up from the intermediate class to take over our table. The answer was two women I'd never seen before and two of our regular male tormentors who had made nuisances of themselves on previous days.

Margaret innocently challenged the women as they took their seats. "I'm sorry I think you'll find two other ladies normally sit here for the intermediate class"

"That's okay," said one of the men. "Lily and Rebecca were both very ill last night and we had to call the doctor to them. I didn't feel too good myself."

Even now he looked awfully pale and grey. He also seemed to be visibly trembling.

"Nothing serious I hope?" I said.

"No, I think not. We think it was food poisoning" he uttered before gesturing that the conversation was over and he headed for the toilets, again. I made a mental note to strengthen the concoction as it appeared that it was only a partial success this time around. We went for elevenses and attempted the daily ship's crossword while sipping coffee.

Soon it was noon and we joined the choir for today's rehearsal. Lorcan recorded our efforts as we sang each song that we have rehearsed thus far and he will narrow down the selection by the next rehearsal, which will be in three days' time as we are two days' docked in Bermuda. We achieved one "gorgeous!" and he said we were so good that he considered keeping all the songs in the show. This decision will probably exhaust whatever limited goodwill we may have with our fellow passengers.

After lunch we retreated to the cabin for a rest. I awoke with a start at 16:10. We ran up the stairs to Lawton's where a patient Anita and Brian accepted our apologies and we played a few hands of mini bridge. Midway through our session Brian spoke.

"I heard that a woman died last night" he said, absentmindedly, as he studied his hand of cards. My ears pricked up.

"Really?" said Anita. "What happened?"

"I overheard two men talking in the lounge while I was waiting for you, my dear. Seems she'd been taken ill the day before and, despite moving her to the medical centre, she passed away overnight." Brian still scrutinised his hand. He laid down the Ace of Spades on the table and looked me straight in the eye.

I jumped out of my skin and must have looked flustered. My initial reaction was that he knows something.

But then I got it.

I'm his partner.

His look in my direction was checking that I understood his action. I shouldn't try to win this hand as he's got it won already with his cards. Just throw away something, any old card. That's what his card was telling me.

Christ, that was unnerving.

I nodded in agreement and duly tossed down a two of Clubs and the game proceeded.

At dinner, our table was one down as Jill was poorly and Frank ultimately disappeared towards the end of the meal with a plate of food for her.

I had turned to spying in recent evenings and the table of four, on the other side of the pillar next to us, have been fascinating me for some time as they sat in silence every night. There had been a brief exchange this evening where one party spoke to the other. The response was a negative swing of the head and that was the extent of dinner conversation. Two hours later they rose and left. What a sad way to waste an evening.

Across the ship in the Gaiety Theatre, the Topstars presented *Dance around the world.* We sat in one of the front rows and the show was one continuous burst of colour and high octane energy. They sang and danced brilliantly and the lighting and sound was superb. The performance is truly West End theatre standard.

We sat next to a Swedish couple, Oscar and Agnes, who had flown from Stockholm to join the cruise in Southampton.

"English passengers," Agnes said, "have so much more luggage and clothing to wear than I have, as, like you, we had flights to catch and the airline's baggage restrictions to comply with."

Margaret nodded her agreement. It wouldn't be long before a bit of re-using of her limited wardrobe would be required.

"One English woman had boarded with fourteen bags and one of those was just for her shoes," Agnes added with a laugh.

Day 10

Thursday 12th January.
Docked in Bermuda.

Bermuda is a collection of one hundred and eighty islands in British hands, six hundred nautical miles off the east coast of the United States. The seven largest islands are linked by causeways and bridges. The Bermudan population is a mere sixty-four thousand souls.

Bermudan dollars are the local currency, which is equal to the US dollar, however I was warned not to get stuck with them as they are worthless outside the islands. We have $100 US dollars and hoped it might be enough for two one-day travel passes and the odd cup of coffee.

I wanted Margaret to have breakfast in bed, and after showering, visited the restaurant, returning to the cabin with hot milk, porridge draped in honey, a plate of croissants, cheese and slices of cold meat. This was no mean feat, as it involved a walk across an open windy deck, the forcing open a heavy sea door, taking a lift ride followed by traversing interminably long corridors before eventually reaching our cabin.

The ship docked at Kings Wharf at 09:00. It had followed the Cunard ship, Queen Victoria, into the dock. Disembarkation was set for 09:30. We visited the Palace restaurant for coffee while we waited and chatted to a couple, Matt and Irene, with whom we shared the table.

"So, where is your cabin?" Margaret asked while polishing off a hot buttered croissant.

Matt cleared his throat. "On deck 7 is where we are now and have been since day three."

"Yes, it's mid-ship," said Irene, "and so quiet."

"Sounds like you landed on your feet," I said with a hint of envy.

Matt wiped his mouth on a napkin. "It wasn't always so. We started the cruise in cabin F103 but we had two really rough nights and I got to breaking point and rang reception at 04:30 on the second night. I said to them that the clanging and banging was not the ships normal movement but was unsecured equipment rolling about. I said we hadn't got a wink of sleep in forty-eight hours and we were absolutely exhausted."

"And they moved you? Just like that?" I said incredulously, almost dropping my toast. "We were three doors away from you, had the same noise and had our cabin flooded twice! We complained and failed to get moved!" The injustice of it all really irked.

Matt shrugged his shoulders and bit into another plump sausage skewered on his fork. "Not only that, Luke, but we were moved to a peaceful external cabin for one night and then to passenger heaven, cabin A200, a spacious cabin with a bath in the middle of the ship."

"A bath" sighed Margaret, "how lovely."

The gangplanks were put in place and the first passengers had disembarked by 10:00. A long queue formed at the bus and ferry ticket office so we walked on and into the British Naval Shipyard where a shopping centre with a clock tower offered us the first glimpse of prices in Bermuda. They seemed not too outlandish in some shops but vastly inflated in others.

We queued, for twenty-five minutes, to buy four bus/ferry coin tokens which enabled us to visit the island's capital city, Hamilton, and return to the ship. The journey takes one hour by bus and only thirty-five minutes by ferry. Just as we neared the front of the queue, the woman immediately in front of us turned her head and beckoned six other passengers to join her at the desk, which irked at the time, us having stood there for almost half an hour.

But the lost time would prove more costly than I expected. Due to the delay collecting the tokens, we missed the once hourly ferry sailing by just twenty feet. We stood helpless on the jetty and watched it pull away, the steam from its funnels rising up into the clear blue sky. At the back of the ferry waving happily were the woman and her friends.

Resorting to Plan B, I got directions to the nearest bus stop and joined a women and her wheelchair bound husband, waiting for the next bus. When it finally arrived, I saw further passengers approaching the bus stop at speed, so I brushed past the slow-moving couple and we boarded the bus ahead of them squeezing into the last two available seats.

Someone near the front of the bus gave their seat to the woman's husband when he was finally helped on board the bus. I felt a bit of a rat but sometimes it's dog-eat-dog out there and Margaret's arthritic hips benefited from the padded seat.

The bus takes the scenic route to the capital and, peering through the dusty window, I could clearly see how the causeways link and combine the multiple islands into one single entity. The roar of the diesel engine drowned out any hopes of a conversation and I settled for studying the countryside as we bounced along the pot-holed roads. The inhabitants appeared to be deeply religious as there were a great many churches scattered about the island. The local school children wore nice old-fashioned navy blue school uniforms with a large crest and letters "BI" on the breast pocket of the blazers. They were very polite and well behaved, even the teenagers amongst them, and even when in groups. On the bus and ferry, the mobile phones kept the kids quiet. Free Wi-Fi is everywhere, except on the ship of course.

The island is extraordinarily green and I overheard a woman saying that they had experienced four inches of rain the week before. Regular rainfall would certainly encourage plant life and luscious grass to cover the land. The pitched roofs had an unusual structure in that the rows of cement tiles were laid like steps, like the sides of the Egyptian pyramids. Also, there was no visible guttering or drains as we have in Ireland. Apparently, rainwater is captured as it falls off the roof and is stored in large basements under the houses. They can store up to thirty thousand gallons in some houses.

There is a pronounced English feeling about the island with many town names like Somerset, Lincoln, Twickenham and Richmond featuring on our bus route. Several towns had cricket pitches. We saw no signs of kids hanging about street corners or graffiti drawn on walls. The society here seemed to respect law and order. It's just a group of beautiful islands filled with stunning white or light blue houses and surrounded by bays with many, many yachts.

When we arrived at Hamilton we stayed on the bus until we reached the terminus in the centre of the town. The terminus was a large concrete and tin-roofed area, heaving with travellers, both locals and tourists. We fought our way through the crowd to the street outside. In warm sunshine, we walked to a nearby Anglican cathedral and went inside the three hundred-years-old building. The church could have been built in England and transported to the Caribbean, stone by stone, so perfectly did it mirror churches in the homeland. The high ceilings, the dark wooden pews, the stained glass windows which flooded the large interior with light, all harked back to its colonial times. The flags that hung from the ceiling were mostly military and related to the two world wars, which are now distant memories. We spent some time reading the inscriptions, remembering those that gave their young lives, all those years ago, before kneeling in prayer.

To our left, two Bermudans sat reading aloud from the scriptures, each alternating with the other. They didn't seem to allow any time for the words to sink in before the other reader read out his next prayer.

Back outside, a homeless man sat by the church gate, his life squeezed into his metal shopping trolley parked next to him. His untended beard and unwashed hair gave away his perilous existence on the edge of society, clinging on grimly. Where does he get the motivation to rise off the church bench and set off around this small city, in a never-ending, repetitive search for food and shelter? It surprises me that even in such a religious, beautiful and well-run island, some people can slip through the cracks.

We walked on further along Church Street and past yet more churches. We got directions and climbed the hill past the Seventh Day Adventist church and supermarket until we found a walkway leading up to Fort Hamilton, a fort started but never completed by the English army after the American civil war had ended. It's suggested the fort which overlooks the bay, had cannon guns that fired one thousand yards out into the bay. However, the guns were made obsolete when ships developed breech guns that fired from three miles away.

We strolled along the harbour frontage a bit further but saw nothing we wanted to buy and so we caught the ferry back to our ship at Kings Wharf. It was a grand experience travelling past the hundreds of yachts rocking on their moorings and coming upon the Cunard's Queen Victoria, a beautiful ship parked behind our own dear SS Azara.

We boarded and overheard that the Queen Victoria was

departing soon so we strode to the top deck and to the bow of our ship. There we listened as the two ships exchanged loud, deep, vibrating farewells to each other, black smoke billowing out of their huge funnels. The Queen Victoria finally cast off its ropes and moved ever so quietly away from the dock, remaining parallel to the dock. It sort of drifted out in a controlled fashion under the watchful eye of *Powerful*, an old English rescue tug that stood by to lend assistance if some were needed.

Dinner was a lively table of good humour and chat. Then afterwards, the Electric girls, Sally and Emma, put on their second and final show in the Gaiety Theatre and with the ship's orchestra backing them and they were fantastic. They did a tear-jerking version of Leonard Cohen's *Hallelujah* and we sat and watched them with Anita and Brian, both tired from a day of walking. Anita missed the last half hour of the show, her head buried in her chest snoring loudly.

Day 11

Friday 13th January.
Docked in Bermuda.

We spent the night docked in Bermuda, but the air con and vibrations experienced when sailing are also present when you are in port, so it made no real difference.

I awoke early, as my body had still not adjusted to the time zone changes we'd experienced to date.

We ate a hearty breakfast and set off down the gangplank. We explored the dockland area immediately around the ship which has been developed as a yacht and retail therapy zone.

We visited a few of the expensive shops and then popped into the Glass Blowing Centre where we watched three men manufacturing a colourful glass fish which would be a table decoration. One stuck a long pole into the glowing yellow heated kiln and removed it minutes later with a glob of glass on the tip of the pole. The next man struck that glass with a hammer flattening it out and then with a set of pincers working and teasing the shape until it resembled a fish. Finally, he stuck the cooling glass on a red-hot piece of glass that would be a base for the object and the job was done.

We walked on and found a sandy beach in a water sports area

behind the National Museum. Finally, we were able to remove our footwear and walk on the bleached white sand and into the cold water of the North Atlantic.

Just a quick dip satisfied the curiosity. The water was freezing!

We spent the rest of the time sitting on a large weathered grey tree trunk that had washed up on the beach and sat enjoying the sun and each other's company. A nearby art gallery contained new works by contemporary local artists and you could purchase prints for as little as $20.

We found several premises offering free Wi-Fi and, along with many other passengers made contact with home.

Back on board, we ate lunch and sat by the pool. Departure was scheduled for 15:00 but had been delayed as a malfunction in the headcount system meant all staff and passengers had to be counted again. I wondered if this "malfunction" was cover for further investigations into the missing entertainments officer. If it was, nothing was to come of it.

For us, it was back to our cabin to be ticked off by our cabin steward and then to await further instructions.

Dinner that evening was uneventful with full attendance. Nothing worth repeating was said at the table and we all scurried off to the theatre where a Frankie Valli and the Four Seasons tribute show was presented by the Unknown Boys, four ex-Jesus Christ Superstar cast members from the West End. It was a fantastic show which also included some Broadway musical numbers. Again the stars of the show were outside meeting and greeting guests as they left.

We walked to the other end of the ship and enjoyed a night of Burt Bacharach music.

Day 12

Saturday 14th January.
Sailing towards Cape Canaveral.

We slept in a bit and awoke later than normal so it was a quick wash, shave and dress and up to the Palace restaurant for breakfast.

Afterwards we lingered about the tennis court until the net and equipment was installed by the crew member.

10:00. Beginner's Bridge Class

It was a largely listening class with the playing of the same hand of cards by all tables. As 11:00 approached the intermediate class appeared just inside the door. But after a while they pressed forward, to line the side walls. Then they proceeded to stand behind our chairs. Their conversation volume level rose as the minutes passed and Brendan's voice became lost in their mindless chatter.

It looks as if my work here is not yet done, I thought, glancing about the room. But do I really want to wipe out an entire class of pensioners? In fairness, not all are guilty but a sizable majority stood condemned. I looked for any ringleaders, loud chatterboxes who talked at the top of their voices while we still had, I glanced at my watch, two minutes and forty seconds of class time, left.

Margaret, reading my mind, followed my gaze and gave me a

nudge in the ribs.

I scanned the intermediate class but failed to find the two women taken poorly by my poisoned cards. One, I can now guess, is dead. I've seen one of their husbands about the ship but, though I'm consumed with curiosity, I daren't ask about their fate.

We had an early lunch and I attended the choir practice. Lorcan is still retaining all the songs that we have worked on and is even talking of adding another. The "Gorgeous!" count was a miserly one today but he did say he had listened to our last rehearsal, as he had recorded it and he had cried! We obviously had sung and moved him deeply. He's such a wuss!

While all the other travellers took lunch, we played more tennis and then settled for sunbathing, tucked in behind the huge funnel. That was until we met up with Anita and Brian for cards. It may be our last game as Margaret is totally browned off by Brian's sssshing of conversation when the chatter is made by others. However, he breaches the rule frequently himself and talks ten-to-the-dozen. He also tends to blame others when he loses. Margaret's had enough of him. Either we take a break or we let the couple loose on each other by making them partners. Something's gotta give.

Back in the cabin, it was time for preparation for the fourth of fourteen Black Tie formal dress evenings. The black suit and dickie bow tie are extracted from the wardrobe and Margaret picks a shimmering blue dress and slips on sparkly blue sling-backs.

Up in the Atrium, which has a wide multilevel swirling staircase as its centrepiece, we see no temporary portrait studio and further along no photographic staff at their desk. The reason for their absence becomes clear when we reach our dinner table. The postponed Atlas Club event with the ship's officers was taking place before our dinner and the cameras were snapping away in the Pelican Lounge.

The table was in good form tonight and conversation buzzed on all sides. Roger had worked as a guide in the Greenwich Naval School and enjoyed leading tourists around the 17th century English ships in the dry dock. Sometimes, tourists would notice the full complement of ships cannons present but noted that there was an absence of cannon balls. "Where are the missing cannonballs?" they would ask. "You'll have to ask the French Navy," was Roger's tongue in cheek response.

We left the table and strolled to the theatre at the front of the ship and found it buzzing, full of finely dressed men and women fresh from dinner. Tonight we had a double bill and what fantastic singers they both were. Lesley Smythe, a slip of a girl from Manchester, sang in French, English and Italian with power and delicacy, songs from around the world. While James Young, an American with Broadway pedigree presented songs by Andrew Lloyd Webber's Jesus Christ Superstar, Sunset Boulevard, Evita etc. Both brought the house down.

Later in a very full Hawks Inn, the Lorcan Bond Trio performed with Chris Whitewell, a saxophonist of remarkable quality and we headed for home.

Day 13

Sunday 15th January.
Still en-route to Cape Canaveral.

We rise and the gentle rhythm of the boat is reassuring and reinforces a feeling of safety and warmth. After a sensible breakfast, we took to the open deck and got in a good tennis session in the twenty-one degrees now warming the deck.

10:00. Beginners Bridge Class

Now that Brendan has distributed a copy of his famed *Bridge Tips*, hopefully, the basics will begin to stick in our brains. This morning saw us exposed to the Stayman convention and Jennifer played the hand brilliantly. Unfortunately, she had to leave the class early and this led to the unfortunate occurrence.

The always annoying intermediate class were even more irritating than usual with their babble of conversation exceeding previous decibel levels. One man came out from the crowd and sat in Jennifer's seat with five minutes of our class to go. He continued chatting to his mates while we tried to play out the hand. The man seemed unaware of his rude behaviour. It's amazing to me, that one can reach the age of seventy and still be unaware of some basic manners.

I stared hard at him and kept a steady gaze going until he looked me straight in the eye. He knew he was being critically observed. Usually, I would look away so as not to invite trouble, to avoid catching their eyes. But this time I sat there, matching his hostile gaze with one of my own.

"What is it, mate?" he said with exasperation and a hint of rising anger. He still apparently didn't know what he had done wrong.

"Excuse me, sir," I said, choosing my words carefully, "our class is continuing and yours won't start for a while, so will you please step away from the chair and let us finish the hand we are playing."

For a moment I had visions of him jumping up and head butting me, but he didn't. He considered my reasoned argument and after a second replied, "Go fuck yourself!" rather loudly.

The rest of the room now became aware of our disagreement. Whispered voices spoke behind cupped hands while we just sat and glared at each other. Margaret didn't know where to look and sat frozen in her seat. The impasse was broken by Brendan, who spoke in a loud commanding voice "Right, that's enough for today. I'll see you all at the same time tomorrow."

Brendan stepped forward to our table. "Luke, can you please collect and pass me the cards from each of the tables?"

I did as he asked, but all the while I knew a rather smug man sat a few feet away and watched me visit the other tables, in silence.

"Now, Luke," said Margaret. "Don't let it affect you. He's a pig and you can't expect manners from a pig, OK?"

I nodded in agreement but I was far from agreeing with her. That man was a worthy list occupant.

We had an early lunch and completed crosswords before we claimed ownership of the tennis court for over an hour. With no practice card games arranged for the afternoon, Margaret took to the sun loungers for a few hours. I wandered the lower decks as the ship cut its way through the endless waves of a deep blue sea. All I could see, in every direction, was sea. No land, no birds, not another ship, just sea.

Strolling along the promenade deck's interior walkway I passed a classical music recital, a ballroom dance class, a lecture on the universe and a live football match, being shown on television in the bar.

Then I saw him. That intermediate bridge player, who took Jennifer's seat earlier, was now in the bar. He sat alone with a pint of lager and a packet of crisps for company. His eyes focused on the large television screen on the wall to his left and he sat on a large couch. Sat wasn't really the right word. He rather poured himself onto the couch than sat on it, his liquid obese body just oozing all over the leather surface and his legs stretched out over the carpeted floor. His arms lolled lifelessly by his side, except for the movement of his left wrist and hand, which seemed to be on autopilot, repeatedly reaching into a large bag delivering a handful of crisps to his gaping mouth. His eyes never shifted from the screen. He was obviously a staunch supporter of one of the sides.

I entered the bar from a door behind him and sat on a high stool where I had a good view of both him and the screen. I waved the barman away and took in my surroundings.

On the screen, Manchester United were playing away to Juventus and led 0 - 1 with twenty minutes gone. It meant he'd be sat there for the next eighty minutes so I had time to formulate a plan.

On cruises like this one, customers rarely have to go to the bar to buy a drink. With his glass almost empty a waiter approached him and he passed his card over and ordered another pint which was duly delivered.

I looked around the bar and found I was amongst an all-male clientele. About eight men were spread around the open bar, sat on high stools and couches, with tables and chairs in the open body of the room. With the sun blazing away outside, only the dedicated fan was inside watching this match.

I checked my pockets for anything useful to assist me with my quickly formed plan to dispatch this individual. The only thing I came up with was a small quantity of my talcum powder. Since coming on board, I had taken to carrying a small sachet of it in my wallet, for just such an occurrence as this. I guessed I had a couple of grams which ought to be enough to knock a dog sideways, but it would be unlikely to kill a large man. It should give him a few rough nights and days.

The question now was how to bring him in contact with the powder? I hadn't the surgical gloves so I had to be careful that I didn't also come into direct contact with the substance myself.

The match on screen was a lively affair and with half-time approaching Juventus manufactured a goal out of nothing. The room groaned as the replay revealed some very poor defending by United and an inspired long distance shot from thirty yards out by the Italian international, Gregato.

"Daly should have closed him down much earlier," cried out one man.

"Typical of United, coasting along and missing chance after chance," shouted another.

"Now Juve are back in it," said yet another.

Five minutes later the referee blew the whistle for half-time. The teams left the pitch and the television channel cut to commercials.

In the bar, conversation broke out and our man rose from his seat. The effect of several pints of lager on any human being is to overload the urinary tract and this man was no exception. I watched him as he trundled out of the bar and into the toilet nearby.

I saw my chance. Most of the men had headed to the bar or the bathroom and the area beside my target's seat was empty. I walked over and stood at an angle, using my body to shield the table should anyone glance around. I quickly drew out and opened my sachet. Carefully, I sprinkled his bag of crisps with the powder and then shook the bag, dispersing the powder granules across all the bag contents. I replaced the bag on the table as I found it.

A quick check inside the bag revealed no obvious signs of white powder. It had mixed in with the salt, pepper and broken crisps. Without looking back I strode onwards and left via the sea door, out onto the deck.

"Fuck you, dick head," I said under my breath.

Swiftly putting some distance between myself and the bar, I was soon back beside a dozing Margaret.

She lay stretched out on the sun lounger, one of more than a dozen neatly spaced along this part of the deck. Her skin glittered with the copious amounts of factor five she had applied, and her flowery swimsuit followed the smooth form of her petite body. Her straw hat threw shade not only on her face but on the book which she had been reading, *The Final Hour* by Tom Wood.

I reached over and removed the book without waking her. She'd only read the first two chapters of this thriller, so I guessed she'd only opened it in the last half hour. Margaret is a speed reader and page turner and would have this book devoured by the end of the day. I read the storyline on the back of the book and it followed the usual format of an agent tracking a vicious murderer for a number of years. The killer would be a nameless hit-man responsible for numerous homicides. Not very realistic I thought but keeps Tom's head above water.

She stirred and became aware of my presence. Her blue eyes opened and focused on me. "What time is it?"

I glanced at my watch. "Just 15:30."

"Gosh I've only been asleep for half an hour. I feel as if I have been here for hours!" She sat up and reached down to slip on her sandals. "C'mon it's coffee time!"

Day 14

Monday 16th January.
Cape Canaveral, Florida, USA.

We docked at 06:00, by which time I was already washed, shaved and dressed.

We rode the lift up to the Palace restaurant and viewed the Walt Disney ship, Dream, tied up a hundred yards away. The huge ship seemed to stretch on forever. Behind it, a stunning red sunrise was unveiling itself and, within twenty minutes, daylight had arrived.

Breakfast in the buffet had an excited bustle about it, with lots of passengers fuelling up before going ashore. Bill and Joan greeted us before heading off to collect their bags for the day. We had our gear with us so we just descended directly to the Gaiety Theatre where we were given yellow badges with 3 on them and sat to the right of the stage with all the other 3s. By 08:20 our group was called to the atrium on deck 6 and with our passports, ESTA'S (US immigration visa forms) and excursion tickets we were on our way into the USA.

American immigration officials were waiting in a large arrival terminal building. All the ship's crew that were going ashore, were in one queue, while the passengers were in another, which was serviced by six immigration officers in glass cubicles. One of the six was dedicated to clearing disabled passengers and the rest dealt with the able-bodied in a slow meticulous fashion. We chatted amongst ourselves until we reached the front of the queue. Then we advanced to desk five where a white-uniformed officer awaited us. Our fear about our non-biometric passports appeared unfounded as he was happy with both passports.

The fear that I might be on some FBI watch list arose from a comment made some ten years ago when I was passing through John Wayne international airport. I was unable to check in online and so I had to present myself to an immigration officer. He stared into his computer screen and though he let me fly he advised me that I should sort it out when I get home. I never did.

No, the sticking point today was an intermittent fault with the immigration department's fingerprint scanner and the official struggled to record all my digits. Eventually, I had both hands fingerprinted and I was photographed and released with a cheery "Have a nice day," ringing in my ears. I confess I was a tad nervous but my ability to keep a low profile while quietly reducing the offenders on board appears to be working well.

Sam, our red-haired, blue-eyed tour guide, was waiting for us outside, next to the line of coaches. She gushed cheerfulness and goodwill from start to finish. Europeans find this instant enthusiasm for people never met before hard to swallow. The cynic in us bubbles to the surface but eventually, we are won over by her relentless tirade of goodwill, information and sincerity.

There is a lot of wildlife in the area of the NASA Space Station and Sam pointed out much of it as we drove towards the space complex. We saw alligators sunning themselves by streams, an eagle's nest, birds of all sorts including spoon-billed birds and small turtles swimming in ponds.

We had paid for the tour that included a visit to the rocket launch pad viewing gallery and the Saturn 8 centre where the Saturn 8 rocket itself is housed. The launch pads, when you finally get to see them, are about three and a half miles away and the gallery we sat in is the closest safe location to watch a launch from. Any closer and the shock wave from the launch would kill you. An IMAX presentation was followed by a visit to a museum that housed many actual rockets, space suits, lunar rocks, lunar vehicles and much more.

A launch of a military satellite was scheduled for that coming Thursday and the next manned mission was scheduled for next year as they test for the Mars landing missions, scheduled to start in 2030.

It was a shame that our visit didn't coincide with a launch but on the plus side the centre was a lot less crowded than it would have been on a launch day.

Then, it was back to the NASA Kennedy Space Centre, which we'd passed on the way in, for further IMAX 3D presentations, a ride in a shuttle flight simulator and a stunning IMAX 3D Heroes and Legends presentation that really felt like you were up in space orbiting the earth.

The shuttle flight simulator had a lengthy queuing system that weaved multiple times as it rose to the ceiling of the complex. It lay bare and devoid of any visitors. We walked briskly to the top of the queue. All along the length of the walkway, experienced astronauts appeared on TV monitors explaining what we might experience and built up our expectation for the ride. Then at the top, we were released into a waiting area and still more explanation of what we were imminently to experience. A final offer was made over the loudspeakers, "If you are of frail or a delicate disposition this is now your last chance to back out."

It was all too much for Margaret, the unfortunate owner of a damaged back. She succumbed to her vivid imagination and their scene-setting skills and at the last moment, she quit the queue in favour of watching the short simulator ride from the control room.

Frankly, I felt underwhelmed when the ride commenced. I can only imagine the sincere astronauts who had eulogised about the ride had more on their mind than the few bumps and rocking movements that transpired in the crude simulation. I've had rougher rides on my lawnmower.

We descended into the complex NASA space centre where real equipment, space suits and moon vehicles were on display. Some you could even touch. Nearby, a recording was running of Glenn Shepherd, the first American in space, being interviewed. When asked why he thought he was chosen to fly the Saturn rocket, he replied; because they ran out of monkeys.

Outdoors, at the back of the centre and behind a park filled with skyscraper high rockets, we found a monument erected to the twenty-four astronauts that had lost their lives to date. Ominously, I noted on the tall black marble edifice, plenty of space was provided for additional names.

The marble monument stood tall on an island surrounded by a lake and could only be reached via a narrow footbridge. A huge alligator sunned himself on the grass next to the water no more than three feet away. An ankle-high fence separated him from us.

We pointed him out to Sam, our guide. "It's no surprise to me," she answered. "There are actually six alligators living in that lake."

I can honestly say I stood there, staring hard at the still dark water in that lake for the next five minutes, and saw nothing that would lead me to believe that five alligators were hiding below the surface. I was still staring into the water when a women and her wheelchair-bound husband arrived, the couple we had met at the bus stop in Bermuda a few days earlier.

They smiled and came over to stop on the path beside me. "What can you see?" he asked.

I explained about the five alligators being in the water while not creating a ripple on the surface.

He peered, like me, into the inert dark water.

"Look over there," his wife said, gesturing to us and all our eyes turned to the right, to a small number of bubbles rising to the surface of the water.

"He's never seen alligators before," the woman said nodding at her husband. It was clear to me that he was fascinated by the possibility of seeing one.

"Let's get a little closer," he whispered to his wife, gesturing that she should move his wheelchair nearer the bubbles.

She disengaged the brakes and grunted as she pushed the wheelchair forward.

Initially, the gentle slope in the ground made further effort from her unnecessary, but within seconds, she was struggling to keep up with the wheelchair, as it gathered its own momentum and slipped away from her despairing grasp. Her husband was freewheeling towards the lake at an alarming speed.

Startled, Margaret and I leapt forward just as the woman tripped and fell, slamming heavily to the ground.

Margaret dropped down to her side and I took off after the wheelchair, which was heading to the very edge of the water.

Fortunately, the slope began to level off and the wheelchair came to a perilous stop. That was until the man in it began to rock about, trying to fling himself out of the wheelchair and to safety. The more he panicked, the more unstable the wheelchair became.

To my absolute horror, the wheelchair began to slowly slip into the water. His feet were already submerged, so the water now crept up to his knees and his terrified screams of desperation filled my ears. Suddenly the wheelchair dipped forward as if the ground below water had fallen away. I reached for the wheelchair and grabbed it by its handles with both hands. I strongly pulled it towards me. Unfortunately, the man had by now released the straps and had turned to face me, effectively kneeling in the chair. My sudden and violent pulling movement merely served to flip him backwards, head over heels, in the opposite direction.

He flew briefly before landing with a splash in the dark water, disappearing completely for a moment before resurfacing, spluttering and sucking in air.

I flew backwards myself landing on the ground, with the now lightweight wheelchair lying on top of me.

"Get me out of here, for Christ sake, get me out of here!" the man hollered at the top of his voice, while sitting upright in the lake, covered in green algae.

I appreciated the urgency of his situation and, pushing the wheelchair aside, I rolled up my trouser legs with the intention of wading into the water and carrying him out, praying the five alligators story was a product of our guide's vivid imagination.

Suddenly, the water area around the man became a thrashing mass of flying spray, shredded flesh and glistening white teeth. A frantic feeding frenzy was in full flow and I could see three if not four alligators rotating around the poor man's bleeding and badly torn body. He very swiftly began to look less like a human being and more like a selection of body parts in a butcher's abattoir. He never spoke another word and strangely his entire being vanished from the lake waters in less than a minute. The alligators each took their share of him and slid silently back under the water.

Within five minutes, the lake resumed its static dormant appearance.

His watching wife gave out a scream and fell into Margaret's arms sobbing uncontrollably. Later, Margaret told me that his wife had picked herself up and would have followed him into the water but for Margaret's intervention. Now the poor woman stood shaking uncontrollably, struggling to come to terms with what she had just seen, the sudden and brutal killing of her husband. It had been a surreal few minutes for all concerned. I don't believe she could process what she had seen and could accept that this had actually happened. It wasn't a nightmare that she will wake up from but a traumatic and tragic reality that had just occurred.

I struggled myself to rationalise how our world had gone from tranquility to Armageddon in a matter of seconds.

"There, there now." The colour had drained from Margaret's face, and I could see her own hands trembling with shock at what she had just witnessed. "Help is on its way. Don't fret now. Look away, c'mon, we'll go over here." She guided the woman through the crowd that had gathered to sit on a bench nearby.

We discovered, a little later on, that the entire episode had been picked up on the centre's CCTV cameras. Although several of their staff had arrived within minutes, there was nothing anybody could do. I offered to stay and assist with inquiries but was told that I was free to go.

The resident doctor sedated the poor woman and I considered asking for a little for myself and Margaret too. We were both totally shook up and Margaret couldn't stop crying.

The collapsed metallic wheelchair was collected by our guide,

Sam, who carried it back and placed it in the luggage hold at the bottom of our coach.

"What will happen next?" I asked her.

"Well, the NASA Space Centre staff will no doubt cordon off the lake and relocate the alligators elsewhere while they drain it down to recover, what there is left to be found, of your friend.

The coach trip back to the ship was completed in silence, many people including Margaret and I remained in a state of shock for quite some time.

Only six dined tonight as our Scottish couple were absent. Food was, as ever, delicious and filling but the occurrences of the day had turned my stomach. Margaret similarly only played with her fork.

News of the death had begun to circulate amongst the passengers and Frank asked me had I heard about it?

"I have, Frank, and what's more, we witnessed it at first hand!" So, without further ado, I summarised our day with Margaret chipping in with bits I'd omitted. I answered what questions I could and had exhausted interest in the subject by the time we rose to leave.

I listened for any news of deaths or illnesses on board from our fellow diners, but nothing was said. The bodies of my earlier victims were probably unloaded here as ship's protocol required the port to be a town with significant mortuary and hospital facilities and Cape Canaveral had both. Now, just thinking about it, I recalled seeing an ambulance at the quayside early this morning as I walked along the deck heading for breakfast.

Day 15

Tuesday 17th January.
Docked in Fort Lauderdale, Florida, USA.

We joined the number 10 grey badge wearers in the Gaiety Theatre at 08:30.

We'd walked along the promenade deck as our enormous cruise liner entered the narrow channel from Fort Lauderdale's coastline to the harbour's inner dock. Our ship moved gracefully past dozens of multi-storey apartment blocks, our height matching that of multi-storey residential blocks on shore.

Then, the Captain ordered the navigation officer to engage the thrusters and the 69,000-ton monolith began treading water as gracefully as a swan before moving sideways towards the dock. Ever so slowly the sleek smooth vessel approached the crude wooden pier with only a row of rubber tyres to absorb the impact should the engines fail to break in time.

I need not have feared as the contact with the tyres when it came, was minimal. The ship's deckhands threw down the ropes and they were caught by dock workers and tied up to large iron knobs located fore and aft on the pier. Within minutes two gangplanks were lowered from the ship and a pair of pop-up marquees with carpet appeared at the foot of them.

Immigration delayed departures from the ship by twenty minutes, but when we eventually disembarked there was no need to produce passports as, apparently, we'd undergone a thorough vetting yesterday. The Homeland Security team had decided that there was no need to repeat the exercise today. So we boarded the coaches having only to display the ship account cards and our excursion tickets.

Jane, our guide, was already on board and we set off for the Everglades once all fifty of us were on board.

The journey took us half-an-hour outside the town of Fort Lauderdale, thus named after a General who had spent less than thirty days' in the town before dying on his return to Washington. It was one of a series of forts built by the United States during the Second Seminole War.

Further stories poured from Jane's mouth, such as the fact Fort Lauderdale is the USA's number 1 destination for college graduates seeking to unwind over the Easter break.

Continuing on with our excursion, we reached the Everglades Airboat tour base

We then stepped onto a lightweight airboat which took about twenty passengers. I brought ear plugs which were immediately put into use as the airboat's engine at full throttle was deafening.

We enjoyed one burst of high-speed travel through the marsh canals of the Everglades and then the boat's captain slowed it down for photo opportunities with three alligators and two iguanas.

I surveyed the sleeping killing machines, their long powerful tails stretched out on the sandy soil and a shiver ran through my body. I would be treating these jagged skinned alligators with new respect, given their species' performance yesterday.

How could I have changed yesterday's outcome? Roger suggested I could have smacked one on the snout or gouged his eyes with my fingers. Possibly, I conceded but what would I then do about the four other alligators whilst I am taking this one on?

The twenty-minute ride was enjoyable, but we really only travelled a very short distance before returning to the dock.

Afterwards, we drove to Flamingo Gardens, a botanical garden and wildlife sanctuary close by.

The coach had us back on board by 16.00 and there was just time for a tennis session before showering and changing for dinner.

Our fellow diner, Craig, had come down with a cold so was missing tonight. We finished dinner and stood on deck as our massive ship bade farewell to Fort Lauderdale in the gathering gloom.

A US Customs speedboat with a mounted submachine gun and gunner up front accompanied us to the open sea. Its amphibious lightweight frame more bouncing along the tips of waves than cutting through them.

Glancing to my left, I saw miles of darkened beaches extending as far as my eye could see. The absolute darkness reached inland too, to encompass the neighbouring roads and building. It all looked a bit odd.

Then the penny dropped. Turtles hatching season. No light pollution to confuse the little guys who need the bright moonlight to make their way to the ocean. Miles of darkened beaches. Now it all made perfect sense.

Day 16

Wednesday 18th January.
Docked in Key West, Florida, USA.

We pulled into the harbour and I watched it all from the television in the bedroom. Margaret was showering as the engines moved us the final inches inwards towards the harbour dock and the cabin walls vibrated.

The ship's upper deck gave us a plum view of the beautiful harbour and town of Key West. It is "Toy Town" tidy and looks just too perfect to be real.

We ate well at breakfast and, once we'd packed our bags, it was off to deck 6 where we trod down the gangplank and onto US soil. We bought a pair of hop-on-hop-off Old Town Trolley Tours tickets and off we went. The trolley looks like what we'd call a tram and travels on the tarmac roads. Painted orange and green, it traverses all of Key West and stops thirteen times, four of which are purely hotel stops so not worth dismounting for.

The round trip takes ninety minutes and is well worth the charge as the drivers keep up a running commentary and disperse local information.

I was surprised how small Key West is—only four miles long and two miles wide with 26,000 inhabitants. It's located closer to

Cuba than Miami and all its water is pumped in along thirty-two-inch pipes from the Everglades. The tour guide explained how it used to be the richest town in America thanks to sales of salt and sponges but then it became the poorest when the depression came, and Utah found salt mines below ground.

Soon we arrived at the West Martello Fort, an old partially demolished fort from the 1780's. It had been turned into a garden by the local Key West Garden Club and had previously been used as target practice for the two other Martello Forts built around the same time.

For over fifty years the gardeners of the Key West Garden Club had added soil and plants and trees to the West Martello tower so to wander around this free to enter garden was inspiring. One of the volunteers led us round and removed a few leaves and scrunched them up in the palm of his hands before passing them amongst our group. The scent given off by the leaves was wonderful, even spicy. "It's actually all-spice," he told us. Outside they had a row of potted plants free to take.

"If only," uttered Margaret.

We walked a bit further and found a long queue snaking back a hundred yards or more. Curiosity got the better of us and, after further investigation, we discovered they were all just waiting to have their pictures taken next to a lump of metal which proclaimed that spot to be the southernmost point in all of the USA.

"You'll hear a lot of that over the next few minutes," our trolley driver said upon our return. "We are now approaching the southernmost house in America and just to your right is the southernmost cafe. The house built in 1860 by Florida's first millionaire, Mr Curry, has twenty rooms but only one bedroom. He built three smaller houses across the road from his own so he had accommodation for his visitors. Each house had a servant's quarters."

In 1982, Key West left the United States of America and declared its independence as the Conch Republic. It then immediately surrendered without a shot being fired and as an independent and third world subtropical nation applied for fifty-two million dollars of foreign aid. The flag of the Conch Republic still flies on buildings today.

We took the trolley back to Mallory Square and returned to the ship for lunch. We purchased a Key West traditional lemon and lime cake slice and devoured it in seconds.

In these parts of the world, at this time of the year, sunset comes early. We found a bar near the dock where a sunset party was held every night and I ordered a local beer for me and a rum and coke on ice for the lady and we sparked up a conversation with a couple from New York, who'd escaped the city for a few days rest and recuperation in Florida.

Within minutes, the resident two piece jazz combo of trumpet and xylophone began creating some fabulous soft jazz music and we were there for the next hour. As we sat on our bar stools sleek expensive yachts returned to port and immediately before us a continuous stream of humanity walked by. I ended up being reluctantly dragged back to the ship as our departure time loomed.

"I really don't want to leave this place," whispered Margaret as we stood on the upper deck and watched the gangplanks being removed and the security team exiting the dock.

"Neither do I," I said. "Neither do I"

We missed the formal dinner and stood again on the upper deck watching the lights of Key West fade into the distance.

Day 17

Thursday 19th January.
At Sea in the Gulf of Mexico.

I awoke a little earlier than normal this morning. I'd finished off the laundry run last night but, flying solo, I had cocked up the dryer settings so the clothes I collected at midnight were still damp this morning.

The bow camera showed daylight from the minute I flicked it on. The screen was just blue sea and lots of it.

We caught breakfast and waited by the tennis court until the deckhand appeared and erected the net. We were only just starting to play when Vicky appeared and sought to join in. We'd seen her before. Apparently, her husband doesn't play so she was alone again today. We played a game ourselves before inviting her onto the court to knock up in a two-against-one game, with me being the one.

Vicky, a tall, yet heavy, woman played twice weekly with a group of women, when at home in Sussex. Her trained shots at the net showed her familiarity with the game. She did, however, not endear herself to Margaret by attempting to hog both sides of the court and I had to intercede several times to get her to stick to playing one side only.

Steam was coming out of Margaret's ears as she glared at

Vicky's back while Vicky continued to play all shots as if I hadn't spoken.

In the end, I resorted to lobbing the ball over Vicky in an effort to reach a stranded Margaret at the back of the court.

Vicky, by her own irritating behaviour, was putting herself forward to membership of a most unwanted list but she ranks at the lower end of the bad behaviour spectrum.

We fled the court to join our bridge players, Jennifer and Jimmy, for a largely note taking class, dealing with conventions around bidding before we finally played one hand. Brendan, having belaboured the conventions for forty minutes, gave an identical hand to all tables which had nothing to do with conventions. Give me strength!

With our session concluded the intermediate bridge class pupils swept into the room and surrounded the tables. My two card playing victims were noticeable by their continued absence, not only at the bridge classes but also around the ship The two women's husbands have not been seen either so I suspect they all disembarked at Cape Canaveral, the cruise ending prematurely for them. No sign, either, of the loud-mouthed Manchester United football supporter whose crisps I'd flavoured in the bar. I truly hope now my job is done with this group of people and we can all look forward to a stress-free, learning environment.

The next port on our itinerary was New Orleans so we thought we had better educate ourselves on what would be the biggest city we would be visiting. We attended a lecture on what to expect and are looking forward to the experience.

An hour later we were back in the Gaiety Theatre for our choir rehearsals and I thought we were better than the one, "Gorgeous!" scored today.

Once that practice was over we travelled by lift up to the Hawks Inn for a lunchtime concert *Jazz at Vespers,* where our New Orleans speaker, Chris, appeared now in his role as a clarinettist featured with the Lorcan Bond Trio.

They played a medley of gospel songs with the largely white audience singing the choruses with gusto. They started with the *Battle Hymn of the Republic* moved onto *Just a closer walk with thee,* and then Chris featured in a *Hymn to Freedom,* written to commemorate the murder of Martin Luther King. *Amazing Grace* was given the jazz treatment but lost none of its emotional power and then the black gospel number, *Down by the riverside,* which doubled as an anti-war anthem with the chorus, *Ain't gonna study war no more.* Next up was; *What A Friend We Have in Jesus,* an old Salvation Army favourite that Margaret knew from her childhood. No lyric sheet consulted singing that one.

As befits a ship drawing closer by the day to New Orleans, the traditional jazz standard, *When the Saints Go Marching In,* finished the concert in a rousing fashion and the musicians received a prolonged and thunderous ovation of applause.

We descended to our room and changed bag contents dumping the bridge handouts and choir lyric sheets and replacing them with towels and swimwear.

I set Margaret up on a lounger by the pool and we had a light lunch.

Afterwards, I headed to the gym, where there was a scattering of people like me who cared about their bodies and were prepared to mix up the holiday pleasure experience with a little work-out pain. They were prepared to counterbalance the days of excessive good living with a few hours of exercise.

I recognised some of those present as musicians in the ship bands and one or two passengers looked familiar, but there are thousands on board so I wasn't surprised to see mostly strangers working out.

The gym was well equipped with free weights, dumbbells and skipping ropes, a modest yoga area and a large selection of aerobic equipment. I plucked a running machine from a line of six and keyed in the setting before starting off on a 5 kilometre run. The sea was relatively calm now and I was able to run with confidence looking out a porthole at the sea flashing past.

After a short while, I became aware of a tall thin man, about my age, who was supposedly, working out too. In reality, he was sat at the foot of a weights machine, chatting loudly to two women wearing leotards and carrying yoga mats.

I tried to block him out of my mind, but he sat directly in front of the porthole and one of the women with him had a shrill laugh that cut right through me.

Ten minutes into my run I found that I wasn't as fit as I first thought. The pace I'd set of five minutes thirty seconds a kilometre, was proving too fast for me today. Seventeen days of living the high life had taken its toll. This irritated me somewhat and I grudgingly reduced my pace on the machine. Minutes later I had to adjust downwards again and still, the chatter continued. By now I'd been half an hour in the gym and this guy hadn't exercised anything other than his vocal chords.

As I entered the last kilometre of my run, the sweat was running like a stream freely down my face, my breathing was laboured and my legs began to wobble. Add to that the constant cackle of this woman and you can imagine I was not in the best of moods.

I finished the run and grabbed a towel before making my way to the dressing room and jumping in the shower.

While I was drying myself, same man walked in and opened a locker to retrieve his own towel.

I finished dressing and as I left, I spotted him enter the sauna. After he'd passed inside the unit I grabbed one of his shoes and wedged it, at one side under the external door handle and forced the other end of the shoe under the towel rail that hung out of the door frame.

He must have heard someone messing about with the door as I heard a banging on it coming from inside. "Hey what's going on out there?" he called.

I wasn't going to identify myself to him in any way, so I ignored his shouting. Even standing just the other side of the door I found his speech garbled and distant. He had zero chance of anyone hearing his cries outside of that room. In a parting last sadistic twist, I turned the temperature gauge up to its highest setting, 100 degrees centigrade and left the dressing room.

Almost immediately, I passed another male passenger in the corridor outside and, looking back, saw him enter the dressing room. My sauna prisoner would, it would appear, escape with a mild scare. Hopefully, he would link this brush with death to his loud manner earlier, but probably not. *Manners maketh the man*, and a lack of manners can certainly piss people off, I concluded, as I walked away.

That evening we attended the formal black-tie dinner and we were eight again. We decided to skip the theatre show which featured a ventriloquist and a singer, and opted instead for the Topstars ABBA tribute show, *Thank You for the Music*, which was in the Pacific Lounge.

We split for our cabin and decided to have an early night. The SS Azara was set to sail up the Mississippi River for the next nine hours. Outside shards of lightning lit up the sky while rain fell heavily.

Day 18

Friday 20th January.
New Orleans, Louisiana, USA.

Margaret and I rose early enough to watch the sun slowly rise. The information channel told us the ship was travelling up the Mississippi River at a stately 11 knots but outside, a dense morning mist is covering the water along with all the neighbouring docks and buildings.

We proceeded up the river to our berth next to a major bridge which carried cars and trains into the city. The mist finally disappeared and we played a short game of tennis on a still wet court after our breakfast.

Once we'd cleared the security area around the ship, we emerged onto tram tracks and a street overlooked by several very tall buildings.

"Remember that building," Margaret said and pointed at the Hilton Hotel. "It will be our landmark for finding our way back to the ship."

We stopped to help a pair of well-spoken English octogenarians who wanted to see antiques in New Orleans. Moving slowly using a stick and a walking frame respectively they intended to dine in the Two Sister's restaurant, an expensive but apparently, stunning restaurant with outdoor eating beneath trees in the restaurants garden.

"Damn well left the bally ship without our map," the husband quipped cheerfully, so Margaret gave them ours and off they went. You have to admire such intrepid explorers who have chosen to live life to the full rather than settle for a safe existence watching television from the comfort of an old person's home.

We walked a bit further and crossed several roads. Jaywalking doesn't appear to be a crime in the USA anymore and we saw Americans and tourists readily crossing before the white illuminated man showed. We strode into the city and noticed military veterans standing on street corners armed with collection boxes. They collect for the Veterans Chaplain Core and are on the streets all year round.

Walking around a group of tap dance street performers, whose admiring audience snarled up the footpath, we nipped into a branch of Walmart Supercentre to buy some cream in order to treat an insect bite on the back of Margaret's leg.

Finally, we reached the tourist's area of the French Quarter and wandered around the external fencing of Jackson Square, a small city park. The park was bordered on three sides by performers, artists and psychics who had set up stalls in the streets. The remaining side; horse-drawn carriages gaily decorated with colourful flowers awaited paying passengers. Their drivers shouted their itinerary to the sea of tourists who constantly flowed past. We set off to find Bourbon Street; the most popular tourist street in the city. We overshot it at first but that's okay as we discovered some beautifully decorated houses, dressed ready for Mardi Gras.

Witchcraft and voodoo appeared to be a big part of the city's culture and many shops sold related articles and trinkets such as facemasks and sculptures.

Anyway, once on Bourbon Street, we found that it was long and noisy as hell, with music coming from many locations, but none of it was the jazz I wanted to hear. It was still only noon but I fully expected to hear jazz music emanating from the city at all hours of the day.

The noisiest vehicle on the street was a de-commissioned fire truck that had been draped in colours of red, white, and blue. A party on board was already in full swing with people dancing and waving to pedestrians while singing patriotic songs broadcast from large loudspeakers carried on the open back. Many on board appeared to be military veterans and the music they played drowned out the music from the businesses they slowly passed. We began to tire after a couple of hours walking and sought out somewhere to rest our weary feet. Wafting towards us, carried on a cooling breeze, was a rocking bluesy version of the Animal's classic hit, *The House of the Rising Sun*. Like a powerful magnet, we were drawn to the music. We followed it inside the Big Easy bar and found the three-piece band set up at the rear.

We sat at two empty stools and waited for service, but it wasn't as forthcoming as I'd like it to be so finally, I went up to the counter but was ignored. Waiters came and went but none took any notice of me except to ask me to move as I blocked the service end of the bar. In frustration, I gestured to Margaret and we decided to take our business elsewhere.

We crossed the road where we found an upstairs restaurant and claimed an outside balcony table. We sat and listened to the same music while sharing a delicious large shrimp platter with chips, washed down by two Hurricanes each. The Hurricane, along with the Hand Grenade, are two local cocktails delivered in tall glasses with ice and a slice of orange that New Orleans is famous for.

Thus fed and watered, we rejoined the streets and came across a busking jazz group on the side of the street playing inspired music. We walked a little further on to a covered but open-sided market where tourists wandered aimlessly from stall to stall. Margaret bought a couple of New Orleans jazz CDs. And a poet, Charles Garrison, caught us examining his bookmarks for sale and recited one of his poems to us, then and there.

"The Strength to Face the Day by Charles E Garrison," he announced in a loud voice. A crowd gathered in around us to listen to him too.

The dawning of a new day
A new day has come my way
Full of joy or sorrow
I know I cannot say
But whatever be the challenge

I know that if I pray
I'll have the power that I need
And the strength to face the day

No one knows what the day will bring
It may be sunshine or it could be rain
But whatever be the problem
Whatever be the pain
If I sing and if I pray
My Master will give me the courage
and the strength to face the day
so my friend you too by Grace
have a brand new day
Filled with joy or sorrow and
Hope for a brighter day

If you start out singing
And never cease to pray
Almighty God will give to you
The strength to face the day

He smiled warmly and took a bow as applause rang out. We bought several bookmarks which carried this poem and shook hands with Charles and wished him well. I felt fated that we should meet and that I should spread his words further afield. He wrapped the bookmarks in a piece of paper that revealed him to be a pastor as well as a poet and on the back of the page was a story about life being an empty mayonnaise jar and be sure to fill it with the right stuff, cause if you don't, you may not have room for the right stuff.

Finally, we set about returning to the ship and walked along the concrete promenade which led almost to the ship itself. Local police have been invisible to us today, yet there is a feeling of being safe about the town. Even the motorists driving huge shiny cars and chrome covered trucks move about cautiously. Lots of polite and courteous behaviour can be observed among strangers.

But there was one exception to the rule. A tattooed, lean punkish white woman with anger in her eyes cut through the crowd and her eyes lit upon my T-shirt, a white cotton garment carrying a water coloured sketch of green leafed swirling palm trees that stood proud on a small desert island.

"Fuck your T-shirt," she spat as she swept past me and in that same moment, she grabbed Margaret's wicker bag, wrenching it from her shoulder.

Margaret struggled to retain the strap of the bag, but the girl was too strong and was moving away at speed. She dragged Margaret off her feet and along the pavement until Margaret let go of the strap. Once released, the bag and the girl vanished, lost in the swirling crowd, in moments. I stood frozen. My feet were glued to the pavement. I'd been taken completely by surprise.

Two tourists stepped forward and helped Margaret to her feet. She appeared dazed and with a cut knee but otherwise OK.

Maybe the girl was on drugs or mentally ill. I'd heard her outbursts of anger earlier in the day, but, in the bustle of a crowded street, I'd not got a glimpse of her. Something snapped within me and I set off after her leaving a shaken and surprised Margaret applying a paper tissue to her bleeding knee.

"I'll be back in a minute" I shouted behind me. "Don't move from here!"

A tall black man who had witnessed everything waved to me and pointed at the girl, who, because of her distinct dress sense and hairstyle, stood out in the melee of shoppers. She was still on the footpath but about a hundred yards ahead of me. She was calmly now working her way past the slow-moving tourists, confident that she'd lost any pursuers. She probably hadn't picked on anyone under seventy before because I caught up with her just as she turned off the path and into an alleyway.

I grabbed her by the shoulder and she spun around, eyes glaring, mouth open and teeth bared.

"What the fuck do you want?" she spoke, looking blankly at me. She clearly didn't remember me though we'd met less than a minute earlier. I figured she must be on something.

"Hand over the bag" I said in a calm voice, tightening my grip on her thin, white shoulder.

She moved to put the bag out of my reach, stretching as far as she could away from me and dangling the bag by its straps from her long fingertips. The bag hung open, dropping some of its contents onto the dirty ground below. The girl cried out, in pain, as I increased my grip on her skin. digging into her flesh.

"I'm going to count to five after which point things will get a whole lot worse for you," I said, surprising myself with my steady yet steely delivery. I reached into my pocket with my free right hand and left it there, clenched tight. She could now assume one of two things and if she assumed wrongly she may not live to regret it. She clearly understood my words and I wondered if she felt lucky today.

Seconds ticked past and we stood staring at each other. I worried someone would turn into the alleyway and distract me or turn out to be an accomplice of hers and attack me.

Finally she made the right decision. Margaret's wicker bag tumbled down and joined most of its contents already lying in the dirt on the alleyway floor. I released my grip on her shoulder and she stumbled backwards, down the alleyway rubbing her arm and staring unblinkingly at me.

I kept one eye on her as I leaned down and retrieved all the stolen goods. The walk back to Margaret was punctuated with many sudden backward glances but was also thankfully incident free. I found Margaret where I had left her. The good Samaritans had gone their way and she cut a forlorn figure leaning against the nearest market stall. She smiled on seeing me returning with her basket. I passed it over to her and went to give her a hug but she pushed me away. "Never do that again!" Margaret scolded. "I was worried sick when you dashed off. This is so unlike you, Luke!"

Back in the cabin, we showered and changed for dinner where

only Craig and Mary were in attendance. Many tables at the first sitting were missing the majority of their passengers and the waiters had time to chat at their station, a rare feat. There were evening excursions, quite expensive ones that involved an evening of jazz music and food while you travelled the Mississippi River on a paddle steamer or visited a restaurant in New Orleans.

By 20:30 a New Orleans local jazz combo called *Spare a Dime* had taken to the stage of the ship's Gaiety Theatre and served up a wonderful performance of traditional jazz. Individually and collectively they were brilliant.

It was an excellent idea of the cruise line to bring New Orleans onboard to passengers who couldn't leave the ship. Many of the older passenger couples have one partner who is too frail or lacks the mobility to disembark so these acts brought on board at each port really met a need and ensured the full enjoyment of the cruise for all. Margaret, having walked for hours today and then being mugged, slept through a lot of the show and was sound asleep again within minutes of her head hitting the pillow in our cabin that night.

Day 19

Saturday 21st January.
Still in New Orleans, Louisiana, USA.

We ate a hearty breakfast before heading off for the day. The shuttle bus dropped us at the Old Mint Museum and we went inside. The mint had started printing coins in the 1820s as General Jackson thought it necessary to boost trade in the city. It was briefly taken over by the Confederacy who printed their own coins before the Union side took it back.

Then from somewhere in the bowels of the three-storey building came the sound of a jazz piano being played. At first, I thought it emanated from above and we climbed the steps but only found a Jazz Yoga session in mid-flow. Heading down to the ground floor and into the small gift shop, we came across a male uniformed museum guide playing the most wonderful music. He was about to commence a tour and was gathering interested tourists by playing.

We strolled on into the French Quarter via Decatur Street and there was a definite buzz to the area that was lacking yesterday. All the stalls, shops and cafes were open and busy. We came upon a yard with a set of stalls, one selling just Lego figures, another giant metal grasshoppers, another sold teapots and bone china.

We returned to the ship and got time on the court to play three games before taking a late lunch. Up top, the weather was changing, and we had a swim before dressing for the Jazz Sail Away party in the Crow's Nest. By the time we took our seats the rain was hammering against the ship's large windows and lightning bolts flashed across the sky. The band weren't a jazz combo and, as a result, they sang the songs but without the touch needed to resonate with the audience. Jazz without soul is like bread without butter.

Margaret and I sat next to a window and watched the banks of the Mississippi go by. It had been dark since late afternoon but all along the bank's industrial structures sparkled and blinked like small cities. Periodically we passed ships at anchor, huge container ships and a car ferry, a two-story ship with a flat deck and sloped bow.

Our dinner table of six were in good form following the New Orleans visit. One couple had gone on the paddleboat steamer for their evening meal and a music excursion. The other couple took a different excursion to a jazz restaurant.

We exited the Imperial Restaurant and the safety of indoors and were walking outside up the length of the ship on the promenade and into the teeth of a gale. I was able to play my new harmonica, bought in the Mint, to my heart's content as no one else was stupid enough to be outside in that wind.

Dean Line, a 34-year-old ex-boy band vocalist and self-taught piano player, took to the stage of the Gaiety Theatre bang on time. Together, Dean and the ships orchestra put on a great show based around the music of Billy Joel, Neil Sedaka, Elton John and many others.

With the evening still young, we quit while we were ahead and settled for a glass of wine in the cabin.

Day 20

Sunday 22nd January.
At sea and heading for Progresso, Mexico.

The next morning, Margaret flicked through the TV stopping at the ship's information channel. "Luke, I'm sure a lot of the officers on board have changed. There seem to be a lot of new names I don't recognise. Even the deputy captain, the chief mate has changed."

I wondered whether this was good news for me, that officers familiar with my activities and victims have now left the ship? Would any new officers initiate further investigations or is it all water under the bridge?

We were now back in the Gulf of Mexico and sailing at 18 knots to Progresso in Mexico which is only one day away. High winds have caused the closure of all decks and pools.

Lorcan spent almost the entire choir session trying to make the *Impossible Dream* into something we could perform. No "Gorgeous!" points were awarded but the women were pronounced "Angels," for their heavenly sounding harmonies.

Sportingly, we lads joined in the praise and applauded the women.

We dressed for the sixth black-tie dinner of the voyage. Margaret is now having to revisit her dresses. I, however, simply rotated my three dress shirts and two dickie bow ties. I'd only brought one dinner suit. Sometimes being a man isn't that bad a deal.

We posed for photographs again. This time it was the "Luke the explorer" photograph. You know the one, arm leaning on the balcony looking into the far distance. Then it was Luke halfway down the atrium staircase gazing up at Margaret, my shimmering beauty. And finally, together we stood on the staircase looking lovingly into each other's eyes.

We had our full compliment at dinner tonight and the mood was upbeat and playful. I told everyone about the time I crashed my car in a car wash which went down a treat.

Margaret explained how she was taught to drive over a weekend by Michael, her ex, with a poker and three books to substitute for the car's gear stick and three pedals.

Roger told a good Prince Charles joke and Frank went on to tell us he'd served on a ship where Charles had been a navy helicopter pilot.

Apparently, Charles had eaten in the mess with the rest of the men and told a few stories of the hardships of doing royal tours. We parted company and caught the last few numbers played by the ship's orchestra and the feature act, a consummate cello player.

Then we walked to the front of the ship where an illusionist performed his first show. He bounded on stage and, with a large pad and marker, drew a circle and wrote the words, bowling ball, on it.

Then he shook the pad and out dropped a heavy bowling ball. We were astounded.

There followed a series of audience participation pieces and he finished by inflating a very large balloon and somehow, gradually, climbing entirely inside it. He did look funny bouncing around, at first with his head popping out the top and his feet sticking out the bottom. Finally, he completely disappeared inside it.

That was enough for us and bed called to us loudly. The ship had slowed to 11 knots and the banging that had sounded all day had thankfully stopped so we rocked to sleep with the gentle movement of the ship.

Day 21

Monday 23rd January.
Docked in Progresso, Mexico.

We were booked on the excursion to the Mayan ruins of Chichen Itza and we had to gather in the Theatre Royal at 08:00 for departure.

Despite setting an alarm, I was up and awake an hour before. Outside, dawn had broken and it was a balmy 24 degrees as I set off for breakfast. The Progresso harbour tugs pushed the ship the final metres to the dock and we disembarked smoothly. Seventeen coaches lined up on the dockside, at least ten taking five hundred passengers to Chichen Itza, over two hours away.

We swiftly boarded our coach and headed off along the seven-kilometre long wharf of Progresso, a shallow, working port.

Jose our Mexican guide pointed out that the flat and featureless land is pretty much as the Spanish found it in 1700, dry with rough scrub and jungle. No water sits above ground but sits in a water plate under hundreds of feet of porous limestone rock.

With a few exceptions such as new houses or garages, the passing scenery was entirely miss-able but the roads were surprisingly modern and smooth going.

Chichen Itza itself was fascinating—one of the seven wonders of the world. What makes it unique is the complex design of the main building as a pyramid built over and containing two earlier pyramids. Clearly, the Mayans had studied the stars and had worked out the movement of the sun and moon to create a calendar that is accurate and ran to 2012 even though as a race their flame went out 800 years earlier.

By 13:40 all forty-eight of us were back on the coach which stopped briefly outside Progresso to show us a pink flamingo feeding area. The bird's meat is viewed as a delicacy by panthers who, as it turns out, eat a lot of flamingos. Since both animals are protected species, the authorities couldn't cull either of them. However, they discovered that panthers can be kept away from flamingos by the placing of sweaty human clothes around the flamingos breeding areas and this has resolved the problem.

We pulled up by the ship, now sharing the harbour with the Carnival ship, *Harmony of the Seas*. Back on board, we dumped our bags and Margaret got a bit of sunbathing in for an hour before we played some tennis while the Sail Away Party began just feet away from us at the Riviera pool.

Tonight, the captain announced we were taking the fast route to Jamaica, so we should expect increased ship movement, and there was considerable rocking and rolling as we walked along the deck this evening. An elderly man had toppled off his mobility scooter and was lying on the carpeted walkway surrounded by concerned members of the ship's crew.

I assessed the situation and saw there was nothing I could do to help so we kept walking.

Only six diners attended tonight as Frank and Jill chose to eat Mexican in the buffet restaurant. Roger and Rose had been on our excursion but it says something about the number of visitors because we didn't bump into them once while ashore. The Topstars performed their *Night of a Thousand Stars* in the Gaiety Theatre tonight. We sat in on the early show and got great seats just two rows back. The show was a tribute to the London Palladium and gave them the opportunity to perform dance and songs from the 1920s through to 1970s which they did with their usual high energy and talented singing and dancing.

Then it was upstairs to the Crow's Nest to enjoy a concert by the SS.Azara Orchestra.

Day 22

Tuesday 24th January.
Heading for Jamaica.

Early this morning, I caught a brilliant red glowing sunrise on the ships forward camera.

Margaret and I dressed and walked to breakfast across the open deck, enjoying the balmy warmth with no wind. The ship's movement was now just a gentle sway.

10:00 found us arriving just in time for the Beginners Bridge Class which today focused on a quiz presenting fifteen scenarios for us to determine what our bid would be. Since none at our table had bothered to attempt the quiz yesterday it was a session of learning fast as Brendan went through each hand and justified why he had chosen bid X over bid Y. Some thought he was moving too fast and most felt we should get to play more hands rather than read notes and carry out tests.

At Ships Choir another song was added today, *Delilah*, which becomes our fourteenth song.

We exit knowing we have one rehearsal date left before we perform for our fellow passengers.

Sheila Townly, a rather eccentric astroscience lecturer, gave a lecture on, *What's New in the Solar System*? Although I found it informative and mildly interesting, I have to admit to drifting off to sleep in the warm, dark theatre. Frequently, I woke up to catch a bit more, before drifting off again. She cut an unusual figure with knitting needles stuck in her hair and periodically she lets loose a Tourette's type style of yelp that woke me on several occasions!

Tonight's black-tie dinner must be the last for some time as the higher temperatures normally signal an end to formal dining and the start of Caribbean style clothing. We were a mere six tonight as Craig had come down with a cold and Mary chose to stay with him.

"When I lived in Nottingham I was asked by one of the local gentry to carry the guns for a Greek shipping magnate at a shoot to be held on his land that weekend," said Roger. "Well I turned up and the local squire handed me a pair of shotguns and off we went. My gun was identical to the Greek gentleman's and the weapons and the cartridges were all monogrammed with his initials. Even the hammers on the shotguns were made of gold. I stood directly behind the shipping magnate and when the beaters drove the birds to flight, I would pass a shotgun to him and he simply pointed the gun skyward while staring straight ahead and pulled the trigger. Simultaneously, I fired with the other shotgun aiming and actually shooting the pheasants.

When the shoot finally ended the Greek tycoon turned to me and asked: "How many have I shot?"

"What did you say, Roger?" asked Frank.

Roger smiled ruefully. "I would credit him with all the birds and the tycoon accepted the outcome without question. Apparently, he believed he was such a good shot that he really only had to point skywards to make a kill."

"So Roger, it sounds like you're a good shot" I ventured.

Tonight Roger was happy to answer. "Yes. I'm handy with rifles and shotguns but you don't need much skill to hit something with a shotgun. When a shell is fired from a shotgun, the pellets leave the barrel and begin to spread or scatter. They can spread forty inches at a distance of 100 yards. The further the pellets travel, the greater the spread of shot." He went on. "You see the shotgun barrels have a choke to control the spread so you can adjust that to get the density you want. What's your weapon of choice, Luke?" His question caught me by surprise and I had to think fast.

"I don't own a gun or rifle if that's what you mean."

"No, it doesn't have to be a gun or rifle," he persisted, his eyes never blinking for a moment.

"Then I can answer this one for him," said Margaret laughing "He's dangerous enough with a tennis racquet! Playing doubles last year he caught me in the face with a backhand shot. He missed the ball entirely!"

The moment had passed and, within minutes, conversation had moved on. Well done Margaret.

Tonight we caught Dean Rock's second show at the Gaiety Theatre. He delivered the goods, packing the show with hits from across the decades.

We walked down towards the Pacific Lounge but Margaret felt tired and diverted to the cabin.

I sat in a largely empty theatre watching the Azara's Talent show. No performer was younger than seventy-five years of age. The contestants included several singers, a woman playing a Chopin piano concerto, a performance poet and the SS Azara tap dance class in their entirety.

An act called *The Performance Poet* was a curiosity, as he came on stage with a table covered with props and a rolled-up poem which he read aloud in Ye Olde English, delivered with a thick Geordie accent. He recounted the battle of Hastings in 1066 when King Harold II was defeated by the Saxon invaders led by William the Conqueror. Frankly, he really tried to do too much. He had too many props, tried to play too many characters and frequently lost his way in the monologue but this all added to the charm of his act.

No winner was announced at the end of the ninety-minute show but then how can you judge a winner between such diverse acts? I think they were all just happy to perform and the contest outcome itself was irrelevant.

Day 23

Wednesday 25th January.
Montego Bay, Jamaica.

The next morning, we docked in the harbour, tied up by the jetty. There was no need for the lowering of boats to act as shuttles, moving people ashore, as was the original plan. However, the dock area is very commercial with little of interest for the tourist in the immediate vicinity.

We ate breakfast and then played three games of short tennis during which time the newly commissioned addition to the Octavian fleet, Blade, arrived and docked to our right. It's a much larger ship than the SS Azara and has many more balcony rooms.

We finished the tennis in 25 degrees heat, Margaret snatching victory and both of us dripping with sweat. We weighed ourselves on the gym's scales and I was up six pounds while Margaret was five pounds. Not so bad considering twenty-five days and nights of eating and drinking and making merry. It was back to the cabin for a shower and a complete change of clothes.

Eventually, we were ready to exit the ship and made our way to the gangplank. It was while we were en route to exiting the ship that we met a couple of returning passengers.

"You're not thinking of going ashore?" the guy said.

"Yes. We were."

"It's a complete waste of time," he said. "The free shuttle drops you at the harbour gates and its chaos there. Taxi and shuttle drivers are charging $7 each per trip so $28 return to the town and there's nothing there."

He turned and climbed the stairs. We decided to press on and, stepping out of the lift with the gangplank in sight, we met a stream of returning passengers. They included Jimmy, our bridge partner, wheeling his wife along in her wheelchair.

"Save yourself the bother, Luke," he said. "It's just not worth it."

I looked at Margaret who had harboured security worries about Jamaica before we had even docked. In fact, Octavian Cruises had dropped a security notice regarding the island in our cabin door some days ago.

Margaret looked glum but her mind was made up. We returned to our cabin and locked our passports and dollars away. It was Jamaica's loss as much as ours.

Around the ship there were plenty of passengers who had come to the same conclusion. We sat in good locations on sun loungers by the pool at the stern, the baking heat making me drip sweat even when I had moved into the shade.

In front of us loomed a bank of green mountains visible through a hazy white light. Around us was the crash, bang wallop of an industrial harbour. I traversed the ships upper decks taking pictures before rejoining Margaret. We treated ourselves to two British beers. Then it was into the freezing waters of the pool before retreating to our cabin for a change of clothes.

We returned to the open deck, refreshed from showers, to find that the Sail Away Party had finished and we had already set sail, yet a coach load of passengers on an Octavian Cruise excursion had missed the sailing!

SS Azara sat half a mile outside Montego Bay and launched a boat to go back to the harbour and pick up the passengers.

Our docking slot had expired at 22:00 and forty minutes later, an MSC cruise ship called Opera had arrived to claim her berth. We waved to her as she passed by and we knew it would be another hour before we would set sail for Amber Cove in the Dominican Republic.

Captain Cox assured us that the delayed departure would not cause a late arrival at Amber Cove. Eventually, the ship's boat appeared exiting the safety of the harbour and battling across a stretch of open sea to reach us. Ladders were lowered and the passengers were taken on board and the boat raised to its storage location, outside a cabin on deck 7.

We just had time to visit the cabin once more and effect a change of clothes for dinner. Burns Night, the Scottish celebration was tonight's theme, and, in keeping with tradition, the ship's cook paraded the haggis into the restaurant, escorted by a waiter carrying two bottles of Scottish whiskey and to piped bagpipe music.

Arriving at the centre of the room, everybody stood as a

Scottish crew member, dressed in tartan, recited a Robbie Burn's poem in a thick Edinburgh brogue. Then it was on with the meal and haggis was served as a starter. It tasted much like Irish black pudding to me.

Apparently, in years of old, Octavian Cruises provided free tots of whiskey to passengers, but that tradition is long gone and none materialised tonight.

Day 24

Thursday 26th January.
At Sea heading for Amber Cove, Dominican Republic.

We went straight onto the tennis court and got three good games in before breakfast. Then it was off to the beginner's bridge class where Brendan actually set us loose with a pack of cards.

Each table got identical hands and the challenge was to ascertain what to bid and by whom. It was a game of unbalanced cards so the bidding was competitive and took longer than actually playing the game. Then he addressed the homework from the previous class and cracked through the questions.

Brendan finished a few minutes early and still the intermediate people flooded in ahead of time and pestered us to get us out of our seats. I felt angry about their rudeness.

Angry enough to take another few out? I asked myself. I surveyed the old and decrepit pests that made up their class. If there were just a few key offenders I could select it wouldn't be too bad, but each one seems as bad as the other. As the chatter reached a crescendo and Brendan struggled to be heard I realised the only solution was to wipe out the entire class. With nine tables in use and four people to a table that's thirty-six to kill.

The earlier killings went well I thought. If there was a

suspicion of anything other than food poisoning then I'm unaware of it. Have my earlier victim's deaths just been explained as tragic accidents, allergic reactions, food poisoning, old age or issues springing from existing medical conditions?

This is the whole problem with operating in a vacuum. I just don't know what the ship's officers know and what they are up to. Is anyone looking for a killer on this ship? Is anyone watching me now?

I think I'd know if I was being watched. A quick glance around the room showed that no one was paying me the slightest bit of attention. I have occasionally glanced over my shoulder in recent days but I never caught anyone watching me or suddenly darting out of sight when I turned around.

Taking out the whole class is a step beyond what I have tried to date. I'd have to purchase some more chemicals at our next port of call. I have had to endure twenty-four days of a cruise with this crowd of elderly gangsters who intimidate me and my classmates and try to disrupt our learning of the black art of playing bridge. I can see their motive so clearly. It's so we can't be a threat to them. They don't want any more card players in their class and the best way to keep the status quo is to suppress the beginner class and ensure they never advance in their learning.

But murdering the entire class? I'd have to think about this one further. It markedly ups the ante and the risk of detection. It may be a step too far.

We ate elevenses in the Palace restaurant and Margaret split for our room and a return to sunbathing, while I read the bridge notes in the warm and bright restaurant, before joining the choir for our final practice session.

Lorcan Bond, our choirmaster, shared his running order with us. Fourteen songs were listed starting with *There's No Business like Show Business* and finishing with *Do You Hear the People Sing?* The session covered ten songs but there were poor versions of two sung today that will need revisiting. He set up a technical rehearsal on the 28th and then walked through our entrance onto the stage for the afternoon show in the Gaiety Theatre. Getting one hundred people with varying degrees of mobility on the stage in a particular order is no mean feat.

"The choir on this cruise was a strange one," Lorcan said to me. "We started on day one with fifty singers and now we're almost at one hundred. Normally the numbers go in the opposite direction as the ship enters tropical waters and the arrival of strong sunshine." Today he introduced his replacements as choirmasters for the second half of the cruise. Forward stepped Tony and Alanna both singers and dancers from the Topstars troupe. They will assume responsibilities after the public performance on the 28th of January. I really doubt that many passengers will attend given the public performance as we are now in the tropics and it's a mid-afternoon performance.

Anyway, we dispersed and I caught up with Margaret on deck, spread out on a sun lounger. The heat must have been in the high twenties and we took a light lunch from the buffet with several glasses of water. I sunbathed for a bit, removing my T-shirt for the first time and exposing pure white skin to the sun's rays.

This evening Roger and Rose absented themselves. The rest of us attended the dinner and I enjoyed the tiger prawns on offer while Margaret licked her lips and polished off the lamb cutlets with some relish, leaving a plate so clean the dog couldn't have got a sniff of gravy off it.

We then attended the Gaiety Theatre, taking seats in the front row of the performance of Andrew Shaw, a world-renowned cellist, supported by the SS Azara Orchestra. Together they put on a great show. I keep having to remind myself during this cruise that in my ordinary life back home I could go a year without attending a live musical or theatrical. The ability to go out one night out after another is still a wonderful novelty I attach to cruising and don't think I will ever get over.

We decided to join the Lorcan Bond trio in the Hawks Inn for some soft jazz before quitting for bed before midnight.

Day 25

Friday 27th January.
Tied up in Amber Cove, Dominican Republic.

Amber Cove is a purpose-built port by the cruise line company Cunard and is twenty minutes from the nearest town, Puerto Plata and fifteen kilometres from a beach, by design. It's primarily a shopping centre, secondly, a base for ship organised excursions and thirdly has a water sports complex, which you pay extra to access. It has a sun lounger section where you can relax for free.

There is one beach at Amber Cove but there is also a low concrete wall, multiple large boulders, a mile of barbed wire fencing and a man in a lookout tower to prevent you using it. Signs saying *No Trespassing*, add to the clear and unambiguous message to travellers. It reminded me of the Berlin Wall.

"All that's missing is a minefield" added Margaret as we walked towards the shopping complex.

We have now been travelling for twenty-five days and have yet to set foot on a beach where the water lapping up to the shore is warm.

The Amber Cove complex provided Bic-Taxis, which are bicycles, two passenger carrying taxis who for a donation carried us both from the gangplank, for a distance of three hundred yards, to the entrance to the shopping complex. Once in the complex, we found a large number of well-stocked shops and bars selling all the gifts, alcohol and cigarettes we could wish to buy.

We walked along the white cement pier and enjoyed watching the dappled sparkling sunlight bouncing off the waves and creating a magical effect. Behind the Amber Cove complex, a Jurassic Park mix of vegetation and trees grew over the rolling mountains. Margaret thought of the invisible monster that moved through the forests of the *Lost* TV series from a few years ago and that had been compulsive viewing. There was no sign of the monster today but as he's invisible maybe I shouldn't be surprised.

In the open square area within the complex, a Tours kiosk stood and I approached it with trepidation, but I needn't have worried. By chance, they were selling a tour, leaving in ten minutes that visited Puerta Plata's town square, its Catholic cathedral and a gift shop, before taking travellers to the beach for two hours and all for £15 each.

The first view of the country from the coach as we drew away from the Amber Cover complex was a large refuse tip that covered several acres and sat butted up to the road, a stinking mound of putrid rubbish. Peter, our guide, gave us a smattering of the history of the Dominican Republic and of life in the country today, which is still below acceptable standards, but of course that's not what he said.

We were on the beach by lunchtime and were able to stay

swimming and lazing around on sun loungers for roughly an hour and a half. There was a restaurant which supplied food and drinks, and beyond it, about twenty beach shops. We took a stroll along the clean soft white sand.

Margaret was finally granted her wish and we strode out into the water and rode the waves together in a warm Atlantic sea. Margaret pronounced herself in heaven and we shared a daiquiri sitting on a lounger before slipping back into the sea for another swim.

We arrived back at Amber Cove by forty minutes ahead of the ships departure time.

We attended the Sail Away party which boasted music and cocktails. Margaret had her third swim of the day and we hurriedly changed for a casual dinner. All the team were there and everyone seemed to have enjoyed their various outings.

Day 26

Saturday 28th January.
At sea heading for Guadeloupe.

I ate alone this morning and didn't play tennis. I must have cut a lonely figure in the Palace restaurant, gazing out on the waves that stretched to the distant skyline. Margaret is unwell.

She was bitten several times on the legs yesterday, mostly behind the knees and on her feet. Last night she took the tablets purchased in the New Orleans chemist but they failed to address the itchy swollen bites. Worse still they turned her into a zombie. Having slept badly she'd stayed on in bed reading her book.

For peace of mind, I double checked my Talcum Powder container which still had the lid firmly in place, my hidden clear seal undisturbed. Fortunately, she's not suffering from any accidental poisoning, which I do constantly worry about, but not sufficiently to dispose of my crutch for life.

The full passenger muster, a safety routine required by maritime law, will take place at 10:30 this morning and she must show up for that one. After that, a day of lying by the pool seems to fit the bill.

Today is the choir's big day, their one and only public performance. In truth, I'm not looking forward to it. I'd be happy to rehearse forever. I worried that, as a short person, I may be pushed out to the front of the stage whereas, a position, just behind the curtains, in the wings, would suit me just fine.

Margaret visited the medical centre and the doctor who gave her some medication to address the swelling and itchy bites.

The passenger muster exercise went smoothly and at no time was any loss of passengers mentioned.

I attended the bridge class alone which left our table, one short. Brendan, our teacher, chose to spend this class explaining Rubber Bridge, and Jimmy, my erstwhile partner, rose up and left halfway through the class, in disgust.

"I want to play cards, not just listen to him prattling on," said Jimmy, loud enough for a few tables of players to catch his words.

That just left Jennifer and me to soldier on. We have played very few hands of cards in classes and adding of layers of complexity when the foundations are still settling in, is not helpful. By the end of the class, Jennifer was spouting rebellious words too so our table was near to complete collapse.

The Intermediate Bridge Class massed at the doorway with ten minutes to go and no amount of me giving them the evil eye made them go away. Amber Cove hadn't a chemist in the shopping complex and we didn't stay long enough in the town of Puerta Plata yesterday to enable me to pick up the supplies I needed. Their day is coming, of that I was certain.

I went to join up with the choir who were having their technical rehearsal and we were led around the back of the stage before going onto it.

There were thirty-seven men and we stood stage right clustered around Andy and the piano. The sixty-four women arrived and spread over and into our half of the stage. The men's tenors and bass are now hopelessly mixed together. The women alto singers are pressed in on top of me.

We ran through the two troublesome songs and I thought that we sound quite different now, on the stage. It also seems we can ease off a bit on the volume and concentrate on the diction. Before we left for lunch we all had to sign a form declaring we wouldn't sue if we got injured on stage. That was the least of my worries!

I ate a hearty final lunch before the show that afternoon and then retired to our cabin to shower and change into the black suit trousers, a white shirt and black bow tie.

Together we made our way to the theatre and Margaret slipped into the second row in the auditorium while I joined my fellow tenors in the dressing room.

There, the men and women chatted nervously as Lorcan took to the stage and introduced the choir. As we trooped out I sought out my rehearsal spot on stage right but things had changed.

The piano had moved, and some chairs for the disabled had to be found and brought out front. A lot of alterations and repositioning occurred on stage which ultimately led to me losing my visible, short-person spot out front and ending up three rows back. Margaret would have no chance of seeing me, I thought, and so it was. Periodically I appeared from behind a tall man to wave, between songs, in her direction but other than that I could barely see the choirmaster on his pedestal much less the audience. I saw Anita, who sat with Margaret and who also spotted me, but I was lost to Margaret, in a sea of singers.

The choir sang well, better than in most rehearsals and earned good applause after every number. A few minor errors lost us some brownie points, mainly at the end of lines when there were some singers going up and some going down. After our penultimate number, one of the bass singers, and a regular member thanked Lorcan and Andy for their work and their good humour over the weeks of rehearsal. Applause rang out from the audience and the choir. Then we sang our final number *Can You Hear the People Sing* and it was over.

I asked some of the men would they join up again for the next choir and was surprised to hear some with reservations.

"I'll have to wait and see what music they will be singing," said one older singer.

My, my, what the effect of a little success has on some people.

Within twenty minutes, the glad rags removed, we sat by the pool on deck and stole the final rays from a fading sun.

The dinner tonight was with a casual dress code but Margaret just didn't feel able to keep even the small talk going as she was still a walking zombie so we settled on a meal in the Palace restaurant, the food theme tonight being Chinese.

After a walk down the outer staircases where the air was hot and windy we stepped onto the deck then into the Pacific Lounge where Cantons, a band of five lads from Liverpool, were playing ukuleles to a packed house with standing room only. I thoroughly enjoyed their music and we moved on when we tired from standing at the back.

We got seated in the Gaiety Theatre with my choir buddies, Arthur and Geoff, accompanied by their partners, about five rows from the front. Red Rose featured four stunning sopranos who sing opera and pop music and their forty-five-minute set contained a 007 Bond medley, Queen's *Find me, someone, to love*, Whitney Houston's *I Will Always Love You* and a fistful of operatic numbers. They were backed by the ship's orchestra who were just brilliant. We poured out richly entertained and headed back to our cabin for an early night.

Day 27

Sunday 29th January.
Docked at Point a Pitre, Guadeloupe.

We arrived in euro land again! The ship docked right in the capital city of Pointe-a-Pitre, so that is good news for the independent traveller. The bad news is it is Sunday and a handful of shops will open today.

However, right by the ship are thirty small shops so we could have stopped our visit there and then, but of course, prices are going to be higher there than further afield. We kept walking as we have decided to go to Gosier, the main tourist centre, on the island and only eight kilometres away. It has many beaches to enjoy but today Gosier is celebrating Carnival and is closed to tourists. I was about to give up and settle for the shops next to us on the dock when a tourist information person told us of Sainte Anne.

"There are plenty of beaches there," she said. "Expect to pay 10 euro each one way, if you can find another couple to share the cab with."

We did better than that and found two couples and, together, the six of us sat in an air-conditioned cab and were driven close to a private beach for the Club Med Hotel complex, a few kilometres before Sainte Anne. The first language spoken there is French so I managed to act as an interpreter for the ride. The driver said the public beaches would be very busy but free to use except for the hiring of sunbeds.

He told the truth. We set up a pickup time of 15:00 which gave us five hours on the beach and enough time, if he fails to show, to organise another taxi as the ships sailing isn't till 17:30.

He dropped us off on a dirt lane with a few shanty cafes and I was a bit worried we'd been tricked until we suddenly reached the sea. There we could see miles of magnificent white sand, hundreds of palm trees and a marvellous bay of blue water.

We snaffled four sun loungers, two for us and two for Max and Chris, another couple from the ship, and paid the 10 euro each to the beach boy receiving a black arm tag that enabled us to use the loungers, the hotel toilet and eat at the Beach Hut, which was clearly an expensive hotel.

"Any Wi-Fi?" Margaret asked the beach boy and within minutes she s ringing Rachel, her daughter.

Once settled, we proceeded to paddle in the sea and sunbathe on the loungers.

Max and Margaret took separate walks further along the beach and noted that the strong breeze we were encountering had disappeared within yards of rounding the bend but the beach in that area was heavily occupied so we stayed where we were.

The strong breeze was a great plus for kite flyers, windsurfers and two birds that hovered over the sea near us and repeatedly dive-bombed the fish that swam close to the shore in shallow water. The birds seemed to work together and would fly for yards just scanning the sea before dropping like stones, wings tucked in by their sides as they crashed through the water, only to rise with fish dangling from their long beaks.

Max and Chris reported seeing large iguana's moving in the green undergrowth behind the beach, but Margaret and I didn't see any of them.

We ate at the beach hut cafe a Panini de la jour and splashed out on a couple of bottles of the local beer called Desperate, a red coloured liquid.

I tried to enter the hotel restaurant but was stopped by staff and turned away. "Wrong colour armband, sir," they said politely.

Back with Max and Chris, we found out that Chris was still feeling a bit dodgy about food having been confined to her cabin for six days' with the Novo virus. Four passengers had been flown home from Key West she said. So, my murderous activity could be mistaken for the Novo virus, interesting.

We gathered our stuff together, after we had returned from our final swim and beach walk. Trudging through the soft energy sapping white sand we made our way to the agreed meeting place. The local driver was early so we waited a further ten minutes for the clock to tick round to pick-up time. Our final couple, young loved-up Italians from the other ship in port duly appeared and only then did we find out that two further Octavian Cruise passengers needed a lift in our taxi. Their driver had reneged on their agreement.

Our driver appeared happy to squeeze two more in but felt the need to inform us that his licence was for only six passengers. That was fine we said and we all squeezed in and got back to the ship in good time.

There we met Bill and Joan along with others who had opted to spend the day in the town of Pointe a Pitre and pronounced it a dive and a dead town. "Even the cathedral was closed," quipped Bill.

In the duty-free area next to the ship, almost one hundred passengers sat on rows of wooden benches, logging onto the internet. It's pitiful to watch pensioners and frail elderly folk sit on benches in crude terminal buildings trying to contact their families.

We showered and noticed for the first time that both of us had been sunburnt. Not badly burnt but I had a patch on my forehead and the front of my left hand. Margaret just looked generally reddish.

Refreshed we stepped out on deck and joined the poorly attended sail away party that consisted of a musical duo who were very good but no entertainment team staff to motivate the passengers to sing along or get up and dance.

Margaret was in the mood to boogie so after a table tennis session she danced away and waved to the passengers on the MSV Breeze, a ship which wasn't sailing till after us and who were watching our departure.

Both ships exchanged greetings, ours a deep bass bellow and their horn a tinny slight blast.

We changed again and we joined our dinner table. There were

eight again tonight. Apparently, they'd all gone to the choir's concert yesterday and were ready last night to give me a standing ovation at dinner but we hadn't shown up.

The chat flowed easily across the table.

"I was talking to another passenger over lunch today," Roger said. "He told me it was rumoured that we lost a passenger at every stop."

A few heads nodded and no one seemed surprised. The three couples at the table tonight must have been on over one hundred cruises all told, so if they accept that up to twenty deaths are normal then my few killings will not be spotted.

Margaret then mentioned what Max had told us today about a Novo virus outbreak and his wife's slow recovery. The table went quiet.

Finally Roger spoke up. "Well, that's bad form by the ships officers! Nobody has mentioned a Novo virus outbreak to us, the passengers. I'd have thought that should be general knowledge."

"Funny you should mention that," Jill said. "I noticed yesterday a lot of new hand wash soap dispenser stations are now in position throughout the ship and unusually the crew are actively reminding passengers to use them."

"Yes, I noticed that too!" said Rose. "Of course I didn't think anything of it at the time but it's all now making sense. We should each take steps to protect ourselves against the virus."

Like what sort of steps? asked Margaret.

"Like frequent hand washing, using tissues when opening and

closing doors, not touching staircase bannisters or pressing buttons on lifts with your bare fingers" answered Rose.

"And washing fruit and vegetables. Don't handle shellfish" added Mary.

"So is there anything that eliminates the Novo virus?" I asked to all in sundry.

"Apparently, if you mix water with bleach, five to twenty-five tablespoons of household bleach per gallon of water you can kill the virus," answered Frank. "But, you know, I clean forgot to pack the bleach for this cruise!"

Roger spoke again "It's just not on. This policy of treating passengers like mushrooms, keeping them in the dark and feeding them bullshit is really unacceptable. We can be trusted with matters as important as life and death."

"It's understandable really, Roger," Margaret said "They don't want to provoke panic and have hundreds of passengers looking to be flown home or seeking medical assistance. If it persists I'm sure we'll be told."

"I'm not so sure," said Roger "but I admire your optimism."

We had an hour to kill that evening so we went to the Tiffany cafe where Grieg played the piano for most of the night in the public concourse, surrounded by comfy seats and round tables.

There we sat and played our card game for ten hands, with Margaret winning seven to three.

I watched four stewards gather close by, their conversation in muted tones, their hands encased in surgical gloves, their nose and mouths covered by masks.

A ships officer appeared and led them over to a small table by the window where I now saw an elderly woman lying prone on the floor. As one, they picked her up and carried her to the lift. A swish of the doors and the group were gone in seconds.

Margaret missed this entirely as it all occurred behind her back and I continued to play cards. Passengers were beginning to drop like flies on this cruise.

We finished our drinks and attended a recital by the Damask Duo. They were two girls, one a pianist and one a flautist who played a selection of classical numbers but finished with the modern song, Riverdance, an Irish hit composed by Bill Whelan. They praised the choir's performance of yesterday and afterwards we chatted to them as they waited on the audience to file out. The girls leave the cruise at Barbados and will return to a cold England with an overnight flight to Gatwick.

Day 28

Monday 30th January.
Docked in St. Vincents.

We rose late the next morning which was unlike us.

Margaret pronounced herself clear of the zombie effect of the tablets taken for her insect bites.

We ate a hearty breakfast and took in the volcanic island of St Vincent, as it appeared from the open decks. The full title of this kingdom is St. Vincent and the Grenadines. It is a southern Caribbean nation comprising of a main island and a chain of smaller ones.

We are docked in the harbour of Kingstown, the islands capital city. Next, to our ship, a local ferry arrives in the port and reverses into its mooring location with the ramp at the rear of the vessel already half lowered. The seas are so calm that they can do this without fear of being hit by a wave and sinking. On the quayside, a two-man Caribbean band are playing uplifting music on steel drums to entertain the disembarking passengers who walk past, without a second glance. I'm sure the band are not offended by this behaviour. They'll finish the gig and be gone by 1:00 eleven themselves.

For band and passenger this is a recurring event as a local band is engaged by the cruise line to greet passengers at every port. Clouds are still to be seen around the nearby mountain peaks but the sun is shining strongly down upon us and the temperature is already 27 degrees, even at this early hour.

We opted to play a game of tennis before going ashore and found the court still rain-sodden. The water evaporated quickly and within fifteen minutes the wet surface was a distant memory. Playing tennis in the Caribbean sunshine with the lush green vegetation covering the mountains behind me is one of the lasting memories I will take from this cruise. We retreated to our cabin for a shower and change of clothing before slapping on factor 50 and grabbing a floppy hat for a visit ashore.

Within the hour we were ashore and striding through the crowded duty-free area, that was filled with passengers just hanging about and blocking our way. It turned out to be the draw of free Wi-Fi that was causing the pile up.

We were approached by a squad of orange-shirted men offering sea ferry trips to a white sandy beach, St. Margaret's for $15 per person return. Talking to other passengers we were reassured that it was a good deal and that the beach was clean and had lots of shops.

Simultaneously, two taxi drivers approached us offering tours of the island and visits to the botanical gardens. It was all too much pressure and in the end we walked away from them all.

We slipped through the chain link gates and out of the port harbour area. Yards away we entered into a local supermarket called Massy and saw that prices were displayed in Caribbean dollars.

Prices looked good but we decided not to buy at this stage. No point in dragging rucksack loads of shopping around the town. We continued our walk into the heart of the town which was buzzing with activity, being market day.

About the town, policemen and women directed traffic at busy crossroads managing the endless queues of vehicles going here and there. There was plenty of honking of horns and loud music but no one really seemed upset by the jammed up streets and the slow progress from A to B.

Stalls lined the footpaths throughout and there was constant traffic of people moving in every direction. Many locals stared at us but not in an aggressive or confrontational manner. We seemed to be a curiosity to the locals, with our lightly-tanned skins and unusual dress sense. Most stall holders were selling to local people not tourists because on their stalls contained goods such as vegetables, fruit, clothes, homemade cakes and CDs.

The few that were selling sunglasses, clothing and tourist souvenirs seemed to be relaxed about business and none approached us or pressed us to buy. Through the crowds came schoolchildren dressed in smart uniforms and all of them at least six-foot tall. They looked healthy and were polite and well mannered. Many women walked about in uniforms, to our eyes, similar to those worn by 1960's air stewardesses and others appeared wearing nursing uniforms. Uniforms are definitely "in" on this island.

We kept walking, further and further away from the ship heading around the mouth of wide bay. We came across a large market made up of wooden shacks and corrugated roofs in which lots of locals sat eating and drinking. There were constant coming and goings of local vans and taxis. We reckoned the main purpose of the area was to provide shebeens—cheap drinking bars for the locals.

We walked into the market as far as we dared before turning back towards town. At one point we split up as Margaret had to find a toilet and it gave me a chance to visit a chemist I had seen earlier on the periphery of the market.

"Excuse me" I said to the chemist. "Have you a bottle of 1080?"

He reached below the counter and rummaged about for a minute. I kept glancing back, nervously, to the spot where I left Margaret but there was no sign of her yet.

"No" He said finally emerging, "but I have got something quite similar". He produced a small bottle of white powder with *Kittcha Datcacoll* written on it. "This is a cheaper local version"

"Man, you want to kill a dog or something?" he asked looking me in the eyes. I could see he was mildly curious but hadn't sensed my true purpose.

"Not one dog but several wild ones that have been attacking my hens," I said.

"Ah, a pack of them." he said, correcting my English and nodded. "I'd better give you two bottles then." He grabbed a second from under the counter and wrapped them up in a brown paper bag. "Anything else?"

"Yes, yes indeed" I said scanning the store's shelves. "Can you throw in some of that cream for insect bites and two packets of chewing gum?"

He did as requested and calculated what was due.

"That's 25 dollars."

"Thank you, sir." I handed over the dollars in crisp new notes. "And there is my wife, so I must run, thank you again." I imparted this over my shoulder as I left in a hurry with the bag. The cream and chewing gum were for Margaret and would cover the bag's other contents that I would hide in my bedside locker once on board.

We walked on uphill and found the town's Methodist church, where we were able to sit and rest our feet. It was an unusual church in that the pulpit stood high above the altar. There were no stations of the cross, naturally enough but large chandeliers' with electric lights hung from the wooden ceiling and across the central aisle. To the right and left of the altar were two mounted fifty-inch flat-screen-televisions. Above the altar, blocking out some of the colourful stain glass, windows that beamed in sun, hung a large projection screen. Perhaps the church is used for other purposes during the week, other than prayer? The rows of dark brown benches stood without kneelers, row after row facing the altar. The overriding colour in the church was a light blue, which in my Roman Catholic church at home, would be synonymous with Saint Mary, the Mother of God.

It was gone 13:00 and our feet were complaining from the hours of walking. We turned back towards the ship and retraced our steps noting the poor state of the footpaths and the presence of huge rain drains, some over a foot deep and just as wide, that ran alongside the footpaths. It would be easy to slip and fall into these trenches. Actually, we found later that Mary had done just that and was lucky to only cut her hand, which she had thrust out, to break her fall.

We revisited Massys and picked up several bottles of lemonade and cola to act as mixers. I threw in a small bottle of rum. It all came to less than $10 US dollars. The change was given in local currency so Margaret gave it to three Rastafarian types who sat hunkered on the path, beating out a catchy rhythm from small tin cans. They flashed smiles in her direction.

My overall impression of the capital city was that it had a busy prosperous centre but there also lay a great deal of poverty, just feet away, in the back streets and run-down alleyways.

A new airport is due to open on the island on St Valentine's Day this year and the locals are looking forward to it as planes will be flying in direct from the USA and UK and landing more tourists. Hopefully, the money will trickle down to the poorest of the poor.

We made it back on board and later attended the Sail Away Party, a non-event, as the heavens opened, and rain poured down. We hung about in the Crow's Nest where a pianist kept the music going to the waiters and half a dozen passengers.

That evening we dressed casual and attended dinner with our table colleagues. Roger and Rose strongly recommended the Octavian Cruise excursion in a catamaran to the island of Mustique where they'd lay on an exclusive private beach for two hours before sailing to a small town of Queen Elizabeth. All day, they were fed royally and had many glasses of rum, too many to count.

Another talking point over the meal was when we were discussing astronomy and Sheila Townly's lectures and I asked, purely for scientific reasons, that, if it's a given that mankind is going to populate other planets, has anyone yet made love in space?

"What sort of space had you in mind?" asked Frank and thereafter the tone of the conversation went downhill as we visualised the making of love in a weightless environment where you set off with high hopes but end up drifting helplessly past your partner.

Our wine waiter, Daphne, announced this evening that she is leaving the ship the next day. Rumour has it two hundred of the nine hundred staff are leaving the ship in Barbados. Ruth will be taking her place. Of course, these are Anglicized names and God only knows what her real name is. Both Ruth and Daphne are from the Philippines but from different islands.

We left the restaurant to catch the Cantons band playing ukuleles, in the Gaiety Theatre and I have to say they were brilliant and funny in equal measure. Sitting in the front row we were blown away by their performance. Then it was onto the final performance by Red Rose Girls where we were lucky enough to get seats for their

Stage and Screen show, accompanied by the brilliant SS Azara orchestra.

Since we'd had the afternoon snooze we weren't so tired this evening so we pressed on to the open deck where a *Hoedown Party* was in progress. There was a demonstration of line dancing and country and western music to match which was led by two of the fleet-footed entertainments team. I could only admire their energy.

Day 29

31st January.
Docked in Bridgetown, Barbados.

The ports are coming thick and fast now that we are in the Caribbean. Today we are in Bridgetown which is the capital and the largest city of Barbados.

The ship docked in the deep water harbour which is a good fifteen-minute walk to the harbour gates and from there, a further ten minutes' walk to the Kingstown city centre.

We took the free shuttle bus from the long narrow pier, which today plays host to three enormous cruise ships. Two of the ships are taking on board rations so container trucks are lined up alongside them. Lined up also and waiting patiently to board our ship, are the new crew members replacing those who are leaving for home. Six or nine months on board await the newcomers, people mainly from Goa and Mumbai in India but also some coming from islands as far afield as the Philippines.

The shuttle bus dumped us at the duty-free shop complex. A tourist information official suggests a twenty-minute walk to Brandon's Beach which is quiet and has a shop. We set off on foot and declined numerous taxi drivers and offers from tour sellers as we trotted along the bayside path. However several sellers did warn that we were heading to a dangerous beach. Who can you believe?

One of those was Randolf, who chatted to us as we walked and persisted longer than any other seller of services. He suggested a much nicer, safer beach on the far side of town and offered to take us both there for $10 US, in his Chinese made, bright red Tuk-Tuk taxi which he called *Manchester United*.

We liked his smile and his English was good, as he spends six months a year in England. Our maps didn't show the area he proposed in enough detail so we accepted his offer and climbed aboard *Manchester United* and made it to the beach in ten minutes.

He dropped us at a restaurant called Lobster Alive. Before departing he showed us the changing rooms and pointed out the glorious white beach, which was visible from the moment we arrived and drew Margaret towards it like a magnet. We paid for two sunbeds and an umbrella and purchased three half-price drinks from the restaurant.

The sun came and went as the clouds passed overhead and we settled into our ideal location. It really was a stunningly beautiful beach, straight off a postcard, a postcard normally received by me from some other lucky sod.

We were approached by several local peddlers. One was selling a large slice of watermelon which we bought after the mandatory haggling over the price. Another tried to sell me clumps of the Aloe Vera plant, that looked as if he had just broken off a bit from a whole plant growing in someone's garden. He'd probably picked it on whilst walking down to the beach! He, and his plant looked decidedly dodgy.

"You buy Aloe Vera?" he asked, leaning over me, the strong smell of Cannabis, wafting up my nostrils while he waved the plant about in his left hand. "It's the natural version," he drawled in his deep Caribbean voice.

Since we have twenty pots of the plant in our sun lounge back home I declined his offer.

Another hopeful with a bright yellow T-shirt and an even brighter smile offered us a chance to snorkel with turtles and to visit a shipwreck. We'd travel there, he said, in a glass-bottom boat for an experience that lasted about an hour.

I wasn't interested as I'm a poor swimmer but, to my surprise, Margaret leapt at the chance and she was gone from me in a matter of seconds. She ran to the edge of the shore and was helped on board a small white boat, littered with diving equipment and playing loud reggae music The boat cruised up and down the shallow water along the bay as a team of salesmen rounded up interested tourists. It was clear the boat went nowhere until the requisite number of customers were onboard.

Finally, they gathered enough passengers and the boat moved away from my view. When Margaret returned over an hour later, she was buzzing with the experience. She explained how she swam wearing a snorkel and safety jacket while passing within feet of several large turtles. One swam past her with a blue fish attached to his shell. All around her brilliantly coloured seaweed, fish, and plants fought for her attention. It was sensory overload.

Once she'd settled down, I ordered a large Lobster Bisque and a beer which was delivered to our sun loungers. The soup was deliciously spicy but the amount of lobster in the bisque was minimal. I'd hate to think what the "small" version of the bisque contained.

By 15:00 we'd had our fill of swimming in the beautiful clear water and were ready to move on. We declined many offers from taxi drivers and walked into Kingstown centre, across Independence Bridge and out of town, stopping on the way to look inside an Anglican Church.

Outside, a funeral was in progress and some of the long black mourning limousines flew what appeared to be government flags. Uniformed chauffeurs sat silently behind steering wheels, engrossed in their smartphones.

The mourners themselves had finished the funeral service and had moved outside, en masse, to a corner of the graveyard where the coffin rested for blessing before being placed in the already dug grave.

Smartly dressed mourners stood on mounds of soil and other ancient graves listening to the reverend's words. I'm afraid the wind didn't carry his message of comfort to us.

We walked inside the church and noticed many of the people had left handbags, parcels and smartphones on the wooden benches. What a trusting bunch! We stayed a respectful distance from the large gathering and left the church with the burial still progressing.

Walking on back to the ship we boarded and changed in time

for dinner with just four of the usual suspects. Frank and Jill were on a submarine excursion that was late back so they missed the meal. Roger and Rose had taken the catamaran excursion. Craig and Mary simply wandered about town, on their own.

The meal finished, we walked up on deck to watch our ship ease its way out of the harbour and then pirouette 380 degrees to swing the bow around to face the open sea. It's still amazing to watch an extremely nimble, fourteen storey building rotate and exit small ports at night.

Downstairs in the Gaiety theatre the Topstars presented their *Reel to Reel* show based on the British film successes of the last fifty years and it had already started by the time we had arrived. Inevitably a James Bond medley was included but they also performed *You Can Leave Your Hat On* from the film *The Full Monty,* where at least one of the male troupe stripped naked, his blushes saved by a strategically placed hat. Margaret recognised at least three of the troupe had been snorkelling with her earlier in the day.

We traversed up the stairs to the open deck where a Tropical Music quiz was in progress, run by the Entertainment Team. It's so nice to be up on deck at night with the universe twinkling above you and the temperature still in the high 20's. With two entertainment team members allocated to each side, the competing teams had to outdo each other in various games to win huge value, totally worthless points. Put your hands up when certain words are sung, drum the table when requested, play an invisible guitar, form a conga line, you get the idea. I was surprised by just how many people actually participated but it all came to an end when Sweet Inspiration, a four-piece band took over from the entertainment team. They managed to clear the dance floor in seconds and have people calling it a night in the first ten minutes of their set. We stuck it out a bit longer but their sound simply lacked any edge to it and the blandness failed to engage folk, especially those tiring after a long day of hot sunshine.

Day 30

Wednesday 1st February.
Docked in Tobago.

The shuddering of the ship as it completes the docking usually wakes me up most mornings, but this morning I misread my watch and I had us up and ready thinking it was 08:45, but I was two hours ahead of myself. Half an hour later, the thirty minutes of vibration started and channel 16 showed the bow camera was now pointed into the sunrise, the sun's rays glistening on the ebbing water that rolled on and on to the distant skyline. Already the temperature outside is 26 degrees centigrade. It's going to be a hot one.

Tobago is the last stop on our Caribbean island hopping schedule. We will be at sea for four days, starting tomorrow, before reaching Manaus in Brazil and commencing the Amazon leg of the adventure. Tobago is the smaller of two islands that make up Trinidad and Tobago, neither of which we had visited before.

We headed to the tennis courts after breakfast and in scorching sunshine, Margaret and I played a lively game before showering and heading down the gangplank and off the ship.

We reached the terminal building on foot and met blue T-shirted men selling taxi services around the island.

Margaret had picked up a map and Pigeon Point had been

mentioned as a good place to go so she identified it as our destination. The prices on display were vague, showing value but not whether it was per person, per trip or a return price. It turned out to be $25 per trip but this could be shared by four people. Also, the driver will return at an agreed time to bring you back to the ship for the same fare.

We buddied up with an elderly Swiss couple who agreed to share a taxi and off we went. The driver, Godwin, drove an Infinity car and kept it spotlessly clean. He told us his wife and one of his sons were school teachers and the other son a swimming instructor. We chatted away as he drove.

Pigeon Point is a government-developed beach complex. We paid to enter and that gave us the use of the beach, toilets and access to bars and restaurants. There was also a charge for the sun loungers.

Waving goodbye to Godwin we made our way along the beach. I was amazed to find that so many SS Azara passengers and crew members had been able to find this spot, which was a good twenty-five minutes drive across the island.

In front of our loungers, lying on the white sand were most of the *Topstars* dance troupe. We got chatting to them and they told us they'd spent fourteen weeks' rehearsing in Southampton before joining the ship, in Hamburg. They'd completed nine distinct shows for the winter season.

"You'll see them all on this cruise," one young girl said. The troupe now relaxed in the shallow water and shade of the palm trees. I'm sure these sorts of days making all the hard work seem worthwhile to the youngsters.

The beach itself was idyllic, covered in classic white sand, broken coral and limestone rocks. Tall palm trees swayed gently in the breeze. Some large, black shelled crabs sunned themselves on the rocks nearby and seemed to sense our presence and communicate such to each other. As soon as one ran for cover, under the rocks, they all did. How could they know we were there and that we were a danger as the waves continuously hit the rocks spraying the crabs with water and sand? They couldn't hear us or see us until we stood right next to them and yet they sensed our presence.

Several small shrimp-like transparent fish came close to shore and darted about under our feet. The shallow water stretched sixty feet out and a safety rope and buoys secured the area for swimmers and bathers only. Lifeguards, a first during this cruise, sat by watching over the tourists. Beyond the cordoned area jet-ski's, spouting fountains of water, sped past as did several small boats playing loud music.

We met two very friendly local police officers, one male, one female, and they seemed so pleasant I began to wonder if they really were police officers at all. They wore cycling helmets, open-collared short-sleeved blue police shirts and dark blue lycra shorts. They sat astride two sleek mountain bikes and carried mobile phones clipped to their waists.

"How are you, man?" said the male cop. His dark eyes surveyed me from head to toe. "Where are you from?"

"Ireland," I answered.

"You enjoying your visit to Tobago?" he asked.

"We sure are, officer" I replied. "We are just off the ship, which only arrived this morning and right now are about to experience your stunning beach and seas. Anywhere you'd recommend for lunch?"

"Shaggy's bar over there." He pointed a gloved hand. "They do a mean chicken stew but he doesn't start cooking till noon. Have a beer for now and he'll be ringing a bell when the food's ready for dishing out!" He smiled broadly his gleaming white teeth showing for the first time. Then he pushed down on the bicycle pedal and slowly both police officers resumed their patrol riding through the palm trees along the sandy path.

My name and picture clearly hadn't been distributed by Interpol as they treated me without suspicion. I looked, for all-the-world, like a typical tourist and I made certain that nothing I said or did altered that impression. The absence of any suspicion about the deaths on this cruise was still a surprise to me. If anyone, like the ship's doctor, had spotted a link between the deaths on board to date it has not resulted in either alerting the staff or apparently carrying out an investigation. I thought back to the conversation I'd had with Persel, our helpful cabin steward, just this morning. I'd asked him if the ships doctor was busy as Margaret was thinking of dropping by the medical centre for some painkillers for her back.

"Dr. Matthews is always busy Mr Luke" he'd answered. "We have a lot of old people on this ship. Sometimes they run out of medication, sometimes they fall and hurt themselves, sometimes they get tummy upsets and die."

"People have died on this cruise?" I questioned raising my eyebrows in fake astonishment.

"Yes, Mr Luke, many people have died on every cruise I have been on. This one is longer than most. Even one of the crew died this time" said Persel.

"No! Who?" I dug a little deeper.

"Ahmed Crutz. You probably don't know him."

I felt perplexed. This was not the answer I was seeking. "His name doesn't ring a bell. Who was he?"

"He was a kitchen porter. He'd been on board this ship for the last seven months. He had problems, Mr Luke." He pointed a rotating finger to his head. "He killed himself in his cabin, one, no, two weeks ago."

"Was he your friend?" I probed.

"Oh no, Mr Luke. I didn't know him at all. It's said his mother had died suddenly back home in Mumbai so…" his voice trailed off leaving the sentence unfinished.

"Are you sure no-one else died in the crew?" I couldn't put a name on the tip of his tongue but longed to hear Richard Chad's absence had been noticed.

Persel scratched his head for a moment but eventually replied in the negative. "Maybe, there are others but there are a lot of crew members—it's hard to keep track of everybody. Why do you ask?"

"Just something I heard a few days ago," I replied. "Probably nothing Persel."

"Anything else Mr Luke?" he said, pushing his trolley towards the door.

"No, that's all, thank you." So, if Persel could be believed, I was still in the clear.

We passed three hours, happily sunbathing, swimming, eating some local chicken stew and drinking ice cold beer.

Back at the terminal by the ship, a live band and singers in Caribbean clothing occupied a bandstand hidden behind the market stalls. They performed so well that at first, I assumed I was listening to a CD.

Margaret spotted some nice earrings and matching necklace and bought them for Rachel.

On board, we showered and changed for the Sail Away party and Margaret bought two non-alcoholic cocktails, mocktails, while I added the rum disguised in a water bottle.

Our plans, and that of the ships entertainments team were then scuppered by a heavy rain downpour. We fled inside and found the Lorcan Bond Trio playing to a handful of passengers and waiters so we took a window seat and, clutching our cocktails, enjoyed the smooth jazz right to the end of their session

Outside on the deck night had fallen and we took a walk along the deserted promenade deck. With no-one about, I burst into song and Margaret joined in. Together, under the stars, we crooned a Cole Porter number that he had written for the 1932 musical *Gay Divorce*. The sea door behind us opened moments later and Lorcan emerged, catching us mid-song. We had been singing his last song of tonight's set, *Night and Day* and he smiled broadly and joined in. Now the dance became a threesome, slowly rotating clockwise, and all singing merrily along. It was a magical moment.

The singing ended and Lorcan produced his camera capturing the last images of a beautiful diminishing Tobago, bathed in bright red moonbeams.

Feeling uplifted, I light-footed it down the swirling atrium staircase, Fred Astaire style while Margaret pretended not to know me.

We climbed early into bed with the ship motoring along at 18 knots. The anchor and chain periodically clanging iron against iron as SS Azara pitched and rolled in the turbulent sea.

Margaret took her nightly hip painkiller and we lay in the darkness awaiting the next shudder, crash, bang and then roll. I drifted off but was awoken by the bright light from the corridor beaming into our room. I saw Margaret passing through the doorway in her pyjamas and she was gone in seconds. I glanced at my watch and it showed 00:30.

Five minutes later she was back, with a white-suited officer in tow. He spoke to me. "I have agreed to move you, but I need confirmation from the bridge before it's definite."

"Will you look at the new cabin?" he asked me.

"Can you show my wife?" I responded. "If she's happy then I'm happy!"

We left cabin F100 and travelled wheeling suitcases and

dragging bags along to D179 on deck 8, a location somewhat further back along the ship. I made sure, even in my semi-conscious state that I brought the shaving bag and its contents, hidden deep within my case. We moved through the sleeping ship traversing its long corridors and lifts not meeting a soul.

Within an hour we had relocated and unpacked all our possessions. The room fell dark, with the only sound being the creaking of the wardrobes as the cases rolled gently against their wooden doors. Lying there in the dark, I found it hard to drift off to sleep and wondered why? Then it hit me. I realised I was missing the noise!

Day 31

**Thursday 2ⁿᵈ February.
At sea heading for Brazil.**

My alarm went off at. I turned it off and promptly went straight back to sleep. When we finally awoke properly it was a matter of a short shower, a hurried dress and out. We snatched a quick breakfast before joining Brendan Flood for Beginners Bridge.

An empty chair sat opposite me. Jimmy had made good his promise and had quit the program. Brendan distributed a preset hand to everyone and then sat opposite me at our table. His presence was more than slightly off-putting, but he saw my dismay and gestured to me, in an encouraging manner, to go ahead. I did but very hesitantly and with constant glances in his direction.

Thirteen hands later I had done it. I'd actually won nine tricks. My hands were shaking as I laid the final card. Brendan came up to me afterwards and said "Well played," patting me on the shoulder. These little gestures of encouragement go along way with unconfident amongst us.

The by now infamous Intermediate Bridge Class had begun to gather and I'd normally be getting angered by their chatter but on this day nothing could upset me and I smiled warmly towards them as I left the room. I'm sure they muttered to each other "I wonder what's got into him" as they took their places.

We exited Lawton's with Jennifer and chatted with her before visiting our old cabin where Margaret sought out Persel and told him of our relocation. She passed him £25 as thanks for his work over the last twenty-eight days'. He looked at me. I nodded that he should accept it and he did.

I visited reception and sought an update on our room. They fobbed me off for now and when we met Edgar, our new cabin steward, he had been told that we were there temporarily! Not true. This was meant to be a permanent move for us. The mere thought of returning to F100 filled me with despair.

We enjoyed coffee and then made it to the midday choir practice, the first under the tutelage of Aoife, who firmly took control. Tony, the male Topstars singer/dancer floated about, and the music director, David Dunne, sat by the piano. Aoife introduced our first two songs, *Three Little Birds*, a Bob Marley reggae classic. and *Can't Help Falling In Love*, a slow, lumbering ballad most memorably performed by Elvis Presley. In both, she sought to complicate with harmonies and the reggae tune posed far more challenges, with the typo's on the lyric sheets not helping. We numbered again around a hundred singers but the proof of the pudding, for her, is how many will return for tomorrow's practice.

Aoife operates in a no-nonsense manner, has a powerful voice and brooks no debate, asking that we all give it a try, as the song sounded great in her cabin last night when she first thought of the arrangement. It sounds like she has done this job before on other ships so I'm confident she'll make it work this time.

We ate lunch with Arthur, my Australian choir buddy in the Palace restaurant. He and his wife had been booked on this ship for its next cruise too but have a problem with the room they were allocated. He'd moved three times already on this cruise and was happy with the current room but hadn't been able to change the room allocated to them for the next cruise, a Norwegian adventure.

Lunch over, I took to our room where I updated my diary while Margaret catnapped, making up for last night's lost sleep.

The ship was still pitching and rolling so there would be no tennis today and the clouds meant no sunbathing topside.

We passed a quiet afternoon in the Palace restaurant playing a couple of hands of bridge and analysing the cards and the bidding process.

Yet another formal black-tie dinner loomed for this evening! Most passengers conform but by now are thoroughly fed up with dressing up. We have four more to look forward to. Tonight we took our first malaria tablets. Maybe they have some side effects for Margaret just wasn't herself. She actually asked me to finish her wine.

We had just taken our seats in the theatre when. Benny Mathews, New Zealand's leading tenor of Polynesian descent, bounded onto the stage and delivered forty-five minutes of operatic, New Zealand traditional and classical blockbuster songs.
Nessun Dorma went down a bomb. The SS Azara orchestra accompanied him and, once again, performed very well. Its quite a

tribute to all the performers and musicians that they can perform while the ground moves beneath them, the stage curtains roll from one side to the other and the occasional banging noise sounds in the distance.

We traversed the ship to the Pacific Lounge where Julie Decott changed her show to a tribute to Cilla Black from the soprano based opera and musical show advertised. Maybe she had a vocal problem but she accurately captured the bubbly Liverpudlian's accent and intonations as she sang her way through Cilla's career. It didn't take long, so a few of Cilla's lesser known songs padded out the forty-five minutes.

Amazingly, we learned that John Lennon wrote a song for Cilla and Julie performed it. She also included a song written by Cilla's husband and manager, Bobby Willis. It was instantly forgettable which only goes to prove that there is generally a good reason why some songs never achieve chart success.

Day 32

Friday 3rd February.
Approaching the mouth of the Amazon River, Brazil.

It's early morning and the motion of the ship is that of a steady rise and fall-with-a-slight-twist. The SS Azara is the fastest ship in the Octavian Cruise fleet and has a top speed of 24 knots but is travelling at a mere 18 knots. We are sailing parallel to the South American land mass and expect to reach Brazil and enter the Amazon River sometime tonight.

We are due to spend the next eight days cruising up the Amazon River and visiting Manaus, a city of 3 million people.

From this evening and for the next seven days, the open deck lighting will be dimmed, and passengers are asked to switch off their balcony lights. These steps are taken to minimise the attraction of the ship to millions of disease-carrying insects and flying creatures. Doors must be kept closed to assist the air conditioning system deal with the Amazon's high humidity and heat.

Once again, breakfast was a leisurely affair at the Palace restaurant's buffet. We sat by the window watching the ship cut its way through the undulating waves, the white foam rolling out from under her bow. The brilliant sun is only a warm hazy glow as it's actually on the other side of the ship. No birds appear in the sky. We are too far from land for them.

The room echoed to the babble of human chatter and the clanking of cutlery and plates. The officer of the watch reported our progress and speed and said we will enter Brazilian waters at midday. Around me, waiters in khaki long trousers, aprons and white shirts bustle about offering tea or coffee refills, collecting breakfast detritus or cleaning tables.

Anita and Brian joined us and chatted for a bit. *Free Wi-Fi on board* has been my mantra since day one of the cruise, but today, in Brian, I met someone who put strongly the case for no Wi-Fi. He recalled with horror the intrusive nature of the internet. The days sat on a train or on a bus, close to someone who was broadcasting their conversation to a wider unintended and long-suffering audience.

Anita then remembered a restaurant lunch being ruined by a neighbouring table occupant who used the meal to berate and belittle his lunching juniors and some sorry individuals, also chastised over a loud outspoken conference call. When her lunch was finished she spoke with the restaurant manager and refused to pay for her meal. She also walked up to the neighbouring table and told the man that he was a bully and a horrible person and that the staff sitting around him were ten times the man that he was and she turned on her heels and left!

So maybe the peace and quiet of the cruise would be ruined by the provision of free Wi-Fi. Maybe Octavian Cruises realise that by making it freely available their product, the cruise, would suffer. Maybe the majority of their customers can live very happily without the internet and have no desire to connect now to the internet. It certainly gave me food for thought.

At 09:45 the ships PA system comes alive with Laura, the Entertainments Manager, giving a rundown of today's events, talks, classes, special offers and cinema showings.

"I'm shattered," Margaret yawned. Her poor night's sleep resulted from the absence of the mattress topper on the bed. The topper we had brought to the new cabin had been removed by Edgar and we only discovered this at bedtime last night. This action had led to both of us being awake for much of the night. We'd confronted the miscreant this morning and had squeezed a promise from him to return the topper ASAP. Margaret reckoned he'd removed it out of spite because we'd forced ourselves on him and his rooms and had added to his workload.

"I'm not sure I have the energy to sit through this mornings bridge class" she moaned.

"Well just do your best love" I answered.

The beginners bridge class took an unexpected turn when Mabel, a slightly unsteady, slim white-haired pensioner sought to join our table. With Jimmy gone, we needed a fourth person. Mabel was attending the follow-on session for intermediate players too but felt she needed to rejoin the beginner's classes to clarify in her mind the basics of bridge. Being a current member of the Intermediate Class she was an instant enemy of mine, but I had no logical reason I could explain to the others to object to her presence.

We all agreed to let her join but, although she is now my

playing partner, it will take a while for her to settle in and for me to trust her.

The intermediate class gathered like flies around a large steaming dung pat. This time Mabel remained seated and beckoned her husband to take a chair at our table.

We exchanged pleasantries and I gathered my notes and got up to leave.

He had sat out the beginner's class, reading a book in another corner of the room and now settled into Margaret's still warm chair.

Brendan, pressured by the intermediate class's presence, finished our class five minutes early and then rushed to the door to belatedly hand out homework for completion by tomorrow. He apologised to our departing members and shrugged his shoulders when I queried why he just didn't lock the door.

"No key I'm afraid," he answered. "And if I leave it closed its opened every few minutes by passengers just looking inside to see what's going on in here."

That was the final straw. Tonight I intended to make it my business to find a little time to deal with this lot once and for all.

I opened the door into the theatre and found many passengers already inside, early for today's choir practice. I'd wondered yesterday at how many would return for today's practice having witnessed Aoife's *School Mam* approach to teaching music yesterday. To my surprise, they'd all returned! Aoife continued to spend a third of the forty-five minute class on breathing exercises but managed to add two new songs to the two we'd learnt yesterday.

Both of the new songs were taken from the musical *South Pacific*—*There Is Nothin' Like a Dame* was the men's number while the women were given *I'm Gonna Wash That Man Right Out of my Hair*. First attempts showed the women had got a better handle on their song than the men.

At the end of the class David, the pianist, announced he was going to work with the bass section of men on two numbers, neither of which are in the choir's repertoire at present. I suspect the experienced bass singers have formed a side group for the *SS Azara's Passengers Have Talent* show and were getting assistance. Leonard Cohen's *Halleluiah* was being sung as we left.

After a light lunch, I attended a lecture on the Amazon River by C Lee in the Gaiety Theatre and though it was facts and figures heavy, it was also contained interesting information about the region. Battling against C Lee was the warm room and the all-enveloping darkness. Many attendees fell asleep during his excellent if dry, presentation.

Back in our room, I couldn't shake off the lethargy and switched on the TV to find C Lee's previous lecture being broadcast. This time I fell asleep in our bed watching it. He clearly has a gift for all insomniacs. They just need to watch his CD to get a good night's sleep!

We both took it easy that afternoon until we exited the cabin to find Brian and Anita ready to play mini-bridge. The games are fun and the four of us get on easily. Brian is a bit of a moaning old toad, of course, but no one's perfect.

There were only seven of us at dinner tonight as Roger was cabin-bound with a cold.

Rose turned up and chatted happily, not unduly anxious about her husband. The ship was vibrating quite a bit and caused the cutlery and plates to rattle and dance across the tables. Not sure why this was the case.

In high spirits, we all shared amusing tales of life before the cruise. My contribution had happened a few weeks ago when I decided to go shopping for some new underwear for the cruise. Too often in the past, Margaret would find some timeworn threadbare pairs in the wash and promise that she would disown me if I was found dead in them. As luck would have it, a sale was on before we departed for the cruise and I picked up twelve pairs of medium-sized briefs for six euro, a bargain. I stored them away and into my cruise luggage they went. It was only when I was onboard that I tried them out and found them cripplingly tight. Not in the pouch area but from one hip to the other hip. I persisted with them for twenty-two days by which time I was crippled with pain from both hips and all areas in between.

Finally, I had to act so when we docked in the island of St Vincent I vowed I'd buy some underwear with more room in them. It was market day in the town and many stalls sold underwear but of the boxer variety which I don't like as everything hangs unsupported, if you follow me. Finally we visited a shop that did sell my type of underwear but they only had medium or XXL so I bought three pairs of XXL and returned to the ship where I tried them on. Margaret sat on the bed, watched on with amusement, fighting back the tears. Unfortunately, I discovered I had jumped from the too-tight-to-tango problem to the too-loose-to-lasso problem. The pouch dangled so low between my legs that I appeared to have grown an elephant trunk and the underpants so loosely covered the hips that I ran the risk of them descending with the slightest cough. Well I couldn't go back to the strangulation solution, so I had to continue wearing the XXL or *Liar size* as I like to call them and have tonight binned the other twelve pairs.

Once again tears of laughter were mopped up by thick white cotton table napkins and the men grinned broadly as they could clearly relate to aspects of my story more closely than they'd like to admit.

We exited the restaurant chatting happily and strode, as a group, to the theatre—a first on this cruise.

Colin "Fingers" Hatch took centre stage in the Gaiety Theatre His style was very reminiscent of the sadly now departed Les Dawson. Colin, pushing eighty years old, had over fifty years' experience in show business and was a hard-working trouper who looked destined to die in his boots, doing what he enjoys the most—performing.

Being the fourth comic to work on this cruise, several of his gags had already been told but he got away with giving them his own "special" treatment. He told jokes while accompanying the story with appropriate music on the piano. When he played, his fingers flew across the keyboard. He also had a habit of laughing, helplessly giggling to himself, before telling the joke. As you know laughter is infectious and soon he had the room echoing to laughter.

Two husbands met in Tesco's and had lost their wives in the store.

One said to the other "Lets both look for both wives. What's yours like?"

The other guy said "Well she's 35, long blonde hair, blue eyes and legs to die for. What's your wife look like?"

"Forget about mine. Let's look for yours!"

He performed a remarkable trick, even more, remarkable given his advancing years, of playing the piano while standing on his head. Finally, he finished with a rousing version of Evita's *Don't cry for Me Argentina* accompanied by the SS Azara Orchestra.

Out of the theatre, we were swept along the corridor, trapped in a sea of people walking to the rear of the ship to attend the Keys Duo. They were a saxophone and piano pairing and this evening it was to be a performance of *Movie Music* and featured music by Roger Williams, Henry Mancini and Shostakovich, to name but a few. They were very good and the more accessible set of songs made for a better show.

We exited and headed for bed.

I lay wide awake, yet very still, as Margaret settled into a deep sleep for the night. She slept on her side facing away from me and breathing slowly and regularly. I hit the light button on my watch and a dull glow lit up from under the sheets. The time displayed was 23:30 exactly. We'd been in bed an hour.

Very slowly, and with minimum movement, I edged my body to the side of the bed and slid from under the blankets. I then gathered my clothes and shoes and carried them into the bathroom. There I could dress and straighten myself before creeping from the bathroom and out of the cabin.

I stood in a brightly lit long corridor of passenger cabins that seemed to extend for one hundred yards or more, in each direction. There were doors on each side of the corridor and periodically I passed openings led to lift and stair landings. Not a sound could be heard. Not a person to be seen. This was an adult-only cruise and most if not all of the pensioners were tucked away in bed.

I walked towards the stairs and dropped a level to Lawton's. I walked past the bar and the ballroom which were both deserted save for a few staff tidying up. Lawton's door clicked open and, once inside, I closed it behind me, slipping on a pair of disposable surgical gloves. The room was not in darkness but was softly lit.

I made my way to Brendan's storage area, in a cabinet near the door. I ignored the new boxes of playing cards this time but removed his small portable typewriter and placed it on a table. I snapped a sheet of A4 into the machine and rolled the page up to the top where I commenced typing.

I extracted from my pocket a note that I had I'd cut out of the ship's newsletter some weeks back. So for the next ten minutes, I transcribed the details from that note on to the blank A4 sheet which I headed Intermediate Class Bridge Test.

I spent a minute checking my handy work and accuracy of the

typing before visiting the Library room next door. There I helped myself to paper before running off forty A4 copies on the HP LaserJet that sat next to the librarian's desk. Once done, I slipped the bundle of now hot paper inside a plastic folder and returned to Lawton's placing the typewriter back in its resting place. A quick glance up and down the corridor revealed it to be empty. The door clicked closed behind me and I retraced my steps back to our cabin carrying the folder.

Margaret hadn't moved. I slipped into the bathroom, closed the door and switched on the sink light. There I made up my concoction using the chemicals supplied by the chemist on St. Vincent's and what I had left of my own supplies. Using a damp sponge soaked in the liquid now in my bathroom sink I ran the sponge around all four sides of the bundle of A4 sheets, several times. I hurried on the drying process by applying the hairdryer. Then I had a quick glance into the darkened bedroom which revealed a still slumbering figure in the bed. Once dry the sheets were stored in the plastic folder and slipped in my bag. I shed the gloves after sanitising the bathroom and I threw what chemicals I had left into a paper bag. I'd get them overboard first thing tomorrow. It's too risky to continue poisoning people and to store away the evidence.

Day 33

Saturday 4th February.
Cruising up the Amazon River, Brazil.

Just after midnight we reached the mouth of the Amazon River and crossed the Amazon bar at high tide with fourteen feet to spare. The rich blue sea was replaced in the hours leading up to the crossing by brown fresh water, filled with nutrients washed down from the mountains of Peru.

The impact on sleeping passengers was the end of the vibrations, the strong rock and roll movement of the ship and the start of more gentle motions.

We awoke and made our way to the buffet restaurant walking across the open deck and experiencing for the first time the increased humidity of the Amazon. There wasn't much to see except brown water for miles and some distant green land.

I slipped my paper bag over the railing when Margaret wasn't looking and felt relieved to see it disappear under the waves in seconds.

After breakfast in the air-conditioned restaurant, we stepped back outside and managed a game of tennis. Margaret recorded her first Amazonian insect bite during the game and within minutes displayed a swollen lump on her throat just below her chin.

"Time to slap on the DEET Insect Repellent!" I said and she agreed.

The bridge class was interrupted by the captain's announcement that we would be crossing the equator soon and we did so minutes later. I believe there was a monument marking the point on the shoreline, but I didn't see it.

In the distance I spotted a small town but we were too far away to see much. But that didn't stop droves of passengers thronging to the sides of the ship and snapping away with the cameras.

The bridge class was another good lesson for me because I bid incorrectly, as responder and lost the game for me and my partner. During the game Mabel, my new partner, managed to irritate Jennifer with her shushing noises and Margaret threatened not to attend tomorrow, preferring a church service instead. Mabel is becoming a pain in the ass but I have plans for her.

With class wrapping up and the intermediate class invading the room I reached down into my bag and retrieved the folder and its paper contents. Picking my moment, when Margaret and Jennifer had left the table and before Mabel's husband had sat down, I handed the folder over to Mabel who was sorting out her own bag for the next session.

"Mabel," I said, "Brendan asked if you can hand these out?" It was perfect timing. She was distracted with extracting notes for the next class and storing away the ones from the last class. She had worked herself into a bit of tizz and my interjection just added to her confused state.

She took the easy option I had hoped for. "Yes, certainly, I will Luke. Leave it to me."

I unclipped the folder's clasp and left the documents peaking out, ready for her old fingers to hold and distribute. "Don't forget now." I reminded her, with a smile before vanishing into the milling crowd.

We stopped for coffee before following up a notice in the *Skyline* newsletter that announced that a clothes sale would be held today.

Arriving on deck 6, I spotted a veritable feeding frenzy ensuing, as a crowd of women shoppers were milling about four rails of sales clothes.

I lost Margaret at one stage and had to climb the swirling staircase a few steps to get a downward view of the bedlam and to spot her again. Hangers were strewn on the floor and women rubbed shoulders squeezing past one another with articles of clothing in their hands or allowing them to slip off hangers and fall to the floor. Margaret did her best but returned empty-handed.

At choir practice Aoife and Tony distributed the lyrics for a vinyl record I bought back in 1968. It's called *America* by Simon and Garfunkel and it's actually one of their lesser-known songs but I've loved it from the moment I first heard it, all those years ago. The choir masters didn't cover it today as we were focused on the intricate harmonies Aoife is crafting into the *Can't Help Falling in Love* number.

Afterwards, Margaret informed me that she's feeling excluded in the new choir. "I hate the way that women group together—they make me feel like an outsider."

"Oh, no, that's not good. Why don't you sit with Arthur's wife, Jean?" I ventured.

" No - I don't really know her Luke. Anyway, I'm just saying I might not attend after today"and she turned on her heels and left the room.

With the choir practice over I changed clothes for the gym and pushing lunch back to later in the afternoon, I ran 5 kilometres. I felt good and changed again for the pool where I swam with Margaret.

The Brazilian immigration and customs teams now on board cleared the ship for onward travel and we set off to cover a further eight hundred miles upstream to the city of Manaus. The pilots who will guide us there have now also boarded.

The ship started to move forward at about 16:00 and the captain came over the PA to say that we are clearing the Amazon River bottom by a mere six feet and are moving through the shallow water at 4 miles per hour. Our propellers are rotating so close to the bottom that we are churning up mud and plants from the river bed.

We ate with a full table tonight. Even Roger attended, although he was still bunged up with a cold. Plenty of vibrations at our table caused plates, saucers, cups and cutlery to rattle and bounce about. The other tables in the restaurant didn't seem to suffer as badly as we did. Speculation has it that we were running aground and that the stabilisers were being used to release the ship.

"Did anyone see those people on stretchers near reception this afternoon?" asked Rose innocently.

"No" gasped Jill. "But I did see three people looking very poorly and being taken from the restaurant."

"Now that you mention it, there was a crowd of passengers hanging around the reception area just before we came up for the meal tonight. What do you think is happening?" asked Frank. "Maybe it's the Novo virus striking again?"

The conversation went around the table, but no progress was made. It was all just wild speculation.

I kept my own counsel, although my mind was running riot acting out various scenarios, constantly flipping from one to another. These passengers may well be the first of many who will become ill over the coming hours, thanks to my evil act.

After dinner, we walked to the Gaiety Theatre for the second show from the *4 Voices*, and though they did sing solidly enough at least three of their songs had been covered by other acts in the previous thirty-odd days. Before the act had even finished, I was horrified to watch tens of passengers get up and walk out. While the boys bowed and accepted the applause, streams of people had turned their backs to the stage and were hurrying out the exits. Appalling behaviour!

We visited the upper decks hoping to get a view of the Amazon at night but the top deck was off limits. We settled for a couple of gin and tonics in the Crow's Nest listening to a pianist playing and singing Billy Joel and Eric Clapton numbers while lightning bolts flashed across the sky above the rainforests which bordered the great river on both sides.

It struck me as strange, that we were seated in this little slice of England, enjoying a nice 18 degrees, in a carpeted room with an elegant white piano, enjoying waiter service, paying drink bills in sterling, dressed in our elegant best, while outside the thick glass window it's 30 degrees with high humidity, wild weather and storms gathering in the distance. We were floating past one of the last great untamed parts of the world. The huge rain forests are only yards away, containing dangerous and wonderful creatures and insects. Maybe less than five hundred yards away indigenous natives slept in wooden huts, dressed in furs and hunted daily to find food just to survive. They probably survived for a month on less money than I have just paid for two drinks.

You can view it as obscene that such differences in qualities of life exist in the first place or you can take the view that a shipload of tourists provides a vital income stream for the people of the Amazon and that our visit will do more good than harm. Tourists cannot, by law, buy products made from any endangered species or indeed anything that has ever lived. We were to exit the ship in three towns in the Amazon and had booked on controlled excursions for a limited number of hours. We could, if we so desired, go ashore to wander on our own but most tourists will simply visit shops close to the harbour. All bags are scanned and checked on return to the ship so the chances of passengers encouraging animal killing for the tourist trade is negligible.

We also had to surrender our passports before entering

Brazilian waters several days ago. I'm confident that our imprint on the Amazon will be small and temporary.

However, given the danger in this tropical, steamy, hot environment I think the two thousand geriatric passengers are either incredibly brave or foolhardy to undertake this journey at their age and in their physical state. Margaret and I are viewed as relative youngsters on this floating old folk's home. Even the staff appear to treat us differently. The waiters fuss around the older folk, carrying their trays for them, finding them seats, bringing drinks to their table. If tackling the buffet provides too much of a challenge for them then the Amazon rain forests will be a bridge too far.

I'm sure several will come to the same conclusion and will view the Amazon and its forests from the safety of the ship. And why not? Sure at their age, they can do whatever the hell they like for they may not have many more tomorrows to enjoy.

Day 34

Sunday 5th February.
Travelling up the Amazon River, Brazil.

It's another day on the ship as we continue our journey upstream to Manaus. The impact of the Amazon environment on the ship and its passengers has been minimal so far.

This morning, the breakfast buffet was the usual fayre except for the yellow and red striped fly that landed on the cereal counter.

Startled, I duly killed it with a swipe of a small packet of Special K breakfast cereal. You can't be too careful. Later, I was haunted by the thought that I might have just killed the last of a rare species. Talking of killing I'm feeling a bit anxious about my deadly actions yesterday. Have I overstepped the mark? Only time will tell but what's done is done and there is no going back.

There was just time for another game or two of tennis while bizarrely, sailing up the Amazon River.

Then Margaret went to the religious service, led by the deputy captain, an Irish officer, while I attended the bridge class.

Today Brendan worked through the homework given two days ago. Jennifer went a bit quiet as she hurried to do it now.

Mabel's seat was empty.

I suddenly felt a pang of guilt, but it passed as she really was a most irritating person. In the middle of playing a hand of cards, she'd start whispering loudly to herself as she carried out the computations and calculations in her head. I knew it was unfair handing her the poisoned sheets to distribute, but she had been placed on our table for a reason and I'd like to think this was it.

I sat there squinting at the homework sheet as I'd forgotten to bring along my reading glasses and couldn't see what was written on the page. In truth, I was too nervous to bother with the homework. I was focused on the outcome of yesterday's deadly actions and waited to find out what degree of success I'd had.

I watched the time tick by on the library clock and waited for the hands to settle on 10:50. When they did I looked up at the doorway and found no one standing there. 10:53 and one person had arrived and stood waiting. 10:55 and there were three. They stood awkwardly talking quietly to each other. The noisy buzz of the previous morning was entirely absent. 10:58 and still there was just the three of them standing there, shuffling their feet. 11:00 and Brendan, suddenly aware that there was no pressing need to finish, let our class run on until 11:03. He was clearly surprised and double checked his watch a few times against the library clock. Both timekeepers agreed.

Where were the Intermediate Bridge Class?

He approached the three people clustered at the doorway and, as we left, he was promising to make up a foursome and play a few hands with them.

I gathered my notes and took Jennifer to the restaurant where we met up with Margaret. Jennifer had chatted to one of the Intermediate Class as she'd left the room and they were just as bemused about their classmate's absence as the rest of us. It appears the three who turned up this morning had missed the previous day's class. They'd also missed my poisoned test, I thought to myself.

After coffee, Margaret and I printed off our Aer Lingus boarding cards for the flight home and checked for any emails or messages.

As she'd already mentioned, Margaret opted to skip the choir and so I joined the lads, Arthur and Geoff, for the rehearsal. She headed to a sun lounger beside the pool closest to our cabin.

David, the Musical Director, outlined the master plan for the remaining days which included a few male-only and female-only sessions to work on the complex harmonies. This would be in addition to the normal noon classes.

For me, today was a day of great progress as I discovered I could sing a higher note than ever before! I was amazed to discover this ability so late in life. I put it down to the breathing exercises we now do at the start of each class.

We ran through all three current songs and then started our first work on Tony's baby, *America* by Simon and Garfunkel. With only ten minutes left of rehearsal time he sang it first and then, very remarkably, as most singers were unfamiliar with the song, we did two almost perfect run-throughs. I think the instructors, Tony, in particular, were much impressed.

I met up with Margaret and we lunched on soup and a small

trifle, chatting away with a couple from Sweden before splitting up again. Erik and Elas have met other passengers who have said that there appears to be a lot of seriously ill passengers on board.

"Do you know what the cause is?" probed Margaret.

"Nobody knows for certain," answered Elas "Some people suggest a mystery bug in the food, others think dirty water and yet more suspect the Zeka virus but whatever the cause the medical centre has been overrun with patients."

Just then the captain's voice came over the PA system. "Good afternoon passengers, this is Captain Cox speaking. Can I ask if any passengers who were medical doctors or clinicians in the past, could they make themselves known to the officers of the ship? This is a precautionary measure and will assist us if and when any need for such skills arise. Since we are now in an area of high humidity we will be increasing our anti-bacterial measures across the ship and I would ask you to cooperate fully with the crew whose job it is to enforce these measures. Thank you and do enjoy your afternoon on board the SS Azara."

I noticed, as we left the restaurant, waiters were forcing all passengers to present hands for anti-bacterial spraying.

That afternoon I visited the gym and ran another 5 kilometres and was dripping with sweat by the end. Each run I've undertaken was a challenge and each kilometre required a different mental argument to be won before I could complete it. The hardest kilometre was always the first because I knew there were four more to come. I searched the screen to pick on some positive motivational statistic. Can I complete the first kilometre in under five minutes thirty seconds? Can I build a song in my head based on the rhythmic beat of my runners on the cross trainer? For most of my run, driving heavy rain threw itself against the gym's windows and I imagined running through such a downpour in the nearby jungles and forests.

The gym work out completed, I then sought out Margaret, my queen of the sun loungers, who had sat in and then walked through the same downfall of warm rain, and enjoyed it. We took a swim in the pool and found the water a tad cooler than the air around the pool, but pleasant none the less. The heat is still such that all the fallen water has evaporated and the decks are dry to walk on within minutes.

By early evening the river had widened out and the land along the riverside appeared denser. There are definitely small buildings close to the shore and signs of man-made passages into the forests but no roads are visible. The river is also full of broken trees, branches and grass, all the debris flowing towards us. Pleasingly there are no signs of litter such as plastic bottles, packaging or household waste.

The captain gave us an update at 17:00. "We have covered five-hundred miles and the currents have been strong against us. We will not dock in Manaus until 10:00 tomorrow morning when we will turn into the river Negro."

We visited our cabin and changed for the formal black-tie dinner tonight. By my reckoning, we only have three more formal evenings to come.

The photography team had set up again in the atrium tonight for full length portraits so we stopped and the photographer clicked away taking pictures of both of us.

Roger was still poorly with a cold, so we are seven again at dinner this evening.

"Can anyone figure out what's happening with the increasing numbers of sick passengers onboard?" I asked. It was as if I'd suddenly granted people permission to talk about something that was worrying them, but they all felt they couldn't mention. A plethora of voices spoke all at once and then silence.

Jill expressed the first audible comments. "I don't know how all of you feel but I'm scared of whatever it is, that is knocking people over. I'm still recovering from my operation last year and my immune system is low. It wouldn't take much to finish me off."

Frank responded giving her a gentle protective hug. "You're not to talk like that love, you'll be fine." He spoke calmly and with authority. "I met with one of the ship's officers this afternoon and he confided in me, with what they think is happening. I would ask that you all keep what I'm about to tell you to yourselves, for now."

My ears pricked up. I wasn't sure I really wanted to know what was coming but forewarned is forearmed so I listened intently.

Frank had all our attention and he laid it out, in a low whispered voice, once the waiters had retreated from our table. "In the last twenty-four hours, there have been multiple fatalities amongst the passengers but none amongst the crew. Twelve passengers have died and almost thirty more are in a serious condition. The medical centre has been overrun and the request by the captain this afternoon for retired doctors was prompted by a shortage of trained medical staff on board."

He paused while his words sank in. Nobody said a word and so he continued.

"No one has yet identified what has made these people ill but they all have the same symptoms; severe intestinal pain, vomiting and dehydration. They then develop a roaring temperature and death follows if the temperature cannot be brought down."

Margaret gasped and reached for my hand.

"It's thought the bug is food related," Frank added. "Doctors have taken biopsies and samples have been transferred ashore to a laboratory in Manaus but it will be several days before they know for sure what they are dealing with. That's what's known to date, of course, I'll keep you all posted but remember mum's the word for now."

It was a chastened group that departed early from the restaurant that night. We split-up in the lift area and only then did we find out from Frank that Jill has been in pain from her hip most of the days of the cruise and that the painkillers hadn't worked. At last, we knew why she has been so silent and we assumed moody during the dinners.

We arrived with ten minutes to spare before Ben Mathews final show and what a show it turned out to be. He sang beautifully and then towards the end completed a number with his surprise guests the *4 Voices*.

We sat next to Brian and Anita to watch the show and Brian rudely continued to read his Kindle and ignored us for ten minutes before the show started. He was talkative enough afterwards complaining about Octavian Cruise artists who are paid handsomely to perform and then seek to top up the wages by selling CDs.

True to form, with the show over, Ben was outside signing and selling his CD's. We hurried past and visited the ship's pub, where a quiz based on TV comedy clips was in session.

Unfortunately not a seat could be had so we moved on to chat with Bill and Joan for a short while. Bill confirmed he'd visited a bar in St Vincent and had downed a yard of ale. I'd heard the story from another passenger and suspected it was true. He was on form and was regaling us with a very non-PC type of humour.

We retreated to the Crow's Nest where Lorcan Bond Trio were playing to a good-sized audience.

Lorcan played a song for the choir members in the audience and he seemed sad that he was no longer choirmaster. It's certainly different now and I do hanker for his light touch and gentle humour that was a feature of his reign. I liked his song choice and his mashing of songs. We stayed as long as we could, but Margaret was beginning to yawn and it way past her bedtime so we headed for bed.

Day 35

Monday 6th February.
Arrive at Manaus, in the Amazon, Brazil.

We slept in this morning. Margaret said she felt as if she'd had no sleep and therefore no dreams.

In recent days, since we started taking the anti-malaria tablets with our evening meals, she'd had epic dreams, every night.

Walking along the open deck and past the pools, my gaze fell on the colour of the water. We had turned off the Amazon River and were now in the Negro River. The brown water is gone and we are now cruising through dark, black waters, apparently filled with flesh-eating piranha fish.

It was a sunny day with a smattering of clouds and a strong wind in our faces so it's actually very pleasant on board. Passengers are spotted here and there examining flying bugs resting on pillars and windows. Even though we are now close to the city of Manaus with three million inhabitants and can see the harbour, even our docking wharf, few insects appear to have made it onboard.

We docked at 11:00, a full hour behind schedule due to strong currents against us and the captain's unwillingness to increase speed for fear of sending large waves rippling out and causing damage to other boats.

We ate breakfast and sat next to a couple whose husband commenced emitting lung rattling coughs during his breakfast.

He told us he was on his second course of antibiotics. He'd joined the ship with the illness and thirty-four days' later, he still sounded terrible.

His wife informed us he wasn't contagious but then she would say that, wouldn't she?

We got two games in on the tennis court and then one table tennis match before retreating to our cabin for a shower and a complete change of clothes.

Our visit to the Amazon is a dangerous one for people used to living in the Western world where many viruses and diseases have been totally irradicated over the years. Consulting with our travel agent we had looked up the immunisations needed before departure and so we were inoculated against Yellow Fever, Hepatitis A, Tetanus and Diptheria, several weeks before sailing. Malaria protection was a series of tablets to be taken before, during and after visiting the danger zone.

Now we just had to take sensible precautions with clothing and footwear when going ashore. Margaret opted for, leggings, a T-shirt, long socks and running shoes. Her body was covered by sunscreen and then 95% strength DEET from top to bottom. She had a body that attracted many pests. I should know as I'm one of them.

I too wore runners, long socks, Bermudan shorts and a T-shirt. I used the same combination of lotion and DEET. We both wore floppy hats and sunglasses. Frankly, I didn't care how ridiculous I looked. I was not going to fall ill in the Amazon and that's for sure.

Descending the gangplank, I noticed the line of ambulances pulled up next to our ship, beside the second gangplank normally used to disembark crew. A steady stream of passengers on stretchers descended the plank, carried by medics wearing face masks and gloves. Alongside the ambulances were three taxis into which, it appeared, partners of the sick or dying were being seated while their luggage was being removed from the ship and placed in the boot of the taxis. Everybody going ashore that morning could not fail to see the large number of medical vehicles and personnel arrayed on the quayside and it provoked a great deal of conversation amongst the passengers. We strode along the wooden dock, in silence, just two folks in a long line of slow-moving humanity.

A free shuttle bus service took us to the terminal building from where we then set off on foot.

We found Manaus to be a typically modern city with lots of stall holders and shops selling goods, mainly local goods. Unlike other ports we'd visited prices were not displayed in local currency and US dollars, just local currency, Brazilian Real. Even in C&A, a well-known shop in Britain, the staff told us they didn't accept US dollars. In fact, we didn't find any shop that accepted US Dollars so we visited a local Santander bank branch to try and convert US Dollars into Brazilian Reals.

They had difficulty locating an English speaker and when she appeared, she told us that the bank only carried out foreign exchange transactions for business customers. She directed us to a Bureau-De-

Change some streets away. Two bedraggled American men latched onto us in the bank and at that point all four of us set out to find the Bureau. The younger American's card would only release 100 Reals daily out of the ATM, even though he insisted he had a US $200 daily limit.

The older man was pretty wound up. "Everybody in this godforsaken place has lied to me since I flew in. We're stuck here for the next eight days and nobody speaks a word of English," he complained. He had a point. Portuguese is the mother tongue in Brazil and here, deep in the Amazon basin and on the edge of the rainforests there are probably few English speaking tourists that make it this far, into the wilderness. Certainly, the city shops and vendors are focused on local shoppers, not tourists.

The Bureau-De-Change proved elusive to find and everyone began to get irritable with each other and the fruitless search. Finally, Margaret lost her patience with the edgy pair and thrust our Manaus map into their hands before striding off.

"Give my regards to your Queen," the older man gamely hollered at her retreating back.

"I appreciate the sentiment, but we're Irish, not English," I shouted over my shoulder, trying to catch up with her. We climbed away from the tight city streets and swiftly came upon the Amazon Theatre (Amazonas in Portuguese), an opera house located at the very top of a hill that overlooked the city and just off a large grassy well kept square. Built in 1896 of materials entirely imported from Europe it now stood in its original state, except for the addition of electricity and the modern air-con system that were installed some ten years ago

Our visit to the auditorium coincided with an Octavian Cruise excursion group, so we sat and enjoyed the words from their guide before they moved on. Ben Mathews, the opera singer who performed on the SS Azara, had been at the opera house earlier today with a group from the ship and he sang a few verses to demonstrate the acoustics of the building and I believe the old building resonated with his rich voice bringing tears to many eyes.

We explored the building managing to gain access to the first and second-floor balconies. It was a stunningly beautiful building hovering on the brink of disrepair. We stopped for a snack in the opera house's restaurant and sat at a table outside. From this high vantage point the city lay stretched out before us and in the distance, the SS Azara shone in the sun.

We traversed the square before finding a Bureau-De-Change and exchanged US $40, which was the maximum the bureau clerk was allowed to convert. We visited a shopping centre and walked back in the heat of the afternoon sun to the harbour terminal. A short shuttle ride through the dock and we were back on board.

The ambulances so prominently displayed on the dockside earlier had gone and in their place sat a police car and a police transit van. I couldn't see any police officers so maybe they were on board the ship. I reboarded with reluctance as a part of me, the flight element of the fight or flight response impulse kicked in. I controlled the fear, controlled my breathing and rationalised the situation with an argument that suited my cause. All is not lost. Nothing is certain.

The dress code for dinner that evening was casual. The only topic of the day was not Manaus but the death of fifteen passengers overnight and the removal to hospital in Manaus of nineteen others. The sheer volume of ambulances on the quayside had been impossible to miss. Nothing had been reported through official channels to passengers but stories had transferred through word of mouth.

My thoughts were in a spin. I tried to switch the conversation to the Amazon Opera Theatre but Rose and Roger kept bringing it back to the deaths.

Roger, being an ex-policeman had chatted to the officers of the ship and their current thinking was still that some sort of food poisoning was responsible. No one at the table had yet connected the deaths with any common factor, such as the bridge class, as the victims took ill at various times throughout the afternoon and in different locations around the ship.

The majority of the dead, it seemed, were only found when they failed to appear for dinner last night and stewards visited their cabins. It cast a pall on the dinner and for that, I felt quite guilty.

This evening, we all received a slice of cake baked to honour the Queen. The icing had three layers of colour, red, white and blue. Today marked the 65th Anniversary of the Queen's coronation and our captain, Peter Cox, on behalf of Octavian Cruises felt they had a special relationship with the Queen as she named the SS Azara in April 1995.

We attended an Argentinean three-person dance troupe at the theatre tonight. They were a percussion and singing ensemble who had just appeared on the *America's Got Talent* TV show.

The group split down into a pianist who sang and played a few Argentinean numbers and the two tall male tap dancers/percussionists who performed very complex dance steps, twirled ropes with metal balls on them, in intricate patterns and played drums and boxes. At times the jerks and feet positions held looked very unnatural and incredibly awkward. The show resembled the Irish *Riverdance* show but it lacked a central theme to stitch it all together.

"They would be a good fifteen-minute variety performance slot but a full forty-five minutes, no," said Margaret. We applauded them off the stage and exited the theatre.

To ensure we got seats to the next show, we walked briskly along the outdoor promenade until we'd reached the Pacific Lounge and re-entered through the sea door. Thus we bypassed the slow-moving, determined pensioners who always jam up the interior corridor between the two centres of entertainment. We sat in front row seats and were joined by Jennifer and her travelling companion Gwen. First up was Julie Decott who won the New Faces TV talent show thirty years ago. She is in her early sixties but still has a powerful voice and sang a Maria Callas number along with some Adele songs and a medley of Andrew Lloyd Webber creations. She was followed on stage by Colin "Fingers" Henry who again shone in both joke telling and piano playing.

We headed to the cabin feeling exhausted from all the laughter, a couple of hours later.

Day 36

Tuesday 7th February.
Docked in Manaus, Amazon, Brazil.

We had booked ourselves on the Octavian Cruise excursion Rio Negro Cruise, and we met up with, Jennifer and Gwen, outside the theatre and collected a yellow sticker with a number 2 on it.

The conversation continued to centre on the deaths and sicknesses on board. Several more passengers had recently become bed bound. Simply imagining, I'd guess, that they were suffering from some food poisoning outbreak. It's far more likely that they were dehydrated as the humidity was running at 95%.

Still, *Skyline*, the daily newspaper, had written nothing about the happenings on board and instead continued to focus on the news headlines back home.

I started to complete the crossword in the paper while Margaret chatted away, hoping she might elicit what action the ship's officers were planning to take.

Before long we were on our way ashore and we boarded a small double-decker boat tied up to the same pier as our ship. The way it worked was the first forty passengers boarded and climbed up to sit on the upper deck and the rest, about twenty in number, us included, took seats on the lower deck. Both decks had solid roofs and were open sided giving a clear view of the surrounding area and allowing a cool breeze to blow through. Unlike our previous Octavian Cruises excursions, no ship's representative was on board this excursion and frankly, it showed.

The boat pulled away from its moorings and the cruise guide commenced his talk while seated on the top tier. He may have been giving some historical information about Manaus or the Negro river but his talk fell on deaf ears on the lower deck. Despite two large loudspeakers at the front and the back of the deck broadcasting his words the ship's engine directly underneath our seats won the war of sound, hands down.

I notified the two guide assistants on the lower deck. I said we are hearing some of his words but not enough to make sense. The guides then spent some time trying to improve the loudspeaker volume.

After a short while we pulled in alongside a floating restaurant and transferred from the boat to six ten-seat motor boats, ever so slightly bigger than canoes. The river lapped gently against the low sides of the boats, a mere four inches above the piranha invested water. Our boat had a helmsman but no guide. There were life jackets attached to each seat but no one instructed us to wear them and we didn't. However, later we saw more small boats, like ours and all the occupants in them were wearing their life jackets. I began to feel a bit anxious as we motored at speed through the dark menacing waters. Then the engines were cut and we waited for all the other boats to arrive.

We had reached an area of reeds where gigantic green water lilies grew, their leaves the size of round kitchen tables. In their centre were delicate white flowers. The six small boats lined up to listen to some words, presumably about the lilies and plants that grow there. But once again, we couldn't hear a thing.

We motored up the river and it widened into a broad stretch of water, similar to a lake. Our helmsman cut the motor for no reason I could fathom and we sat drifting in the vast expanse of water.

Suddenly, from within tall reeds on our left, three canoes emerged. They broke cover and raced towards us the occupant's waving long spears and shouting loudly in our direction. It's only as they drew nearer that I noticed most of them were children, in the main teenagers aged six to sixteen. The canoes split up and surrounded our boat, latching onto its sides with their fingers and drawing all the boats together.

In their canoes, the children held wild creatures taken from the river and forests, such as baby alligators, sloths and snakes and, by gestures they indicated they were seeking money. Some people paid to take pictures of the children and the unfortunate animals. Margaret gave money but didn't take a picture.

Eventually, our helmsman started up the engine which signalled the end of the encounter. The kids having extorted what money they could from us rowed away, jabbering excitedly amongst themselves.

A few minutes further upstream we passed what were probably their homes, wooden houses built on stilts where we could see women washing clothes or cooking a meal.

I felt we were unwelcome intruders, voyeuristically gazing into their lives from the safety of our canoes. It was a bit like visiting a zoo but finding the specimens on show were human. Maybe our helmsman lived there? He just looked inscrutable and remained silent throughout the excursion.

A little while later we turned away from the lake and entered a narrow stream that took us into the rain forest, a leafy backwater where we and another boat stopped to hear a lecture on Sequa trees and the Goa gum tree. It was the Goa tree that brought the rubber barons to the Amazon Basin back in the 1890s.

Our guide pointed out the blackness on the tree trunk that extended up for another fifteen feet above the present water level. "In July," he said, "the rivers water will rise to that level and the forest will become a home to many more creatures and fish until the levels drop again in Autumn."

It was astonishing and hard to imagine such a huge change.

"You heard of the monkey fish?" the guide asked.

We all shook our heads in the negative.

"It's a fish that eats birds and will jump up to two metres out of the water to catch one."

Amazing, I thought. The guide didn't manage to produce one of these birds so we'll just have to take his word for it that they exist.

We return to the floating restaurant for lunch and we are given time to walk around a local gift shop. I hesitated to buy anything as, given the warnings we received regarding buying anything, most of the items on sale seemed to breach the rules. There were lots of wooden facemasks, varnished piranhas on mounted plinths, jewellery, children's toys and of course T-shirts.

Luckily the four of us arrived back at the double-decker boat before the other passengers, so we took seats upstairs and enjoyed the commentary we'd missed on the outward journey.

We motored to the meeting of the waters where the black Negro water meets the brown water of the Amazon River. The two, because of varying temperatures and differing mineral content, travel alongside each other for ten kilometres before the Negro water dilutes into the Amazon water.

Once we had arrived at the meeting point, we spotted several pink and grey dolphins surfacing in the Negro black water a few yards from our boat. A rush of passengers to that side of the boat caused some concern but more dolphins were then spotted on the other side so the keel straightened up again. Eventually, we had to leave the unexpected, dolphin show and strike out for home.

On the outskirts of Manaus we passed many barges which were floating petrol and gas stations selling fuel to the passing boats. There are no motorways linking Manaus to other cities so boats and planes are your only options.

"I really enjoyed that," said Margaret as she eased off her running shoes when we had got back in the cabin.

"Me too" I answered. "But what surprised me was the lack of wildlife, especially birds in this part of the Amazon," I said.

"Oh, yes. I didn't notice but now you mention it…" Margaret

commented. She went on "Given the rich nutrition in the water there must be lots of fish. Why the absence of birds? Why no alligators or crocodiles? Are they there but just hidden within the vastness of the Amazon?"

"Good question, you should've asked the guide." I replied.

We played two games of tennis in the oppressive heat and slipped down a level to play a game of table tennis. Dripping with sweat we retired to our cabin.

That night the ship was still moored in Manaus as a sticking fuel pump had delayed our departure. It was a balmy summer evening and although a very heavy downpour had occurred in the last hour, the decks were almost totally dry. The humidity post-storm had dropped sharply and a nice cooling breeze blew across the open deck.

I lay on a sun lounger listening to the Entertainments Manager, Laura, whipping up the enthusism in passengers to dance and clap to the perennial party song *Hey Baby*. She'd been on this ship for fourteen years completing six months of the year on board and six months at home. With a sail away party to lead, on average, once every three days, *Hey Baby* must feature in her nightmares.

Two hours later she and the Entertainments team ran out of inane dances to perform and the DJ packed up and left so a blissful silence descended on the upper deck. That was until the PA system crackled life and we were told that the departure had stalled indefinitely. It wasn't a problem really as the ship was just going to retrace it's way back down the Amazon River stopping in several towns as it went.

We were due in Parantins tomorrow which is just one hundred and ninety miles downstream. I'm sure we could do that on one engine if we had to. Another rumour doing the rounds amongst passengers is that some of the engines have taken in water and need to be stripped down and rebuilt. All the aforementioned proved untrue as by 17:40 the captain had confirmed our imminent departure. The SS Azara emitted three deep long vibrating touts from her funnel and we were off again.

Lying flat on my back on my sun lounger, the world appeared to rotate around me as the ship turned anticlockwise to face back down the river. There was hardly a vibration as the new Manaus river bridge swivelled into my view and still the huge ship turned. On board women emerged wet from the pool, waiters carried trays of drinks and people played pitch and put golf, all seemingly unaware of the ship's rotation. A handful of passengers lined the deck railings to enjoy the experience and changing view.

The sun retreated behind a thick layer of grey clouds and wouldn't be reappearing today so I gathered my things and went below.

Dinner was well attended and we shared a few stories over the course of the meal. The table, and all things on it vibrated throughout. We continued to speculate the reason for the vibrations and the latest theory is that they are caused by the propellers bumping off the river bed below.

I longed to find out what was the latest theory for the sudden deaths of so many passengers was but nobody broached the subject over the dinner table and I didn't want to be the one to show an abnormal interest.

At the Gaiety Theatre the Topstars presented *Stop in the Name of Love*, a tribute show to the music of the 1960s and 1970s. The singing and dancing was delivered in a series of relentless high-intensity sketches that chart the love lives of three all-American teenage couples. Our choir masters Aoife and Tony acquitted themselves very well with the accents, singing and dancing. Tony did a particularly good version of *Me and Mrs Jones*.

Day 37

Wednesday 8th February.
Parintins, Para state, Amazon.

Parintins, founded in 1793, is a small town of 100,000 people located on the Tupinabarana island about 420 kilometres from Manaus. Boats are the most common method of transport for locals, often sleeping onboard, as it can take fifteen hours to travel downstream from Manaus or twenty-seven hours upstream.

The town holds an annual "Boi-Bumba" folkloric festival on 12th June but we are told a smaller version is being put on for our ship this afternoon. Unusually, our captain has mentioned it several times in dispatches so the ticket sales must be slow on the only activity of the day. The town has no coaches or guides so no excursions are offered, except the festival which must be located in a venue close to the harbour.

Today the ship has anchored away from the quayside so we were to be transported ashore using tenders made up of lifeboats from the SS Azara and local harbour boats. It would be a slow affair.

Users of wheelchairs and mobility scooters needed to be assessed by the ship's officers and they would not be allowed on the tender if the passenger lacked sufficient independent mobility.

The ships tender service started early in the day but almost immediately one of the three being used suffered from electrical faults brought on by the heat and was withdrawn. The Fred Olson ship, the Braemor, was docked offshore too and was using two harbour tenders to ferry passengers ashore. They would become available to us when she sailed in the early afternoon.

We ate breakfast and despite light rainfall, got our tennis games in before showering and factoring up for the visit ashore. The DEET that we use, leaves my lips numb and my skin tingles on receipt of the oil which I rub on top of the factor 30 suntan lotion.

We headed to the Atlas Restaurant on mid-ships only to find lots of people already queuing for the tender. After an hour, with no tender and a steady increase in waiting passengers, it's revealed by the hotel manager, that there was a collision between two tenders alongside the SS Azara which had led to several broken windows and both being taken out of service. A passenger was injured so it would be a further half hour before service resumed.

The tenders can seat over one hundred passengers and we piled into one from deck 3 when normal service resumed. It took time to load that number of passengers in the stifling heat. Outside the current was pushing strong against the tender and the river waves were choppy and splashing against the boat's side. Our tender battled for fifteen minutes to get across the river and reach the safety of the harbour pier and I for one was delighted to get off and onto dry land.

Many passengers were due to attend the Boi-Bumba show and the start time had been pushed back to facilitate late arrivals. It was being held, as I suspected, just a few yards beyond the terminal building in an exhibition centre and was expected to run for about an hour. The last tender was scheduled to exit the harbour at 17:00 but we were warned not to aim for that one as it may be full.

Once on the small island, we walked past the stalls and the exhibition hall and walked up a steep incline to visit a green church with a clock tower that supposedly contained an ancient relic. We found it bolted and closed so we proceeded to stroll around the town.

The town seemed poor to our eyes and featured many shops selling cheap clothes, souvenirs and little else. The main form of transport was motorbikes. There were hundreds of them racing along in all directions. Some riders wore helmets but many didn't. Not much English was spoken or shown on signposts or posters but prices in US dollars were widely quoted and the currency happily accepted.

We stopped at a few shops, bought some more underwear for me plus some lemonade and shampoo. Then we rested at a cafe with two ice cold cola's and managed to communicate with two women who appeared to be a mother and a grandmother to a shy black-haired little girl who spent most of the time hidden behind her mother's legs. She gazed out at us from her safe refuge, idly twirling with a small finger, one loose strand of her long jet black hair. She could only have been about three but she's going to be a heart stealer when she grows up.

Aware of the short time window we had, we returned to the harbour. There, a steward on the quayside was giving out moist ice-cold hand towels to mop our brows, wet our faces and generally cool down with. On boarding the tender we found a singer from the Topstars troupe carrying out a new role, allocating the seats on the little boat. It seems they all step in where and when an extra body is needed.

The return journey across the river was much quicker. We left the wharf with passengers queued to the far end of the footbridge awaiting the next tender.

Back on board, we sunbathed. Then there was just time for a swim and down to the cabin for a shower and change for dinner. The captain came over the PA system to apologise for the tender issues and delays and said we would not set sail until 22:00 hours this evening because of the effect the engine's vibrations had on the ship's restaurants. Apparently passengers had complained the night before and he was keen to avoid similar complaints tonight. So we were not alone in suffering. Ali, our waiter, said tables all across the restaurant parallel to us had suffered from vibrations too.

Dinner was for six as Roger and Rose had chosen to pay extra and eat in the Beach House restaurant—part of the Palace restaurant that assumes a separate identity at night and carries a cover charge for presumably better food.

The interest in the recent deaths had now faded so much so that there was not a single mention of it over dinner tonight. The ships policy of not highlighting the occurrence appeared to have worked and unaffected passengers were continuing life on board as if it had never happened.

The age of the passengers I suspect was also a factor in this loss of interest, in that they have reached a stage in life where people are frequently dying and its not front page news for them anymore. Its just a fact of life.

We head to the Gaiety Theatre after dinner to watch the piano artistry of David Dunne, the ships musical director, who at short notice, put together a show. He showed off his own piano virtuosity and then accompanied the orchestra's flautist Rebecca and three of the Topstars principal singers as each sang a different song from the musical Les Miserables. All of them were impressive as they sang with power and emotion. It just shows what they are capable of vocally if they got the chance to shine with their own material. He finished his show by premiering three of his own original piano pieces and they were surprisingly good.

We exited the theatre and went out onto the outside promenade deck where the brown Amazon river was sweeping powerfully past the stationary ship. The skyline was hidden by mist but was periodically lit up by distant lightning that flashed across the sky but was never heard. Along the deck, beetles, giant moths and butterflies landed on the white ship walls. As we walked I could hear crickets rubbing their legs somewhere nearby. They must be on the ship.

Day 38

Thursday 9th February.
Santarem, Amazon, Brazil.

The day is much cooler than we've experienced for a while. It's cloudy and 26 degrees with a thirty per cent risk of showers.

Santarem is five hundred and sixty miles from the open sea, has a population of 150,000 and like Manaus depends on the air and river for travelling as the roads are in a poor state. It's located at a point where the clear blue Tapajos River meets the Amazon River, both flowing in a parallel journey of colours before merging about a mile downstream.

We rose late letting the excursions get away which also meant that the restaurants were quieter than normal. We found seats next to Larry, from the Entertainments team. He seemed to be eating his breakfast in a smart new suit and I watched Margaret's eyes hone in on Larry's yoke dripping from a boiled egg that came within inches of dribbling on his black jacket as it fell from his bread.

"Why the suit Barry?" Margaret asked.

He took his head out of the newspaper he was reading and answered "There is a fire drill happening in a few minutes and as I'm an officer I must attend it wearing my work clothes."

"So in a real fire situation would you have to return to your cabin for a life jacket and don your finest suit before heading for the muster station? Margaret probed further.

He smiled weakly and didn't reply other than to stick his head back into his newspaper. Our conversation was at an end.

"Did you know Richard Chad?" I asked. It was one of those stupid moments when I thought I was just asking myself a question but then heard myself actually asking it out loud. This time he jerked his head up and stared at me with a new interest. Even Margaret looked up.

"Yes, I knew Richard. What about him?" Larry asked.

"Oh, nothing Larry." I started to backpedal and found myself stuttering to buy time while I thought my way out of this one. "I heard one of the stewards say that he'd gone missing on this cruise and wondered if there was an update."

Larry thought for a minute and then replied "No, I don't think he's been found yet. I've gotta say it's all a bit strange. I had to take over some of his duties and I really thought he'd reappear but he never did."

I nodded my thanks and Larry settled back down to enjoy the rest of his breakfast. I couldn't help noticing he'd dropped some of the yellow yoke on his breast pocket as it had journeyed to his mouth. Margaret had spotted it too but we left him in blissful ignorance.

Glancing down from the top deck, we saw the independent passengers proceed on foot along the one hundred-yard pier and turn right past a cluster of gift stalls and out of the harbour complex.

Beyond, a row of taxis sat in the morning sun awaiting occupants.

We walked down the gangplank, with a bag carrying maps and water. We past a three-storey ship that was tied up and getting ready to depart. On the upper deck hung hundreds of hammocks with people already lying in them. Other women sat next to the hammocks chatting away to their occupants. They all smiled and waved at us. On the lower deck, three big storage areas were filled with bananas and bags of apples and other fruits.

We shared a taxi into town with another couple and were dropped near an Information Centre located along the harbour front. We walked over to it and I found half a dozen guys hanging about with identification pouches slung from their necks.

One of the older men stepped forward and spoke with us in English."We've run out of maps in English, so here are some in Portuguese!"

I thanked him and took the map.

"You want Wi-Fi?" he asked.

"Yes, please." Margaret answered.

He pointed to a younger man beside him. "Go with this guy, he'll take you to the London Hotel and get you free Wi-Fi."

We did as he suggested and the young man did all the talking at the hotel when we reached it. Wearing his Tourist Information identification, he took us up to the top floor, through glass doors and out onto a huge balcony which provided a breathtaking view of the large harbour. The heat was intense but the view was so good I stayed out there for a while. He handed Margaret the password for the Wi-Fi and excitedly, she rang home.

Once fed and watered we stepped out and into the streets containing the by now usual mix of shops and high pavements. We walked through the market located in a square in front of a beautiful blue and white cathedral but there were few vendors taking any interest in us and fewer still tourists. We set about walking back to the ship and passed many shops, restaurants and DIY stores on the land side of the road. On the harbour side hundreds of pretty double-decker boats were moored many with people living on them.

We spotted Bill and Joan slightly ahead of us. They'd spotted a couple of large iguanas scurrying between the harbour rocks which rose above the water line. One big yellow iguana just stared right back at us and flicked his tongue menacingly.

We reached a fish market jutting out into the harbour, and discovered that it was made of wood and stood on stilts. The market was now closed but an enterprising group of local men were earning good money, by taking a dollar off every tourist and in return tossing a piece of fish, attached to a string line, out into the water where pink and grey dolphins swam about twenty feet away. There were four dolphins feeding today and they generally got the fish after three casts of the string. I looked around the building while Margaret queued for dolphin feeding. Several cranes stood on the deserted tables that lined the covered market and at first, I thought they were statues, so still did they stand. I was quite startled when one of the birds suddenly moved and flew off.

Back on board we ate in the buffet restaurant and sat by the pool. The clouds arrived and went. We took a swim in the pool and then changed to watch the ship sail away from Santarem, probably the friendliest people and the nicest town of the three we'd visited in the Amazon on this cruise.

Dinner was attended by the full complement and the vibrations had also returned, particularly at my end of the table where Ali had laid an extra table cloth to try and dull the effects.

At the Gaiety Theatre Gerard Benny, another ex-West End singer, delivered his selection of songs. It's amazing just how blasé we have become with night after night of entertainment and formal dining. There is some shock awaiting us on our return when a toasted cheese is served up for tea with a comment of "that's your lot. If you want anything else you'll have to make it yourself."

This evening we chatted at length to Bill and Joan and I was amazed to hear their experiences of rude behaviour from some of the other passengers. Bill reckoned it was his East End accent that prompted the behaviour. "It's snobbery," he said.

"Maybe so but it's still out of order. Point them out to me." I insisted but he declined.

"Forget it mate," he said. "I already have."

At the other end of the ship Robin Essot and Brian Social are performing under the name of The International Piano Duo, an act where two pianists share one piano. They play seated on separate stools and seem to command control of separate ends of the keyboard, alternating their seats for different numbers. They played music by Brahms, Dvorak alongside poignant miniatures by Schubert and Faure.

    I had hoped their playing would include some humorous moments when they tried to play notes located well within the other's part of the keyboard but not so. When such moments arose they simply facilitated each other by swapping seats and the result was some fine music to savour.

Day 39

Friday 10th February.
Leaving the Amazon River, Brazil.

Today is the first of five days at sea as we sail to St Vincent on Cape Verdi. We were due to arrive on Wednesday for the briefest of stays, leaving that very same afternoon.

We ate breakfast and, despite windy conditions, we got two games of tennis in until Margaret admitted she was exhausted and we stopped. She said she thought the anti-malaria tablets were affecting her.

She went directly to the beginner's bridge class while I showered and then joined her there. I anxiously awaited Mabel's arrival but her absence made my morning. It looks like she had succumbed to the poison and I was able to relax as the connection between me and those deadly A4 sheets has now been severed forever. Brendan joined our table again to make up a foursome.

As we finished with the class, I noticed again, the absence of the majority of the intermediate class. Brendan invited anyone who wanted, to stay on for the next class. He got a few takers. I left the small gathering setting up on two tables.

As promised I arrived at the tennis court at 11:00 but there was no sign of Bill. Another four players are on the court so I walked away and joined Jennifer and Margaret in the Palace restaurant where we chatted over coffee.

A little while later, I joined the tenor men for the choir rehearsal. David announced he had four new songs to distribute and promptly launched into them. Konchek, an elderly man who sat nearby in the tenor's section on previous days, sat with us today and I welcomed him in. He stood behind my right shoulder and I didn't hear a peep out of him. Eventually, I glanced over mid-song and his lips were moving but not much was coming out. Possibly praying I thought.

After lunch we sat beside the pool at the stern of the ship and spoke with Jimmy, whom we hadn't seen anything of for quite a while. Apparently, Paula had further breathing issues and struggled to clear air out of her lungs. The ship's doctor wanted her hospitalised in Manaus and she was only still onboard because Jimmy and Paula signed a disclaimer for Octavian Cruises against any death or insurance claim. While we chatted, Paula lay on a sun lounger nearby. Jimmy reckoned she wasn't up to chatting, so I left her alone.

The *Crossing of the Line Ceremony* is held every time SS Azara crosses the equator and its an initiation rite for sailors who have never before crossed the equator. The Entertainments team had scheduled the ceremony for 14:00 at the Riviera pool.

Laura, the Entertainments Manager joined King Neptune on chairs located on the stage behind the pool. Before them, two teams were to fight it out over five rounds for the right of SS Azara to cross over into the Northern hemisphere.

King Neptune's team of Shellbacks were black dressed pirates and competed with white uniformed ships officers called Pollywogs, in a series of games held around the pool. The sailors who have already crossed the equator are called Shellbacks and the rigged contest ended in a points tie.

Meanwhile during the contest, the weather turned nasty. Torrential rain began hammering down on the deck scattering passengers in all directions. We stayed until the end when the ship's team captain defeated his opposite number by knocking him off the greasy pole straddling the pool and into the water. Both teams and the adjudicator then hopped in the nearby hot tub and were covered by buckets of colourful paint. The ship was now able to sail on to Southampton!

We visited our cabin and shed the wet shoes and clothes. Together we headed upstairs to the Hawks Inn to play cards and read. Entering the lounge, I noticed a large number attending the Water Colours with Diane painting class, a daily occurrence while at sea.

Similarly, on the other side of the lounge, ran the Craft Workshop with Janet Nichols. Both occur in the morning and are repeated in the afternoon.

We played a hand of cards and discussed possible strategies but I noticed we had attracted filthy looks from a man reading a book nearby. We lowered our voices but Margaret was peeved.

"It's not a library," she hissed before closing her eyes and going to sleep in the comfortable chair.

It certainly sounded like a library with the rain beating down on the window outside and a silence that had covered the lounge like a blanket inside. It stayed wet and cloudy for the rest of the afternoon. About 17:00, the *Inspiration* music group arrived and carried out a sound check for their pre-dinner show and we trotted off to change our clothes.

Tonight's the food at dinner was delicious and we went cold turkey, without wine, for the first night in weeks. When the evening acts were discussed Rose and Roger thought they'd seen John Stevens previously and were not up for seeing him tonight. "Too many singers singing the same bloody songs," said Roger sourly.

At the Gaiety Theatre John Stevens, a mature, gentlemen who was seventy-five, if he was a day, stepped on stage in a smart black suit and red handkerchief in his breast pocket. From the word go he showed why we should give him a chance to impress. He displayed his sharply honed voice and stage manner and was the consummate professional.

The SS Azara Orchestra really swung with his version of *Summertime*. Hairs rose on the back of my neck. He really threw the kitchen sink at the audience and they responded with a standing ovation.

We chatted briefly after the show as he stood by the CD stand. He told us he'd taken ill upon boarding the ship but you couldn't see a trace of it tonight. John was the best performer so far. I was looking forward to his Sinatra Tribute show coming up in a few days time.

We walked down to the Pacific Lounge where the Topstars were repeating their ABBA tribute show *Thank You for the Music*. They were exhausting to watch and the quick costume changes, clever choreography and great dancing made the show work.

In Tiffany's Bar later that night we saw Jimmy, Paula and Betty seated in the plush lounge and joined them.

"Jimmy told you what happened to me in Manaus when they tried to get me off the cruise?" Paula said when we had taken our seats. We nodded.

"The ships doctor tried everything for me after I took bad. I was kept three days in intensive care but they still couldn't get to the bottom of my problem. I'd been fine for the first few weeks of the cruise and then I had to have the oxygen tank for a week but I got over that didn't I Jimmy?" She fell back into her seat, exhausted from the effort put into talking. She gestured him to continue.

"You did love" he said. He turned to us and spoke "She was as bright as a button up until the week before we entered the Amazon river. It all kicked off again with Paula struggling for breath, having heart palpitations and then really vivid scary dreams at night. The ships medics were very good and managed to stabilise her condition but the ship's doctor and the other senior officers were putting pressure on us to disembark in Manaus. It was touch and go but we managed to sign the forms and get to stay on the ship. Then two days ago I realised that her bad turn coincided with her starting to take the anti-malaria tablets. So we stopped taking those and she's getting better in leaps and bounds."

Paula leaned forward again. "I'm on enough tablets as it is," she said firmly. Margaret patted her knee and Paula held Margaret's hand tightly.

"I can't die so far away from my kids and grandchildren." Tears welled in her eyes. "And I'm not having Jimmy with his heart issues landed with me and our bags thousands of miles from home in a third world country. The humidity would kill me anyway."

The conversation was interrupted by the piano player who called over to Jimmy to sing a song and Paula urged him to stand up and do so. "Sing for me" she whispered to him.

After a moderate show of resistance he rose to his feet and sang *If I Were a Rich Man*.

"He's got a lovely singing voice," Paula said, and he did.

Jimmy, a slight bespectacled man, fuelled by a gin and tonic or two sang in an easy, steady voice and we all joined in the chorus.

The three of them headed for bed shortly afterwards, Jimmy wheeling Paula to their cabin and Betty following with her mobility frame.

Margaret and I ordered another drink, played some cards and thanked our lucky stars we were not living life in their shoes.

Day 40

Saturday 11th February.
Refuelling in the Para river en route to open sea.

We were now on the Para River, a tributary of the Amazon River and heading for Bolem to refuel. This would take four to six hours. The information channel informed us that there was a high chance of rain. Temperature wise, it was 27-29 degrees on the river today.

Breakfast was followed by tennis and then into the beginner's bridge class. I knew, looking at Brendan's wife, Shirley, that something was wrong. She told us Brendan was ill and she was standing in for him. I could see she'd been crying and that there was more to it than she was saying. Her eyes were red and her hands trembled. Normally she sat behind Brendan and read a book or prepared hands of cards for distributing. I'd never seen her take a class.

"We will, from now on, just play games," she announced. Our first game was in its infancy when I summoned Shirley over. I needed her help. She basically took over my hand and guided me to victory. She was counting the cards, calculating who had what, was prepared to lose a few tricks and generally she controlled the game. I was too nervous with her beside me to actually engage the brain, even for a moment.

When it was all over I turned to Shirley. "What's up with Brendan? I hope he's not too ill?"

She seemed relieved to be able to talk to someone about it and out it came. "He's not really ill. He was interviewed by a ship's officer last night, about the spate of deaths and illnesses that have decimated his class."

I was shocked and sat glued to my seat trying not to show my horror.

"Why did they come to him?" Margaret probed innocently.

"Well Brendan had gone to the ship's captain two days' ago when he found that a very poor turn-out of his bridge class attendees had coincided with the food poisoning outbreak. Brendan actually said to the captain there may be some link between the absentee card players and the illnesses but his suggestion was dismissed at the time."

"Good Lord!" Margaret said under her breath.

"So do they now believe there is a connection?" Jennifer asked.

"Apparently so," went on Shirley. "We were in our cabin last night when a ship's officer turned up with two armed crewmen and told Brendan there was now some evidence that supported his theory and they took him away."

"So do they suspect Brendan had some hand in the poisoning?" Jennifer pressed Shirley.

"I'm really not sure. Brendan returned at midnight and he's

been confined to our cabin until further notice."

"But if he did poison the passengers he's surely not going to approach the captain and draw suspicion to himself?" Jennifer uttered.

"That's right" echoed Margaret "I'm sure Brendan is innocent and I can't imagine why they think otherwise. Why I suspect the ship's management are desperate to attribute the deaths to someone other than themselves and their crew!"

Shirley seemed reassured by Margaret's definite statement of support and reached across to squeeze her hand. Jennifer leaned over and gave her a hug too.

Shirley returned to the podium and continued the class and I felt really bad that she was suffering like this for something I'd done. Of course, not bad enough to surrender myself to the authorities but that's life. It's a shame the link has been found but I may still escape capture.

I left Margaret chatting to Jennifer after the class and I joined three men on the tennis court.

With an hour of tennis completed I nipped downstairs and showered in the cabin before finding Margaret lying by the pool. I had just enough time to gulp down a quick snack before joining the choir for our men-only practice. It followed on a session for the women-only and they sounded good.

At 14:00 the SS Azara Regatta, a passenger model shipbuilding and performance competition, was held. It had been previously cancelled because of rain. Four ships were paraded, of varying standards. The ship models were walked around the Riviera Pool with their creators and then the boats individually examined and tested in the pool. Tests like withstanding a mini-tsunami were carried out. Two sank in seconds. The one looking like an oil rig made of four empty water bottles strapped together could have survived if some water had been inserted in the bottles. Instead, it flipped upside down immediately. The winner was a replica of the SS Azara and built to scale. It looked the part and the judging panel of ships officers had no problem declaring it the winner.

We spent the rest of the afternoon by the pool. Rose won the deck quoits daily competition again and has now a collection of Octavian Cruises gold tokens that can be surrendered to buy goods from the ship's shops.

Next to our pool hanging out of a white painted pipe about ten feet above the ground was a large butterfly. He had an eye on both of his wings. He was about five inches long and unaware of the hundreds of pictures he will feature in when folks get home.

The laundrettes are causing trouble again. This time the *Skyline* newsletter announced that no washing machines could be run as the ship was short of fresh water, given the limited local facilities available and this was expected to be the case for the foreseeable future.

Margaret states a hand wash is imminent as she may be knickers-less within two days'. So, just before dinner, she commandeered a dryer and gave her hand washed items a good seventy minutes of drying.

Dinner tonight was for eight and all were in good form. The SS Azara is still refuelling and so there were zero vibrations over dinner, which was nice.

After the meal and the courteous goodbyes from Ali and Hamoud, our waiters, we made our way to the Gaiety Theatre where Paula Amzar the *Virtuoso de Valencia*, a flautist of international standing took to the stage with an interesting multimedia show. After the show, we made our way out and down the external promenade deck to slip into the Pacific Lounge but we weren't fast enough to beat those competitive pensioners and to get seats and left to find entertainment elsewhere.

There were plenty of alternatives to choose from, the Bond Trio were playing soft jazz until midnight in the Hawks Inn, the film, *The Accountant,* was starting a quiz was going on in the Bulls Head, Gregory was tinkling away on the ivories in Tiffany's and Inspiration were providing live ballroom dance music in the Pelican Lounge. DJ Benny was due to start his late night sounds at 23:30 till late in the Pelican Lounge and of course the buffet was open all night. Decisions, decisions, with too much choice we simply slipped off to bed.

Day 41

Sunday 12th February.
At Sea, just off Brazil's coast.

We were motoring along at 19 knots in calm seas this morning. The temperature on the open deck was 25 degrees and dry but overcast. Though the seas are reported as calm, because the ship is speeding along, there is enough rocking to set the anchor and its chain off again. Fortunately, it's a distant clanging and banging noise from where we now sleep but it still woke me up. Margaret heard it too and she is eighty per cent deaf. After breakfast, we stepped onto the netted tennis court and battled swirling winds and a swaying ship and court. We could've coped with all that and even soggy balls but then the heavy rain came and we fled indoors.

The morning Beginners Bridge class was just us playing cards and we had a few lively hands with me leaking information to all, but particularly my partner, so that all understood why I bid the way I did. Mabel's replacement, Susan is an elderly but mentally agile woman. She is also a natural card player and she felt I was giving too much away in my preambles. So in future, I'll just have to wing it, bid and be damned.

Each day Susan checks that we are happy for her to play with us. She is a bit bossy and gets up Jennifer's nose at least once a session but for the greater good, Jennifer had bitten her tongue and agreed Susan could stay. It turned out Susan, though bossy, with us in cards, was under the thumb of her retired GP husband and when she plays with him, she doesn't utter a word. It's hard to believe but there you have it.

Once it had stopped raining I left Margaret and nipped up to the tennis court where Alan, Phil and Terry were playing two against one. I evened the sides up and we had a good foursome going when the rain returned and though I proposed we play on through a monsoon downpour the others displayed some semblance of sanity and left me standing alone and drenched on the court.

I was left with an hour to kill before choir rehearsal so I visited the gym and ran 5 kilometres. With the gym located in the bow of the ship and on an upper deck, the heaving and pitching forced me to run with both hands holding onto the treadmill's handlebars. I wanted to quit several times and had to play the usual mind games to stay to the bitter end. By that time I was dripping with sweat. The running machine's rubber floor was saturated and I had to towel down the whole machine and mat.

Margaret had a trifle dessert and some water awaiting me, after I showered in our cabin. I gulped it all down before grabbing a handful of tissues and a glass of water. I headed off to the choir male-only practice session arriving in good time.

Tony, as good as his word, stood next to me and gave me a few tips including how to snatch short breaths between lines. He informed Geoff he was really a bass singer and should perhaps join

Arthur with the bass ensemble.

Arthur, still suffering from a sore throat, an allergy thing, was noticeably quieter than normal.

Konchek, back after yesterday's absence, was present if silent as a church mouse.

The afternoon was a blank canvas for us as the rain fitfully fell on the open decks. We sat in the Palace Restaurant and practised bridge hands before changing into togs and having a swim in the Pool that was pitching and rolling in keeping with the ship's motion but not quite as badly as earlier in the cruise.

A quick shower and into the lift we went heading for our cabin.

On the ride to our floor, a man in the lift let slip that the washing machines were back in action. He said they won't be telling anyone until tonight when passengers will read the good news in the *Skyline* Newsletter. "Keep it to yourself!" he cautioned.

We all put fingers to our lips in conspiratorial silence and didn't tell the next woman entering the lift. This news is gold dust.

Tonight's dinner was a formal black-tie affair, the first in several days. We were handed a glass of Prosecco as we entered the restaurant and were told to await an announcement once we were seated. The Hotel Manager came over the PA system and announced that the captain had declared that all should have a free drink in compensation for the vibrations suffered at dinner in recent nights. The announcement was greeted by applause and the drinks duly imbibed.

We, despite our reservations visited the Gaiety Theatre and gave Gerard Benhitly a chance to shine. It's more than half full and he is working hard but for the first time, we decided not to stay to the end of his act. He's skipped in favour of an empty dryer which we found on deck 11. How low can you sink in the entertainment world?

We revisit the laundrette later and find someone had stolen our laundry bag but the clothes it contained were still in the dryer and still warm. I told you the font of all evil on a cruise is the laundrette.

Day 42

Monday 13th February.
At Sea heading to the Cape Verde islands.

Once again, the SS Azara is powering through the water at 22.6 knots but into a strong Northerly wind of 25 knots so the upper decks are closed and there is no tennis for us this morning.

We suspect the altered schedule is to facilitate refuelling and the delay in refuelling meant the captain had decided to put the nautical boot down and we were close to this ships top speed of 24 knots.

It was 26 degrees centigrade onboard and dry but cloudy outside. Our TV channels finally work and we can tune to channel 16 to watch the ship's progress from her bow camera but there is nothing but sea to see.

It's the eve of St Valentine's Day and I need to do something to mark the occasion. I planned to work on a poem. Maybe I'd draw a cartoon on a card. I will have to get my creative juices flowing.

We ate breakfast in the small Al Fresco restaurant to the fore of the ship. It's a smaller version of the Palace with a somewhat limited range of food but they make omelettes on demand. We eat late and attend the beginner's bridge class and find there are only three of us. Susan's seat is empty. Shirley, Brendan Flood's wife, fills in for Susan and is a welcome addition as her wisdom leads to a good lesson in how to play the game and the mindset needed at different times. She's also very social and chats away with ease but I could sense something was playing on her mind.

"What's the latest on Brendan?" Jennifer asked Shirley at the end of the class.

Shirley hesitated and then spilt the beans. "Brendan has been accused of murder and attempted murder based on the discovery of the poisoned A4 sheets, typed up on his typewriter. He can't explain how his typewriter was used and why someone would do such a thing. He's been moved to a cell in the bowels of the ship and will be handed over to police on our return to Southampton. It sounds pretty cut and dried but he still pleads his innocence and has offered to take a lie detector test.

Margaret and Jennifer sat silently with their mouths open.

"I'm going to stand by him," Shirley said defiantly. "I know him and he is not capable of these acts. We'll get the best lawyers in the land and fight this case all the way."

I feel pretty bad about this turn of events but dammit if Brendan hadn't gone to the ship's officers and made the link for them between the deaths on board and his absent bridge class he'd be fine. No-one would have thought of the relationship between the two. He's the author of his own downfall and that's for sure. Thank God I am the devious arse covering individual that I am. Even now I believe my escape is still possible.

We leave a worried Shirley to tidy up the desks and we meet, by chance, Susan's husband on the promenade deck.

"Is she OK?" Margaret asked him.

"Yes, she's still poorly but has improved and is currently in our cabin resting. She's stopped taking the anti-malaria tablets."

"About bloody time," muttered Margaret as we walk away. "He is too cock-sure about what's good for her," she added, "Even if he is a General Practitioner."

Jennifer and Margaret were happy to chat over a coffee and the three of us sat in the Palace restaurant discussing matters until I needed to attend the choir practice. I used the time to order from the ship's reception a single flower with a note saying, "It was always you."

The choir was reunited for a combined male and female session and David, our music director, showed signs of stress and irritation. His personally annotated music sheets had been either stolen or mislaid. We raced through the breathing exercises and then he ran through many of the songs declaring today was the last day for new joiners to the choir. No more after today.

Geoff was absent as he and his wife were attending a Caribbean members club special meal this lunchtime. Arthur is present but his throat is worse, despite having gargled in salted water. Konchek is back but still singing quietly. Bye the bye, he has the worst case of halitosis I have ever had the misfortune to breathe in. I had to move and stand further away from him. I plan to bring lozenges tomorrow and offer him one. Let's see if that works.

Back in the Palace restaurant, the two girls were still hard at it, as the blue Atlantic sea just races past their window.

Jennifer leaves and we sunbath near the pool for an hour or so. The sun comes and goes and we get a game of tennis in and follow it up with a swim.

Back in our cabin it's a shower and quick change for the casual dress dinner. We arrive to find Frank and Jill have opted to go Indian on us and eat at the Spice restaurant. Geoff, my choir colleague, on a neighbouring table is still rolling out his extensive and colourful wardrobe. Patent leather brown shoes, bright yellow trousers, a plain white shirt offset by a rainbow coloured tie, white jacket and medals on display. Geoff looks quite the dandy.

He proudly explained that he had lots of clothes made to measure, on a visit to Hong Kong a few years ago. He'd been measured up and chose the material on a Monday and collected the completed suits, jackets and shirts on the Wednesday. I took my mouth organ to the dinner table, for comic effect, and it generated the required laughter. Food was lovely as usual but I have to question the need to eat for £16 per person extra at the Spice Restaurant when we can eat such marvellous food here. Each meal has five starters, eight main courses and five desserts to choose from. Surely that's enough for most people?

On to the Gaiety Theatre where Gerard Benhitly failed to wow last night's audience. Tonight we see the swift return of the flautist, a beautiful and talented Spanish girl who presented an all-new show and left to a standing ovation. Passengers liked what they saw and applauded all her songs warmly. She finished with the Flight of the

Bumble Bee completed in one minute seven seconds.

We rounded the night off with a drink in Tiffany's where Gregory was playing, amongst other tunes, a medley of Beatle songs. We caught Betty on the way to bed and she said Paula was much improved and she and Jimmy had left the bar only minutes earlier.

We were fast asleep in bed at midnight when the PA speaker in our cabin came loudly to life. "This is the Officer of the Watch calling all crew and passengers. Will a first responder first aid unit go to the front kitchen compartment of deck 6?"

Two minutes later he was on the PA system again "This is an announcement for all passengers. You need to take no action. I repeat you need to take no action." Five minutes later the loudspeaker crackled again into life.

"This is your captain, Peter Cox. Please be aware that all is now well and I thank you for your cooperation and wish you a good night's sleep."

I wondered what all that was about?

Day 43

Tuesday 14th February.
St Valentine's Day. At Sea.

I awoke with the ship somewhere in the mid-Atlantic, at sea and en route to Cape Verdi's island of St Vincent. The SS Azara was still steaming along at close to top speed. The high northerly winds had put the top decks off limits again. It was dry but cloudy and all pools and spas were open.

When Margaret wakes, she finds my sketched Valentines card on paper torn from a pad of the ships headed paper.

When she was fully awake I read the first poem and let her read the second. She laughed in the right places. I checked furtively the post box outside our cabin to see if the ordered red rose had materialised but it hadn't.

Later, while Margaret is heading to the bridge class I visit reception and see what has become of Margaret's missing rose.

"Yes Mr Granger, the florist has it ready but you only specified a day for delivery and not an hour so he was going to deliver it sometime today."

So a lesson has been learned. The order form omits a line where I can specify the hour but passengers familiar with the ways of Octavian Cruises will state a desired delivery time. Maybe they should change the bloody form? I fume silently.

I took the beautifully presented tall glass vase holding the single red rose from the florist and strode up the atrium staircase to Deck 8 leaving a trail of havoc in my wake.

"Oh look at thoughtful man with a rose for his wife."

"Now there's a true husband for you Geoff."

"Isn't that beautiful Ron? Where's mine? "

I blushed as red as the rose with the unwitting attention seeking walk through the shops and lobby area and hot-footed it to our cabin. I now see why the florist was normally the person who delivers the flowers!

The beginner's bridge class was slow to start as we gave Susan a chance to appear. However, with the news that her husband was now unwell, we guessed she'd be a no show.

Shirley again filled in and we played three interesting games.

The hour between cards and the choir rehearsal was filled by chatting to Jennifer, who continues to be, at a bit of a loose end as a lone passenger.

The sun shone and the pool areas were busy with bathers lounging about and displaying copious quantities of flesh. Some passengers are now as red as berries but they still seek more of the sun's rays.

The choir rehearsal today was a combined male and female class and David announced the performance date as Monday 21st of February, the afternoon before we arrive in Southampton.

Aoife was conspicuous by her absence and no mention of her

was made. David was now leading the project with Tony just doing the admin, handing out music sheets, doing a bit of coaching and leading his one song, *America*.

Our small tenor team of Geoff, Arthur, Kotchek and I, were all present but Arthur was still struggling with his throat. Kotchek sat behind me and as far as I could smell, the halitosis of yesterday was mercifully absent. I came armed with sucky sweets to offer around to all, if necessary, but they stayed firmly in my pocket. Tenors number about thirteen, bass about twenty-five and the women about sixty in number.

"Singing falsetto, like Frankie Valli does, does not diminish your manhood," David said. "It's been proven from scientific research carried out on wild birds that the male bird increases his chances of mating and woo-ing the female bird when he sings a wider range of notes. Of course, he also uses his colourful plumage."

"C'mon men, surely you want to increase your chance of mating?" he addressed the bunch of septuagenarians and older. Several of their wives sat across from them and laughed rather too enthusiastically.

It was mid-afternoon and the Valentine's Day Chocolate Buffet at the Imperial restaurant was already in full swing. I entered the room and found that there were cordoned avenues by which to approach the chocolate buffet. These were policed by smartly dressed waiters. I chose the left-hand route and was guided to tables on both sides laden with chocolate treats. Hundreds of chocolate desserts of all shapes and sizes had been placed around a fifteen-foot tall chocolate fountain that continuously gurgled while producing an endless river of liquid chocolate.

The idea was to choose a dessert, then the waiter would submerge the already chocolate coated cake slice, bonbon, biscuit or tart under the thick stream of dark chocolate. The calorie-laden plate was then returned to you for consumption.

Margaret had chosen to skip this indulgence so I ate with strangers all too pre-occupied with their desserts to make conversation.

I joined Margaret at the pool where she was chatting with Jill, a woman from London who was awaiting a knee operation. Her husband, Ray, lay sleeping beside her.

Jill was aware of the deaths of two passengers on board, both very elderly. She also knew of a couple, the husband of which had suffered a stroke in November but hadn't consulted a doctor for fear of being told not to take the cruise. He subsequently suffered a second and more debilitating stroke on board and was still on board but now cabin bound.

I left them chatting and took to the treadmill in the gym and did my best time so far running five kilometres. We just had time for a swim in the cold water of the Crystal pool and then down to the cabin for a quick change of clothes.

Tonight's dress code was black-tie. I noticed, as our hands were being sanitised at the entrance to the restaurant, that the women were being given long stemmed artificial red roses.

"What about us?" I heard several men protest, muttering black words about sexism. I also spotted pink balloons bedecking the entrance pillars from floor to ceiling. Once inside I saw that all pillars in the restaurant had pink balloons attached. Our smiling waiters stood by our table.

How do they do it? Greeting the guests so cheerfully for two sittings, night after night, following long days of working in the other restaurants and communal areas from early morning, snatching a few hours break along the way. They should be well remunerated but maybe it is just as well that I don't know their wages.

The camera team entered the restaurant to capture diners. We were asked, as couples at the table all were, did we want pictures taken? The other's seasoned travellers and presumably with bulging albums of pictures from other cruises declined but we agreed.

"Look at me" said Fiona, our photographer clicking away. "Now look at each other," and finally, "Go on–kiss each other."

In front of our friends, it was hugely embarrassing. Of course, during the meal, Margaret mentioned my first poem and they insisted on hearing it and, after some weak protest from me, I read it out. I think it achieved its aim of making it relevant to all and having a bit of humour thrown in.

During the meal Roger spoke at length to Frank and I about a disaster that befell the British army in 1850 at Hawkes Ridge.

"I must admit Roger, I can't recall what happened at Hawkes Ridge!" said Frank. "Tell us more."

I was glad Frank had said that as I hadn't a clue myself.

Roger continued "You see, it was at Hawkes Ridge that the

Zulus wiped out a regiment of 1,500 men. However the next day they attacked again but this time they were repelled by a well organised second detachment, who numbered less than three hundred and who only lost thirteen men themselves."

"I wondered to myself why that was and what I found out was very interesting," Frank went on. "Part of the reason for the huge Zulu's losses was their tradition. Once they felled a soldier they always stopped to kneel down and disembowel him there and then. This meant leaving themselves wide open to being shot. If they had just kept running men through with the spears and coming back later for the trophy taking they would have done much better."

"And," I asked. "the other saving grace for the British soldiers was?"

Frank smiled and added the missing factor. "Though the Zulu's had captured a large quantity of British weapons the previous day, they hadn't the understanding in how to load, focus and fire them so the lethal weapons proved to be of little use to them in the end."

In his telling of the story I could see a sharp and analytical brain still functioning. He liked to know things. He liked to figure out why things happened as they did. There was always a reason and he sought to find that reason.

"How about the outbreak of deaths on board this ship a few days ago Roger?" asked Frank. "Have you any further news from your contact with the officers?"

Before Roger could answer Margaret interrupted him. "Have you all heard that our Bridge Instructor Brendan has been placed under arrest?"

"No, I haven't," "Roger said." Tell me more."

And so she did. The table hung on her every word and it seemed Roger's contacts on board had let him down on this one.

"Good grief," said Frank visibly surprised. "So it wasn't food poisoning after all?"

I got a sinking feeling in the pit of my stomach and I had a strong urge to go to the toilet and puke my guts up.

"Shut up, Margaret," is what I longed to say, but I had to sit there po-faced and expressionless as my antics were brought to the attention of the whole table. When she'd finished there was a stunned silence.

Finally, Frank spoke. "Why did Brendan do it then? I can't see the motive."

"No," pondered Roger. "Neither can I. Something just doesn't fit together in this jigsaw. It's just so bizarre."

I could almost see the cogs moving in his brain as he rotated the facts in his consciousness, trying to make them fit better. The only silver lining in this happening was that I had never shared my frustration with the intermediate class over any of our previous evening meals. Margaret saw my frustration with them only once and as I am her boring steady retired accountant husband, it would never cross her mind that I could be responsible for all those deaths.

The conversation went on and on until it was chuck out time for the restaurant and the waiters ushered us to the doors.

We went straight to the Gaiety Theatre and found two seats in the very front row for John Stevens' show. We were wedged between Geoff, Sarah, Bill and Joan. I'd enjoyed his first show so much I wondered if I was expecting too much of him for the second but I need not have worried. He sang brilliantly and the orchestra were on fire. The only faults were when some video clips failed to materialise when requested and John, manfully adapted his program and worked around it. He finished with a unique version of the *House of the Rising Sun*, an Eric Burden and the Animals hit from the 1960s. There was plenty of Frank Sinatra, Matt Munro, Nat King Cole and many others. He did a duet with a Dean Martin stand-in, aka Brian Koran, *The Lady is a Tramp,* which was probably the weak spot of the show.

At one stage he asked the audience to turn the person sitting next to them and say "I love you," given that it was St Valentine's night. Bill caught me by surprise. Ignoring Joan, his wife, Bill turned to me and said, "I love you, Luke" And accompanied the words by delivering a big wet kiss on my stunned lips.

Day 44

Wednesday 15th February.
Island of St Vincent, Cape Verde.

We'd docked in the deep-water harbour of Mindelo, the main town on St Vincent island, one of the nine main islands that make up the Cape Verde islands almost four hundred miles to the west of Africa. The five largest islands in the group are also known as the Barlavento or the Winward islands. The deepwater harbour is made from a volcanic crater and though the name of the islands are Verdi, meaning green, there is no green to be seen on these imposing volcanic mountains that rise up around the harbour.

We played tennis for an hour or more onboard before disembarking on a cloudy windy day. Octavian Cruises had arranged shuttle buses to transport all to the town centre. We met Marge and Rob and went with them as they been here last year and knew the town.

Beggars approached us as we exited the bus and walked up the hill. We turned right into a small square and saw a church at the far end of it. Outside the church and on the steps sat many people and dogs. The people didn't beg until we were leaving the church which was simply decorated but had a certain beauty about it. Things looked a bit grim in this town.

We walked along the street until some familiar faces came towards us. Joan and Bill advanced with warnings of passengers being robbed of bags and laptops and we were told to be on our guard. Looking about I saw there was no sign of any police presence either.

Bill had, however, made friends with the local kids by buying them sweets. "I'm missing me grand-children," he confided to us.

"You'll change your tune next Friday when you've been back home for a few days," I warned. "You'll be begging for another holiday, mark my words!"

In the large market square, the area had been split into two raised zones, both accessible by steps or ramps. Two circles of cafes were in the centre of one area, where the customers, all locals, sat at tables outside. There was no Wi-Fi in these cafes. All around the market and neighbouring streets groups of men hung about with nothing to do. There were phone repair stalls and stalls just selling clunky running shoes. We spotted plenty of passengers out and about but Rob and Marge took a protective interest in a frail couple whom they spotted were struggling with getting about. Both were well into their eighties and they had somehow made it to the market square, her with the tell-tale Parkinson's tremor and in a wheelchair and him pushing her along and looking very, very tired.

We all helped to get her wheelchair down off one section of the market where there wasn't a ramp and up onto section where there was. In a poorly thought out way, the ramp only partly did the job and left the wheelchair wheel dangling eight inches above the road.

We visited the naval museum which was located on the harbour front and it was a lovely old four storey whitewashed building that offered beautiful views at several levels, including a roof-top view of the harbour. It's collection of maritime historic fishing equipment reminds us that Cape Verdi was a major whaling community and at one stage in the 1820s, three hundred and twenty-nine ships set sail daily to searching for whales. Not to admire these huge animals and photograph them, but to capture and kill them. They'd spear the whale in the head, strap it's body to the side of the ship and with a roaring furnace fire lit on deck, they'd melt the whale down to blubber, oil and salt it's meat while still at sea.

Outside the museum a large group of men and women gathered under a roofed, open-sided shed, playing cards and gambling. Beyond them, further along, the frontage, fishermen were repairing their boats and women sat on street corners with plastic basins of small silver fish for sale.

With time running out, we rode a shuttle back to the ship, handing our change in escudo's to a beggar near the shuttle bus. Back onboard the sun shone and we sat on sun loungers for an hour or more lapping up the rays until clouds arrived.

Once again we met up with our fellow diners in the restaurant. The meal was an extravagancy of fine food and, as usual, I felt obliged to eat every one of the five courses on offer. A crash diet will be called for once we return home.

"Your table has been booked in the Spice restaurant for 18:30

tomorrow night," Ali told us. He'd asked that we book all other meals through him and we did, hoping he'd benefit.

"Luke, the Chivas Regal blended whisky sampling is happening again tonight at the atrium," whispered Frank.

"Count me in," I said, enthusiastically. So, once again, I went with him and sampled the whisky, one month on from the last sampling. I was no closer to spending £32 on a litre of the blended whisky.

"What do you think, Craig?" I sought his opinion as Scotland is renowned for its whisky and I'd seen him sip on a glass, at dinner, earlier in the night.

Not surprisingly he was scathing in his opinion of the whiskey on offer which though crossing his lips never got down his throat. He spat it back into the glass in disgust and pulled a face as if I'd poisoned him or given him a spoon of foul tasting medicine.

"Ach, Luke. Don't go near that blended crap! If you must buy what they have on board then stick to pure malt whisky" and then he added "If you want my opinion, I recommend Glenfiddick." With that, he wasted no more of his time on the matter and headed for the theatre.

The Gaiety Theatre featured Jimmy Juttle of Jimmy Juttle and the Renegades, and he went down a storm. Forty years on from his only chart hit *Alone with You* he is still making a living from music. He is a rather stout, short, bald, black man with gleaming white teeth and a gentle manner. Born in Newcastle he was part of the Northern Soul circuit of the 1970s and his light shone for a fairly brief period of time. His act tonight is based on the music of true soul giants, the Temptations, Smokey Robinson, Stylistics, the Drifters, Gladys Knight etc so we all knew the words and all sang along, clapping to the beat. His vocals sounded delicate and I thought his mike needed the volume turned up a tad but the SS Azara orchestra's soul train of musicians got into the groove and carried his vocals beyond what he could reasonably expect. He got called back for an encore and sang Gladys Knight's *Portrait of My Love,* which was a rather low-key number to end on but to be fair he does have a second show to perform tonight.

Outside, a clamour of female fans were waiting to speak with him, many only teenagers when he was at his height, fame-wise. He kindly took the time to speak with each one.

Margaret was tiring and in pain with her back and hip. Having taken all the permitted painkillers the only option was bed and sleep. She'd also forgotten her hearing aid for the entire evening so the meal and any spoken words by Jimmy Juttle had passed her by.

Today we'd taken the last of our anti-malaria tablets so maybe Margaret's tiredness and vivid dreams will end after tonight.

We'd had the first notification regarding the end of the cruise this evening and it's always a sad moment. We were given deadlines for specifying a time we want to disembark at when we dock in Southampton. If we wish to make an early start and can carry our own baggage, without assistance, we need to keep all our baggage in our own room the night prior to docking and we need to notify reception by noon this Sunday.

Day 45

Thursday 16th February.
At sea heading for Tenerife, Canary Islands.

Margaret had another rough night. I woke and snuck into the bathroom, showered and shaved before dressing quietly via the light from the bathroom. The cabin door clicked closed behind me and I left for breakfast on my own.

Sitting at the foot of the atrium stairs, I slipped my socks and runners on. It was 07:30 but I could hear no movement around the ship. Down in Tiffany's Bar two waiters were opening up the bar and a couple of passengers sat by the window.

I strode down the long-carpeted deck past Lawton's where we will be in our bridge class and coincidentally I spotted Brendan Flood, our bridge teacher, approaching me, as I took a photograph of the Chaplin cinema entrance.

"I'm a keen photographer myself," he said. "when no one's about."

"Good to see you, Brendan." I shook his hand. "Is all that confusion cleared up for you? Are you a free man?"

He nodded. "I'm free for now anyway. They released me yesterday after I'd spoken with a solicitor who intervened on my behalf and is going to represent me. I'm free subject to further investigations and I've promised to co-operate when we land back in Southampton."

I pushed my luck a little and probed a bit more. "Tell me, Brendan, what do you think went on?"

He scratched his head and removed his glasses wiping them with the front of his cotton t-shirt. "I think it was food poisoning myself but the poison on the paper is hard to explain. Apparently, the poison used was a type sold in the Carribbean for use on animals. I mean how in God's name did that get on the copier paper? I'm rightly confused by all this. The one positive point I can take from this nightmare is that there are none of my fingerprints on the sheets of paper so they can't prove it was me. Anyway, I must fly. Speak to you later." And off he went.

I felt a weight lift off my chest knowing an innocent man was now free. Maybe this will be the end of it?

The Palace Restaurant was a very pleasant place to dine and one that lives in a parallel universe to the 09:00 version. At 07:40 there were no queues, very few people and you take your pick of tables. I chose one by the window. The sun shone brightly in the sky, spreading its beams in an ever increasing arc across the rippling blue sea water. It warms my arm and is too bright for me to look directly at. I just admire the strong shadows it casts and enjoy the steady gentle rhythm of the ship as it cuts its way through the sea like a knife through butter.

Margaret was up and dressed when I entered the cabin. We

went straight to the tennis court to get a couple of games in before bagging two sun loungers and heading to bridge class.

Susan turned up late only to tell us she was not going to be with us in the beginner's class from now on, a relief for all parties.

Afterwards, I sat with Margaret and Jennifer for coffee and then we all went our separate ways. Margaret set off to find a free washing machine and I went sunbathing for a while. Noon came too soon and I reluctantly joined the lads in the choir for a men-only rehearsal.

I can't say I hear much improvement in the singing. *Can't Help Falling in Love* still puts the tenors into falsetto territory and I suspect David will gloss over it by having Tony sing with us on the day. *America*, a song we had a good grasp of has gone bad with the harmonies now added in and sounds dreadful.

David asked and got four volunteers to sing solo in *There is Nothin' Like a Dame*.

We exited as the registration for the passenger's talent competition was starting and I knew Geoff planned to go solo with a song for that and the men's bass team were giving it a bash too. Up top, on the open deck the sun was shining but the pools were still cordoned off.

At 14:00, at the pool, the ship's departments competed against each other in a tug of war.

At 15:00 in the netted cricket court the ship's crew played the passengers in a challenge cricket match that the crew won easily. Both events attracted large crowds of watchers.

We sunbathed the afternoon through and eventually headed for the cabin. On the way we visited Reception and registered our wish to self exit at 10:10 on Wednesday.

For a treat and to find out why anyone would pay £16 each extra to eat there, we'd booked an early bird at the Spice restaurant, the ships Indian restaurant. With the special offer, we were given a free bottle of Octavian Cruises house wine. The restaurant and staff are dressed differently to mark them out from the normal restaurants and obviously the menu was different if not superior to our normal food. We ate with brass cutlery and two hours later we rose from the table, stuffed to bursting. Jennifer and Gwen had come in after us and, looking around before leaving, I noticed the restaurant had filled up since our arrival. The ship's officers occupied two tables. The International Piano Duo had discovered partners for at least a meal and who knows what else.

Afterwards, we had a choice between a classical female in the Gaiety Theatre or the three West end leading ladies performing in the Pacific Lounge. We chose the girls and played cards to pass the time until they appeared.

Singing to backing tracks, they covered music by the Andrews Sisters and the Beverley Sisters and sang songs from musicals they had had leading roles in such as Grease and Les Miserables. From the off, they sought audience participation and three men were enlisted to dance and then another three were dragged up to sit in chairs and be flirted with. They finished with the *Rule Britannia* and *Land of Hope and Glory* and the room became a sea of waving

Union Jacks while the passengers bellowed out the songs ingrained in their memories since birth.

Despite other offers we quit for bed. The clocks advanced once more overnight and we will soon be back on GMT time. It was also the first night without anti-malaria tablets. Hopefully Margaret was heading for a peaceful night.

Day 46

Friday 17th February.
At sea and heading for Tenerife, Canary Islands.

Margaret, was a bit frosty first thing this morning. "I told you to wake me at 08:00, not 06:30!"

I hugged the icy one and she falls back to sleep until I press the defrost button at 08:06 and gently wake the slumbering grouch. Once showered, dressed and ready for the day Margaret is her usual bouncy self. Especially when we get three games of tennis in and she wins all of them.

The beginner's bridge class goes well despite my poor play and everyone seems happy. Shirley, Brendan's wife is very chatty and we learn a lot while she plays on the table. Brendan himself is teaching the class and is largely back to his old self, which could never be described as cheerful. Several class regulars approach him afterwards to say just how pleased they are to see him back and he thanks them for their words.

Afterwards, we have coffee with Jennifer who is happy to chat and for the company.

We eat lunch and were sunbathing in the secret area in front of the gym when the PA system announces that the afternoon variety show would be starting in fifteen minutes in the Gaiety Theatre.

So, with myself dressed only in flip flops, pink shorts and a flowery T-shirt and Margaret in a swimsuit, we attend. The theatre is surprisingly full. The show consists of the SS Azara orchestra, and the Topstars singers. I must say they were all brilliant. David, the musical conductor, played one of his own compositions in a solo slot and I could easily see his music being featured in nature documentaries, for example. I couldn't help noticing that a lot of people were dressed in long trousers and jumpers, for the first time in almost fifty days.

We made our way back outside to the open deck and the oasis pool with its remaining four sun bathers determined to savour the last rays of the todays sun. Down we stepped into the pool which was unusually warm, as if to reward our persistence and we lingered there as long as we dared, for the final days of the cruise were coming into sight and it would be many months before we enjoyed this experience again.

We exited our cabin in our finest, for the final black tie evening dinner, the fourteenth on this cruise. We stopped in the atrium for the photographic team to pose us and take a few pictures. Then it was on to the dinner gang and our three ever smiling and dutiful waiters.

Most of the table plumped for Marco Pierre White's full meal menu which featured half a lobster in the main course. It was a filling meal and the conversation was lively.

Margaret brought Brendan's good news to the table. "He's been released and was at the bridge classes today!"

"Fantastic" said Mary "You know I spoke with him once when we shared a coach to the NASA space centre and he seemed a lovely man."

"Yes," interrupted Roger. "He's been freed all right, but I've an open mind about the matter." And he left his statement hanging about for a moment before adding with a shrug of his shoulders, "All the evidence still points his way... I'm just saying."

"Does his release mean they have someone else in custody?" asked Jill. Good question I thought.

Before Roger could answer, the PA system crackled into life and, for the next ten minutes, the dance song *I Got a Feeling* blasted out as the thirty plus cooks that prepare seven thousand meals a day appeared, filing through the large restaurant in their white uniforms, chef hats and aprons. They were applauded all the way but I just wanted to hear Roger's bloody answer.

Who is now in the frame for the murders?

"No, it doesn't," answered Roger eventually. "But I have been told that the Octavian Cruises Head of Security boarded in Parintins, several days ago now and he is intending to interview all the passengers and crew before we dock in Southampton."

He glanced around the table. "It appears from all your faces that he has yet to interview you."

"So has he started then, Roger?" asked Frank. "Interviewing I mean."

"Oh, yes," said Roger. "I believe he started with the crew and I expect we'll all be called in over the next day or two. He's interviewing on board because the killer or killers are definitely still on this ship, right now. Secondly, if the interviews were left until we'd landed he'd disrupt the onward travel arrangements of thousands of passengers and crew. Just a few minutes given up now will save a bucket load of hassle later."

"I wondered why the Brazilian authorities hadn't halted the cruise in Manaus," said Frank.

"Ah, good point, Frank," answered Roger. "It appears the Brazilian authorities were told by someone in Octavian Cruises that the crime had occurred in international waters and so not within their jurisdiction. Now, I don't believe that is the case at all but it would have been hugely expensive to Octavian Cruises if the ship was held up for days in Manaus. It would mean paying compensation for passengers as certain stops would just be cut from the remaining cruise and worse still if the delay was much longer then the ship, crew and passengers could all be in the wrong place by the end date. This could threaten the next cruise that starts the day we return to Southampton and, of course, it would mean flying passengers home."

This was indeed bad news from my perspective, but, on the plus side, the detective doesn't seem to have any leads to follow, other than Brendan's foolish yet accurate link of the deaths to the bridge class. The lab tests may give some understanding as to the nature of the poison used, but any connection to me has been flushed away through the ships waste system or is floating in the sea a few thousand miles behind in the wake of the SS Azara.

My mind was racing, but I think I managed to keep up appearances and focus on the night in hand, parking the worrying until later.

We trooped out of the restaurant to review the latest crop of photographs from the ships photographic team. Then we joined an endless stream of smartly dressed folk walking to the Gaiety Theatre for Jimmy Juttles second show. He didn't disappoint and neither did the SS Azara orchestra. He may not have a powerful voice but he has that unique soul phrasing in spades. His small chat between numbers was awkward, particularly trying to imply that David, the musical director, was drinking all afternoon. David then threatened in joke fashion to walk off the stage. Though Jimmy's singing was smooth and sincere his nervousness was obvious. "You'll have to help me with this one," was regularly spoken to the audience and of course they did, every time.

With Margaret still awake and in good spirits, we relocated upstairs to the Hawks Inn where the Lorcan Bond Trio were providing a gentle wind down to the day with a jazzy piano and smooth vocal sound delivering timeless classics to the black suit and sparkly dressed mature audience.

Lorcan though under the weather and reaching for a hanky frequently, performed without a sniff or sniffle. With his white five string bass strapped high to his chest, he sang in his own high pitched voice while plucking the strings with nimble dexterity.

Thomas, the pianist explored the deeper off key recesses of the white Steinway piano that his fingers flew over, and Ray on drums provided that rhythmic backbone all tunes need.

Day 47

Saturday 18th February.

Docked in Santa Cruz, Tenerife, Canary Islands.

The Canary Islands are just off the west coast of Africa and sit in the Atlantic Ocean. We are back in Euro land.

During the night I had a bad dream. It was set in my parent's home. The house was empty, just as we had it in the last days, before the legal completion of the sale. In the dream, I knew that both my parents were dead several years and I was alone. I gazed out of a bedroom window yet I looked out onto the view I'd actually have got from standing in the kitchen. The concrete patio outside the window looked freshly laid and someone had stepped on the freshly laid concrete leaving a single large boot mark. I could see the grooved tread of the boot now engraved forever into the concrete. I then turned and was now in the hall, outside the bathroom and there, just appearing from the study, came a huge, menacing man. I've never seen anyone like him in my life but I knew he was here to kill me. I tried to scream out loud but what came from my mouth was merely a whimper. He saw me and, rather than advancing towards me, he turned to go back into the study and I knew he was seeking a weapon to kill me with. I turned away, my heart pounding, to see what I could find to defend myself but the bedroom behind me was empty. I woke up in the bed of our cabin, my clothing saturated with sweat.

I decided to get up and sit in the bathroom until I felt I could go back to sleep. Two and a half hours later and I was still there.

Maybe I did have some side effects from the anti-malaria tablets after all?

Or maybe Roger's news of the detective now onboard has affected my subconscious?

The ship docked in Tenerife just as dawn was breaking. We showered, dressed and played a few games of tennis after breakfast, before heading for the town. The harbour contains three large cruise ships and a Frank Olson car ferry. Down the gange plank located in midships we went and then boarded a shuttle bus that drove to the terminal building and dropped us beyond it at a nondescript grey building. We got out and walked forward, in the wrong direction, as neither the coach driver nor Octavian Cruises had bothered to indicate which direction the city centre was in. There had been a lot of building work in the harbour area and new roads and building had made the area unfamiliar to us, even though we last visited it only eighteen months ago. We eventually found the main shopping street and a bistro with Wi-Fi. We sat outside and enjoyed two tall glasses of ice-cold lagers. Geoff and Sarah found us there and sat down for a chat and a drink. They knew the town well and were off to meet their son Andrew for lunch. We talked about the eventful cruise now almost over.

"Its been an extraordinary cruise by anyone's standards" said Geoff.

"And you take that any way you want too" added Sarah. "I mean the sights, the rough seas, the passengers and the huge number of deaths. I've never known a cruise like it."

"When we signed up for this cruise" Margaret said "I specifically chose Octavian Cruises because of their renowned safety record but look what's happened? Outbreaks of the Novo virus, large scale food poisoning, lifeboats crashing into each other, passengers left behind as we sailed. It's been one disaster after another. I certainly won't be recommending Octavian cruises to my friends anytime soon. They should be renamed Calamity Cruises!"

"Have you two met the detective yet?" Geoff asked easing back into his chair and watching the passing shoppers.

"No, not yet. Have you?" I asked leaning forward to take a sip of my beer.

"No, not yet but I heard he's been busy and has been working his way through the crew. He's been given an office near the Medical Centre I believe." Geoff answered, before glancing at his watch and gesturing to Sarah. "C'mon old girl, finish up that coffee. We must get cracking. Andrew will have a fit if we're late for lunch."

We go our separate ways and we pick up some T-shirts for our neighbours back home as gifts for minding our car and house. By 14:00 with most of the shops closing for a siesta we head back to the ship.

We eat lunch on our return and I played some serious tennis with Arthur, Bill and Harry. Harry is seventy-five years old and a regular tennis player. He challenged me, twenty odd years younger, to a singles match which he proceeds to take deadly seriously. I had to run like a demented rabbit to subdue this stubborn older player.

Afterwards, I join Margaret, Jennifer and her friend Gwen for the final half hour of the Great British Sail Away, which involved *Last night of the Proms* type sing-alongs. The Union Jack flags were waved vigorously and passengers bellowed out Irish, English, Scottish and Welsh songs as we sailed out and away from Tenerife. The party ended with Queen's *We Are the Champions,* and Status Quo's *Rockin' All over the World.* I knocked back a couple of cans of John Smiths Bitter as I had an enormous thirst following the hours of tennis. Passengers broke up into smaller groups still dancing and singing to their own songs as the party wound down and people began to slip away.

Dinner tonight was casual and we dressed quickly. I took a seat next to Rose and she was happy to chat about her knee and hip operations, both successful. Roger talked easily to Margaret. Frank traded jokes with Craig. Mary and Jill chatted quietly about knitting.

"I met the detective today," said Frank.

"Me too," said Roger

"And me," sparked up Jill.

"Snap," said Rose "He's moving fast isn't he!"

"He'll have to be," said Frank. "He's got a lot of people to see."

"What's he like?" asked Craig.

"An older man, coming up to retirement I'd reckon" said Roger. Frank nodded his head in agreement. "Looking back on it, I reckon his approach was to just ask a few questions and then sit back to see what I would say."

"Questions about what?" asked Craig. I'm so pleased he was taking the lead here because he was doing my job for me.

Roger spoke up, "Well he had my passport details and the ship booking details in amongst his paperwork, which sat on the side of his desk, so he focused his questions to me on where I was on the day before the poisoning and on the day of the poisoning. It's now so far back in the cruise that I struggled to recall.

Frank butted in. "Yeah, all the days at sea tended to merge in my memory too so I answered a bit vaguely. I mean who keeps a daily diary these days?"

I hoped Margaret wouldn't drop me in it. I glanced in her direction but she was now deep in conversation with Mary and Rose and hadn't heard Franks comment.

"I don't know anyone anal enough to record daily life on a holiday cruise with a bunch of pensioners." said Roger. They both laughed at the absurdity of such a pointless activity.

"Really!" Frank added. "C'mon – I mean give me a break! It's just expecting too much for pensioners, which I must remind you Roger we both are, to recall activities on specific days when they have been onboard a ship as long as we have."

"Aye," said Craig. "But he's a job to do and he needs answers so I'll have to put my thinking cap on and remember my movements."

"Listen to him," uttered a female voice from the other end of the table.

"More likely I'll be doing the remembering," added Mary, her eyes twinkling with mischief. "This lad would forget his trousers if I didn't lay them out on the bed each morning!"

The table erupted in laughter and Craig looked suitably chastened.

Frank then sparked up, leaning forward conspiratorially to whisper across the table "He did ask if I'd seen anyone acting suspiciously or acting out of character." He paused the bastard, shamelessly milking the drama of the moment, for what seemed an eternity, before adding. "...but I couldn't think of anyone and I said so."

"How long did the interview last?" Margaret asked him.

"About fifteen minutes max," said Roger.

Frank nodded in confirmation. "He gave me his ship phone number and asked me, to contact him if I remembered anything."

"What's the detective's name and what does he look like?" I asked. I realised that my question may be showing a tad too much interest but I felt an urgent need to know who to look out for around the ship or loitering behind me, I needed to put a face to this man.

"You'll be seeing him soon enough," laughed Roger impishly.

"It's telling, isn't it that no further deaths through poisoning have occurred since that day?" Frank threw this out as an afterthought and it hung there in the ether for a while but no one responded, least of all me.

It was 20:30 and we arrived with minutes to spare at the Gaiety Theatre and took seats in the front row. Tonight, Roger Bever, a comedian, was the act scheduled to perform but before he started, we had a parade of representative staff from each of the departments on the ship. Deputations from the cooks, the waiters, the cabin cleaners, the restaurants, the entertainment team, the administration and the money earners (photography, excursions, cruise reservations, reception) filled the stage. In all, about sixty of the circa nine hundred staff accepted the applause from passengers, no doubt hoping the goodwill would be reflected in the gratuities left by the parting guests.

Then Roger Bever appeared and from the start, it was clear he was a joke comic armed with quick one-liners and some quirky eccentric humour thrown in. He thrived in thinking on his feet and worked his way along the front row of the audience asking what their names were, where they were from and what they used to work at? He'd craft jokes based around the answers he got.

We were sat in the front row and inevitably he reached me and I gave my career as an accountant. Next to me sat Margaret and she also admitted to being an accountant and then he came to Roger who identified himself a retired copper.

"Christ, lads, have I interrupted a raid?" he asked.

The crew talent competition is on again tonight in the Pacific Lounge but we chose a different location on the ship to spend the latter part of the evening.

Back in our cabin, at midnight the banging and crashing is both audible and vibratory but also a distant distraction.

Day 48

Sunday 19th February.
At sea, off the coast of Africa.

We woke and checked the information channel. We were sailing at 18 knots in rough seas and the temperature was 16 degrees centigrade. The ship's heaving and throwing motion could unbalance all but the fittest and most agile.

By 08:30 we're dressed for the day. We exited the cabin and stepped into the empty lift when its doors slid open on deck 8. Inside I selected deck 12 but instead of displaying our requested stop, the button lit up bright red and the lift panel then went blank. I tried to press it again but the power was cut to the panel. Suddenly with a jolt, the lift began to rise, swiftly. It rose past deck 9, deck 10 and deck 11 and came to a halt on deck 12 but the door wouldn't open. We pressed and pressed the panel's buttons but got no joy.

Just when I began to panic, the lift took off again and rose to deck 13 and then, deck 14. I knew there was no deck 15 so I was bloody pleased when it stopped. Then, without any instruction from us, the lift set off at pace downwards. It hurtled down past the floors, 14, 13, 12, 11, 10, 9, 8, 7, 6 and was heading for 5. I suspected 5 was the lowest it could go, and it was. It duly reached it with a shudder and we came to a sudden stop. We were both sent sprawling across the floor. Margaret cried out "Luke you have to do something!"

Before I could stand up, the lift had set off again. This time we travelled upwards. For the next few minute's we sailed up and then down the lift shaft, passing floors without stopping and then reversing the journey. All the time the ship was rocking and heaving from side to side. I was terrified.

Once I had time to assess what was happening, I flipped open the metal cover and pressed the alarm button hidden inside. I could hear the shrill bell going off outside the lift but nothing else occurred and our terror ride continued.

Then I pressed small patterns of morse code—dit, dit, dit, pause, dit, dit, dit, pause dit dit dit, on the alarm button. This is the morse code entry for SOS – emergency but no one reacted. No call from a control centre or the ships bridge. The loudspeaker within the lift remained stubbornly silent.

As the minutes passed and the violent lift movements up and down past the floors continued, our anxiety grew. I increased the frequency of alarm button pressing until finally, my finger was permanently on the button.

Margaret was in a panic. Eyes wide, mouth open in a silent scream, she stood ramrod straight upright jammed into the far corner to support herself. She felt around the smooth silver metallic wall for a handrail or something to grip but found nothing to cling onto.

Eventually, the lift stopped moving but we were still trapped inside it. I heard a voice from above shouting something to us but I couldn't make out what he was saying. The lift remained static at deck level 5. A short while later, that seemed to us an age, a technician opened the lift doors. We stepped out shaken but okay.

"All out?" the man asked from somewhere above us.

"Yes. It's just the two of us."

The green jump-suited technician jumped down from the lift ceiling and joined us in the lobby.

He smiled and said "I was walking past when I heard your alarm bell and I've been chasing the lift up and down the floors for the past five minutes or more."

It didn't inspire confidence. What if he hadn't been passing? What then I thought?

"There are loads of safety features on this lift," he informed us. "You would never have fallen to the foot of the shaft."

I wasn't so sure.

We walked up the stairs to deck 12 and sat in the restaurant. Neither of us felt like eating so we settled for two cups of steaming hot tea. Upon leaving half an hour later we walked past the lift and I didn't see any, Out of Order signs. Not only that, the lift appeared to be continuously in use. I went to reception and made a formal report of the incident, verbally to an officer.

"Yes, we had reports from passengers of a lift sailing past floors without stopping," he confirmed.

I said "I would have been reassured if, upon my pressing of the alarm button, someone in the ship's crew had made contact with me via the PA system or from outside the lift as we have just spent a considerable period of time yo-yo'ing between seven decks unaware that anyone knew we were trapped."

He shrugged his shoulders. "I can do no more than register your comments, sir."

"Well don't say I didn't try to warn you – that lift is a death trap!" I said loudly and I turned on my heels and left, fuming.

It's a sea day so the Beginner's Bridge class resumes today, and Shirley has again made up our four. The session was uneventful save that I played out two contracts losing both, one quite convincingly by -3 tricks. Brendan again conducts the class and seems subdued but able to park his problems and deliver a good lesson.

Too soon, I had to leave for the Choir practice and, lo and behold, the return of the prodigal daughter! Aoife the Topstars Irish vocalist attended the first session in over a week so maybe she really was ill. She picked up where she left off and revisited her three songs, accepting that there is now no time to change or correct. One practice class remains.

The men give their song a blast and Geoff performs his solo line much better. Overall I thought the performance today compared to previous efforts had slipped again. We were asked by a woman's representative to run the idea of men wearing Caribbean shirts to add colour on the day. David, the musical director will put it to the men tomorrow.

David also confirmed rumours that the French half of the International Piano Duo, Robin Essen had been left on the dockside at Tenerife when his bag was stolen. He was actually left stranded at the foot of a volcano by his taxi driver who took off and he missed the ship sailing by the matter of a few feet. With the SS Azara having sailed without him, he'd rejoin it in Southampton.

I caught up with Margaret in the Palace and we decided to take in a movie, *Inferno*, starring Tom Hanks which was showing at in the Chaplin cinema. I am ashamed to say I slept through ninety-nine per cent of the movie. I'm a bit stressed and haven't slept well these last few days. This morning lift ride of terror just about put the cap on my day.

We made our way to the Imperial restaurant for dinner and found all the team in good form and chatty. Obviously, I shared our news. "I've started writing a new book called, *Trapped in a Lift on a Sinking Ship*, and of course my new song, *I Left My Pianist in Tenerife*, is due out next week!

Frank reported that International Piano Duo, remained a duo, for this afternoon's concert because the multi-talented ships music director David had taken over the empty seat of the unfortunate Frenchman and performed an exciting selection of Hungarian dances, some pieces by Eric Satie and Ravel's masterpiece La Valse.

We strolled up to the Gaiety Theatre for the first show by the Magpies, a group of four men in their thirties who play rock n roll hits from the 1950s. They put on a brilliant show with Vinny the singer/guitarist fronting the group and showing off his powerful voice and slick guitar work. The lad on the lead guitar replicated some of the greatest guitar licks of Chuck Berry, Elvis Presley, Buddy Holly and Hank Marvin. The drummer and bass player provided a steady tight rhythm for the others to shine. For forty-five minutes they stood playing some of the best songs ever written and were true to the original recorded versions.

We met Bill and Joan after the show and chatted for a while before taking a stroll outside on the Promenade deck, the dark sea looked menacing and the wind blew a gale. We were returning to winter in the UK and Ireland.

We sat down in Andersons Bar with them and another older couple Roger and May. Bill has a huge personality and a wicked sense of humour and he is deliberately un-PC and calls things as he sees them. He's the granddad kid's love but parents are fearful of. Leaving the kids with Bill and Joan for a week probably meant they'll see the inside of every pub in the area and quite possibly would taste some alcohol along the way. I even bet that when the parents came home Bill showed them pictures of the kids. "Here's one of Gilbert, asleep in the Frog 'n' Toad, there's one of Alex eating crisps in the Bulls Head, there's another of Gilbert in the Duke of York."

Bill said that Joan had a letter from his hospital consultant that detailed what treatment Bill must get immediately if he falls ill on the cruise.

"No, I ain't got it," said Joan. "It's in the cabin".

"That's just great," said Bill. "Thing is if I fall ill this letter needs to be produced. I read it yesterday and noticed someone had written in pen, in big letters: DO NOT RESUSCITATE!"

We left them bickering pleasantly and turned in for the night.

Day 49

Monday 20th February.
At sea, halfway up the coast of Portugal.

Last night's sailing was through choppy waters and the Captain said he expected a calmer day today. This morning we were travelling at 18 knots, experiencing temperatures of 15 degrees centigrade and the upper decks are off limits. The sunbathing days have gone for good. Those lingering Bermuda shorts would soon disappear from around the ship and long trousers and jumpers will become the order of the day. The upper decks are off limits all day which means no quoits and no tennis or cricket.

Last night, along with the *Skyline* newsletter, was an invitation to a Captains Farewell party and an Octavian Cruises Customer Questionnaire in our cabins mailbox. The returned forms for this cruise will not make easy reading in headquarters.

We ate breakfast and Margaret then tackled the launderette, a sure fire way to ruin her day.

The Beginner's Bridge class members were gathered around a large screen watching Brendan demonstrate a computer-based program that can help sharpen your skills, and which he, by good chance sells. We settled for a few more hands of cards with Shirley again explaining and tutoring us.

Coffee with Jennifer revealed she had booked next year's cruise yesterday as it gives her something to look forward to. Her home life, as a retired worker and now widow, sounds a rather empty affair and I do feel for her.

The final choir practice was with David. He was alone as his Topstars assistants were in rehearsal for this afternoons show. The choir were in mixed form, some sung better, some sung worse. He dropped complicated harmonies and dropped a song he'd failed to get to, off the running order. I feel right now he is just eager to get it done. The ambition to make us the best choir ever had retreated as the hours passed and reality had begun to kick in. Geoff nailed his solo but the song America was a minefield of uneven lines and breathing patterns.

We ate lunch and practised bridge in Lawton's with twenty plus tables of experienced players quietly competing in the vast carpeted and dimly lit room.

That afternoon in the Gaiety Theatre the Topstars presented, *We'll Meet Again*, a nostalgic show that featured over a hundred songs from the WW2 period. Remember the majority of this audience were in their twenties when WW2 occurred. These songs were their pop music of the time. The dancers and singers began the show with a ten minute medley of songs most of which I knew but a significant number I'd never heard of. First up was Aoife, our Irish blonde who sang *The White Cliffs of Dover*, made famous by Vera Lyn, who is still alive as I write and is over one hundred years of age. Then on came the other singers and dancers who rattled through so many songs, with their timing being just perfect and their energy levels high. The elderly man sat next to me knew most of the songs and sang along with them. The show finished with the rousing *Rule Britannia* and *Land of Hope and Glory* at which point, we all stood up and waved our Union Jack flags. All except Brian, our fellow Irishman, who sat next to Margaret and not only didn't wave a flag but chastised Margaret for joining in! What a sour puss he'd turned out to be. When in Rome do as the Romans!

Up in the restaurant a short while later Roger pronounced it the best performance of that type of show that he'd ever seen and he's a veteran of many such shows.

We visited our cabin and donning the suit one more time, we left to visit the Captains Farewell drinks party in the lounge. We queued to have a photograph taken with him and Margaret thanked him for safely guiding us over the last forty-nine days. Passing down into the lounge, I took a gin and tonic and Margaret settled for a glass of white wine from the waiter's tray. Arthur and Jean beckoned us over and we sat chatting until Captain Peter Cox made a brief speech and we all trotted off to our usual first sitting meal. There Ali and Hamoud stood waiting to greet us and, at the end of the meal, they passed over to us forty-eight days worth of menu's, the top one signed by both of them and wishing us well. Unfortunately, the sheer weight of the menus means all but two of them will end up in our cabin bin.

At the Gaiety Theatre, Roger Bever, comedian, was back for a second bite at the audience. It was really just more of the same. He interrogated the front row seeking out their basic details, names and previous careers. For such basic information, he found it remarkably difficult to come by. Several audience members either froze or deliberately avoided giving him a direct answer. He fished in the same pools as last time. Hasn't the world gone mad? Didn't we have a tough childhood? What do you think of the Middle East?

We cut the night short at this point and headed back to our cabin.

Day 50

Tuesday 21st February.
At sea, halfway across the Bay of Biscay.

The wind force had dropped to a northerly force 4 so the upper decks and all the pools were open. The temperature was a mere 10 degrees centigrade and the SS Azara was sailing at nineteen knots. The ships own movement was rhythmic and gentle. Long may it stay so! We were due to clear the Bay of Biscay by 14:30 so one known area of rough sea was safely behind us..

We took breakfast in the Palace restaurant and I managed to play some tennis but had to cut it short as Roger Bever the comedian, was lecturing on the 1942 assassination of Rheinhart Heidrich, thus showing he had a second string to his bow. A packed theatre hung on his every word and he took questions from the audience at the end.

We attended the final Beginner's Bridge class and exchanged hugs and thanks to Shirley and Brendan Flood for their twenty plus classes and handouts. I felt certain that Brendan's good wishes would be swiftly withdrawn if he knew how I had framed him for the deaths.

Coffee with Jennifer was a nice affair as we three relaxed and discussed life while the blue sea rushed past the window. We checked in with reception who claimed no interest or obligation to assist us with a train strike in England. *You're on your own son,* I was effectively told. I asked if they could find out the current status on the strike and they promised, with poor grace, they would do that.

We completed an employee exceptional service nomination for Ali our table waiter whom I had noticed had displayed great humanity and kindness to many of the elderly passengers he encountered around the ship.

At noon the choir's technical run through began in the Gaiety Theatre. Getting one hundred singers on and off the stage safely is a challenge and I get a position in the front row with Geoff. The tenor rows are in front of us and the bass boys take up the last three. We commit our position to memory and will file on and off in a set sequence. David runs through the songs and draws Aoife and Tony in to take charges of their numbers. We break for lunch and promise to be back at 15:00.

My stomach is still unsettled with the imminent performance playing on my mind and the detective onboard doesn't help so it's just a cup of tea for lunch for me. I heard from Margaret that Craig and Mary were interviewed by the detective this morning. He is getting close and I'm hoping my deep sleeping partner Margaret will still be a solid alibi when I get a chance to give my ha'pence worth to the curious detective.

I still, have no idea what he looks like and I have begun to scrutinise every face that I come upon asking, is that him? Or is that person staring at me? A degree of paranoia is settling into my brain and I must get a grip on myself. One more day will see me ashore and safe. We spend an hour or more in the ship's health club spa enjoying the hot tub, the steam room, and the sauna. It takes my mind off the show and other things.

We men don Caribbean shirts for the show and I loan Geoff a spare one I have with me. We gather in the last three rows of seats in the theatre until it's time to troop on stage via the dressing room.

Unlike previous choirs where I was lost in the crowd, I this time stood in the front row of men but unfortunately behind the black piano so at best I was visible from my waist up. I spotted Margaret and Anita in row two and gave a rather limp nervous wave, which was acknowledged by smiles. Once settled on stage I have a habit of burying my head and reading the lyrics and notes. I end up singing down to my feet rather out towards the audience, at least that's what Margaret says and I've no reason to doubt her.

The theatre is about two thirds full and we get a standing ovation at the end of our ten song program. People are very generous but its just possible we sounded good. Certainly, with several songs we glided through tricky waters and I thought *America* was a massive hit.

We poured out of the theatre elated, the adrenalin pumping through our veins. Margaret said, "I was so proud of you I cried."

Elation carried us on a wave to the Palace restaurant and we were joined at our table by the two Topstars choirmasters, sincerely pleased with the outcome, which one hopes reflects on them too. Geoff, eighty-seven, was in ebullient form and had sung in the lift on the way up and showed no sign of deflating or shutting up anytime soon.

We visited reception for an update on the strike but they hadn't kept their promise and appeared disinclined to even browse the internet to find if it was still on.

Just before dinner the PA crackled to life in our cabin and the disembarkation timetable and actions were communicated to all:

"Please be out of your cabin by 08:00. Breakfast is served in the Palace restaurant up to 08:30 and waiter served breakfasts will be provided at 07:00 to 08:00 in the Imperial restaurant. Self-evacuating passengers should disembark between 07:15 and 08:45. Thank you."

The announcement came to an end and we relaxed in the cabin, with not a stitch packed. Outside our cabin, the corridors are filled with hundreds of suitcases, locked and bedecked with cabin tags. They await the ship's crew to move them to a central location overnight and then to carry them ashore in the morning. I can see it's a logistical nightmare as some passengers will be retrieving cars, some will be booked on coaches or taxis and others, like us, will be starting a long journey home independent of Octavian Cruises.

We dressed for the final dinner which carried a casual dress code. The vibrations rattled the cutlery on the table yet again and it was hard to hear conversations on the other side. Finally, the food was eaten, the coffee drunk and we had one last round of joke telling before embracing, promising to keep in touch and telling each other just how much fun we'd had sharing the table over the last fifty days.

Postponing our case packing we attended the Magpies second

show which confirmed them as the most popular entertainment act of the cruise as it was standing room only. Finally, all good things do have to end and we left the theatre.

Grudgingly we faced up to the packing which took over an hour at the end of which we had the two large and two small cases filled plus my rucksack bulging. Our portable weighing scale certainly was a comfort.

We set the alarm for 06:00 but neither of us expected to sleep much that night. We'd only been in bed less than an hour when I answered a knock on the cabin door. I'd almost forgotten the interview with the detective and had, as time had passed, begun to believe I might escape interview.

A ships officer was standing in the corridor. "Please accept my apologies for disturbing you and your wife at such a late hour, Mr Granger. But can you both get dressed as quickly as possible and come with me now?"

"It's a bit late, officer," I complained in a mildly irritated tone. "We have a long day of commuting ahead of us tomorrow."

"I appreciate that and I'm sorry sir, but the detective has asked to speak with all the passengers before the ship docks and the interviews are over-running a-bit today."

He noted my continued resistance and confided. "There are more passengers to be seen after you tonight."

"I suppose it could be worse then." I acknowledged. "Can you give us a few minutes? I'll have to wake my wife." I pointed to the prone body covered by blankets and still oblivious to the light beaming through the open door.

"Certainly, sir," he replied, "I'll wait out here."

I woke Margaret gently and once she was compos mentis she slipped on a tracksuit and a pair of flip flops and was ready. I wore similar and ran a brush through my hair before passing it to her when I'd done with it. Together we left the room and walked to the lift in silence with the young English officer trotting along ahead of us.

He escorted us downstairs to deck 5 and left us sitting on a bench outside a small room whose door was closed. He knocked on the door and entered, closing it behind him. I could hear some conversational noise but it was too blurred to make any sense of. Moments later he reappeared and smiling at Margaret said, "Don't worry. This is purely routine. You'll be back tucked up in bed in twenty minutes, I promise you. Thank you for your cooperation. I'm off to collect more passengers." and with that, he was gone.

We sat another minute or two lost in our own thoughts. Eventually, a deep voice boomed out, "Enter," and we rose as one.

I opened the door to let Margaret into the room first. Extending a hand of greeting from across a large desk, a stout grey haired man allowed the briefest of smiles to rest on his face before gesturing to us to sit in the chairs opposite him.

I thought it strange that he'd see us both together but I suppose it was all he could do, given the number of people to interview. I did a quick calculation of hours needed to interview 2,800 people for twenty minutes each while working eighteen hour days. I came to forty-seven days' and he only had, by my reckoning thirteen days if he started interviewing on the day he boarded. He had to cut corners so there was a certain method to his madness.

He fell back into his padded chair and, reaching out, flipped open one of the two brown folders on the table. Around the room were strewn many archive boxes filled to the lid with similar folders. On his desk a small notebook and pencil sat next to a mug of steaming coffee and an old fashioned grey telephone.

"Mrs Granger?" He looked up and she smiled. He glanced down again and after a long pause he said, "Margaret?" He was clearly tiring and the effort to stay focused was written on his face. He took a swig from the mug and rolled the liquid around his mouth before swallowing.

"Yes, that's me, Officer," Margaret confirmed.

"Right," he now briefly examined the other folder and glanced at me. I could see the image from my boarding card on a photocopied page and saw he was checking my face against it. "Mr Luke Granger?"

"Yes, sir," I answered and like Margaret, I smiled. It wasn't returned because he was now reading further through the folder and had his head down, eyes fully engaged. Finally, he read the last page in the folder and picking up the two folders he dropped them unceremoniously into the archive box at his feet. The noise startled us both. We now had his full attention and he took a deep breath before launching into a spiel he had already recited hundreds of times over the past two weeks.

"Good evening, folks. My name is Gary Matthews. I'm a

detective based in Southampton and a fulltime employee of Octavian Cruises PLC. My job is to investigate unusual and often criminal activities that occur during cruises run by the company.

I have been assigned to investigate the death by poisoning of a large number of people on or around the thirty-third day of this cruise which was, to jog your memory a bit Saturday the 4th of February. That was two days' before the ship docked in Manaus, a thousand miles up the Amazon River in Brazil."

I nodded. "Okay."

"Seeing as that was seventeen days ago I appreciate it may be hard for you to recall that specific day but do your best." He paused, "What were you both doing on that day?" He reached across his desk and pushed the ship's *Skyline* newspaper for the day towards Margaret who, picked it up and began to read it.

"Well, officer, we had breakfast and attended the Beginners Bridge class at 10:15 and then we went for coffee. I'd be pretty sure Luke attended the choir practice at noon." She looked at me questioningly.

"Yes, that's how it was," I ventured. "We split up at noon as I recall. Margaret went to the clothes sale in the atrium and I attended the choir practice."

He seemed satisfied with our answers. "Did you see anything untoward occur in the bridge class that morning? Was anyone ill during the class or was there any falling out between attendees of either the beginners or the intermediate classes?"

"Not that I saw," answered Margaret, promptly and with a

smile.

I merely shook my head. It was great that we were being interviewed together and that she was taking the lead. Long may it stay that way!

"Mrs Granger, what was your profession before retiring?"

"I can answer for both of us officer, we were both accountants," Margaret was playing a blinder and I think was treating the interview as a quiz show and she loved quizzes. She seemed to relish the question and answer format. This answer produced another dead end for our detective whom I couldn't yet decide was either just going through the motions of an investigation or was cunningly appearing not to care but playing with us like fish, wriggling at the end of his line.

"Did you study chemistry during your schooling, Mr Granger?"

His question came like a bolt from the blue. In switching his questioning from Margaret to me, just like that, he had caught me off guard. I'd switched off, I'd relaxed.

I couldn't be sure what he knew about me? How much of my life was laid out for him in that folder? I made a decision and decided to answer honestly.

"Yes, I did, Mr Matthews. It was a compulsory subject in Ireland up to our intermediate cert examinations, equivalent to your English "O" levels. We both studied chemistry to a basic level because we were schooled in Ireland."

Margaret agreed and Gary Matthews seemed pleased that he

may be onto something. "But I dropped it fast the next semester as I was useless at it. I was able to switch my studies to economics for my final two years in school. I sat the Leaving certificate, an equivalent to your English A levels in English, Irish, lower lever mathematics, economics, business studies, art and French."

"Cripes," said Matthews "we only sit exams in two or three subjects for the A levels in England. You guys had it tough!" The detective then switched his attention back to Margaret. "And you, Mrs Granger, did you continue your chemistry studies?"

"No, detective. I left school after the intermediate exams and I became an articled clerk in a large accounting practice in Dublin where I stayed until I qualified as an accountant five years later."

Another lead withered on the vine.

The detective glanced at his watch–00:05.

I guessed he'd been hard at it for about thirteen hours today. God only knows how many more passengers he had to interview before he'd finally hit the sack. Time was on our side.

"So, did you two go ashore at any of the islands before you sailed to Brazil? Did you visit any of the Caribbean islands? To refresh your memories they were Jamaica, the Dominican Republic, Guadeloupe, St. Vincent's, Barbados and finally Tobago."

"Now I can be certain we didn't get off at Jamaica," Margaret answered. "We probably visited the others but I can't recall for sure." She looked to me for help.

"Why don't you check the ship's card reader scanner's as they capture and record all embarking and disembarking," I volunteered.

"I'm sure the records can be made available to you."

"I have those records Mr Granger but I like to hear independently from passengers too." A check question included to test out passenger honesty had been rumbled.

"Did either of you visit a chemist while you were ashore?" I stepped in to reply before Margaret could answer.

"No, Officer" I said.

"No?" said Margaret. "Now that's not right, Luke, we did visit a chemist when ashore!"

My heart sank as Mr Matthews leapt. Margaret wasn't finished and I was helpless to stop her.

"I had some chronic insect bites, Mr Matthews. They kept me awake for nights on end until I said to Luke I must get something for them when we next get ashore." Margaret paused to draw breath.

"And where was that, Mrs Granger?" asked the detective, his pencil in his hand, poised and waiting.

"Ah, it's come back to me." smiled Margaret triumphantly. "It was the Walmart Chemist in New Orleans. Luke, do you remember?"

"Yes, that's right," I answered, mightily relieved she'd forgotten the chemist in St. Vincent's. Margaret couldn't ever lie and as such a person she was brilliantly believable. She rattled on about her bites, the failure of the treatment and her visit to the medical centre on board.

Detective Gary Matthews was already opening the folders for his next passengers and the knock on the door was followed by the ship's officer entering the room.

"Well, thank you both for your cooperation this evening and I wish you a pleasant onward trip tomorrow." Detective Gary Matthews shook both our hands as we slipped out of his office and out of his clutches.

Day 51

Wednesday 22nd February.
Docked in Southampton, England.

The ship had arrived in the early morning and unusually I hadn't heard any of the docking noises that normally had accompanied our arrival in port. The SS Azara was definitely stationary and her bow camera showed a darkened Southampton dock and terminal with just the odd flash of coach lights as they passed on the road nearby.

Outside our cabin in the post tray sat our final ships account statement and it would hit our credit card unless we queried it immediately.

Up at 06:00 we showered and dressed before heading up to deck 12 and the restaurant for breakfast. The cold English winter air cut through my light clothing and we huddled together as we walked into the face of a cold wind. We ate heartily but I couldn't wait until we had got off this ship. I was haunted with a fear that Margaret may recall the chemist visit I made in St Vincent and go to the detective's office and land me in it. Not deliberately but these things happen.

We made our way back through the atrium and spotted two men laying out piles of newspapers and magazines. They didn't look like ship staff, so I asked if they had any news about the Southern

Rail strike? They had! The strike was over and they insisted on giving us a bundle of newspapers and magazines for free!

Back in the cabin we packed the last of our possessions into our hand luggage. I recognised several items would not be coming home, such as several pairs of my teeny weeny underpants, one washing machine tablet, shampoo, toothpaste and the dregs of our brandy.

By 08:00 we were dragging along the corridors of the ship two cases each, all with wheels, along with my rucksack and Margaret's handbag. Down at the gangplank the ship account cards functioned one last time and the electronic voice said an emotionless "Goodbye."

We wheeled our four bags through a terminal ground floor now filled with thousands of suitcases from the ship. We walked on and through the border police and customs section where benches sat awaiting use, but no officers were to be seen. Suddenly we emerged into daylight and onto the path. Outside a long row of taxis waited for passengers.

"Oh, Luke," Margaret said, turning to me. "I really loved this cruise but there was just one thing wrong with it."

"What's that?" I asked genuinely confused.

"Fifty days' just wasn't long enough," she answered. "Let's do one hundred next time!"

THE END

About the Author

Mark Rice has kept daily diaries for years, but started publishing short stories and novels in 2014.

At about the same time, he started a blog weirdorwhat.wordpress.com where you can find many more stories and postings. He is also on Facebook and other social media sites.

He lives in County Wexford in Ireland and is happily married with grown-up children.

Hobbies are gardening, photography and running.

He is a member of the Gorey Writer Group based in County Wexford, Ireland.

Other Titles By Mark Rice

Murder In Maspalomas

This is a fast-moving novel that takes you on a journey to the sunny Canary Islands. A couple are forced to flee Ireland with the hope that a Dublin drugs gang will not follow for a paltry debt of €50k. How wrong they were.

Amusing Short Stories

Life observations and humorous musings (Volume 1)

Fur Coats and Other Short Stories

A set of lively, humorous, yet touching stories of life in current times.

ALL TITLES ARE NOW AVAILABLE ON AMAZON

COMMUNICATE WITH MARK RICE

Mark welcomes all questions, suggestions and feedback.

Feel free to contact him as follows:

Email – markrice10@gmail.com

Blog - https://www.weirdorwhat.wordpress.com

Printed in Great Britain
by Amazon